BONDS OF FIRE AND FURY

A FLAME RIDERS NOVEL

JAMES A EGGEBEEN

Bonds of Fire and Fury

Copyright © 2025 by James A. Eggebeen

ISBN: 978-1-949833-03-4 (Paperback)

ISBN: 978-1-949833-02-7 (Hardback)

First Edition: October 2025

To my granddaughters, whose boundless imagination lights the spark for every story I tell and every dress I create. Your dreams of soaring dragons and bold adventures have woven themselves into the fabric of this tale, inspiring the fiery spirit of Karzul and Kin'tara. With each stitch and every word, you remind me that the greatest magic lies in the love and wonder we share.

N
DARESH
THERA–DARESH BORDE
CHAYAK
THE
ANCIENT MINE
THERA
THE
CITADEL

Thera

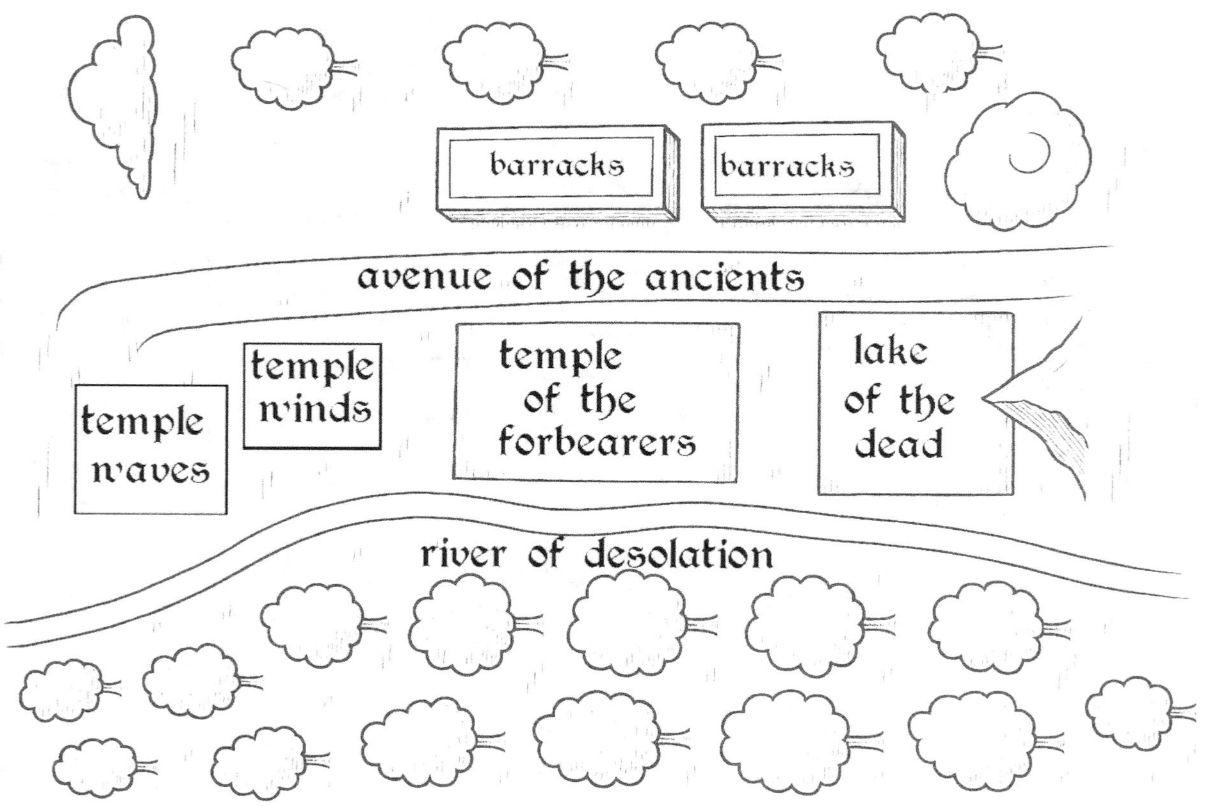

The Forbearer's Mine

PROLOGUE

Kin'tara stirred. It had been half a millennium since she'd fallen into the slumber of mindlessness. Following her instincts as nothing more than a hungry wyrm, she'd waited, huddled together with those like her who inhabited the high mountain caves, departing only when hunger drove her forth. But mostly, she slept, and she dreamed. Dreamed of uncountable past lives bonded to humans. Each dream offered her new insights into reality, new emotions to process, new ideas to mull over.

Soon, it would be time. Time to choose a new human. Her final bonding. It would be her last metamorphosis. At least that's what her dreams told her. But dreams were fickle things. Prone to interpretation, to change, subject to the whims of fate.

A tickle teased her senses. The image of her death. It was distant, vague and undefined, yet it was there. Her next human would be essential to the fulfillment of her dream of metamorphosis. That much was clear. Soon.

But not today.

She glanced around at the rough granite walls, shot through with crystals which held no power or light, and longed for a past, another cave, one filled with light and magic.

But that too was in the future.

She laid her head on the rough granite and let the warmth seep from her.

No hunger drove her.

No call to bond.

The time was near, but not yet upon her.

As exhaustion claimed her, she let out a deep sigh and surrendered to sleep.

1

DRAGONFALL'S GAMBIT

*I*n the heart of the mountains, high above the placid plains, jagged peaks pierced the clouds. When people spoke of it in hushed whispers, they named it Dragonfall. A narrow stone bridge extended in a precarious embrace across a fathomless cavern. Hewn from weathered gray granite, it told tales of aeons past; the bridge standing the test of time, a narrow thread giving a singular view to the jagged cavern where the dragons slumbered. Gusts like ethereal fingers caressed the stone, threatening to sweep everything from its path into the bottomless cavern below.

The bridge seemed to sway beneath Karzul's feet, but he pushed the thought away. Stone was stone. The narrow span had stood firm against the ravages of time. It had been there even before the forbearers created their long forgotten marvels. It did not move. It did not sway. It was solid, no matter what his gut told him.

He suppressed a shiver. The morning was cold, but not yet the freezing cold of winter, just the damp penetrating cold that lingered after the rain washed the smoke from the air.

Pain shot from his foot to his hip as he stepped on a blade of rock. He reminded himself to be careful. No sturdy boots for him. Not today. Today, he needed to feel his way. And feel, he did. Every loose stone and change in camber registered beneath the thin soles of his moccasins.

He glanced over at Nephim standing there in her crisp uniform. That dragon rider's uniform was a masterpiece in both form and function, designed to withstand the rigors of flight and the ferocity of battle. Sleek black with gold piping, the uniform bore the emblem of a dragon on each sleeve along with intricately designed spells of protection and agility. The pants were tucked into thigh-length black leather boots that glimmered even after the long trek up the mountain.

When he'd first met Nephim, he'd assumed her crisp uniform was because she was born to the manor, but he'd learned this was the garb all riders wore. He himself would be dressed the same if he succeeded this day.

"Choose." Nephim's words were barely discernible over the whistling of the wind. She stood at the edge of the span, sheltered from the gusts by a small outcropping. Her loose-fitting cloak rippled in the wind, exposing a layer of fat surrounding her belly, the sign of wealth and privilege that only those raised in the manor retained past childhood. Half a hand of summers into her womanhood, Nephim was already famous, or infamous, for she'd had the great fortune to survive what so many before her died attempting.

It was said that on her day of choosing — an event infamous in its own right — Nephim had arrogantly selected the largest dragon she could find. She'd leapt from this very bridge and landed squarely on the massive creature, legs clamping around its neck before it realized what was happening. But before she could form the bond, it had thrown her.

What must that have been like? To fall through the sky, a stone haphazardly tossed from the span, careening off the walls toward the knife-sharp rocks below?

That was the thought that gripped Karzul as he stood frozen in place. What if he missed? Would he be as fortunate? Would the gods smile upon him as they had upon her?

No.

There would be no dragon driven into his path. No second chance.

Not for him. He wasn't among the fortunate ones. Fate never favored him. If he missed, or failed to create the bond with the creature he chose, he would plummet to his death.

"I can do this." He spoke the words aloud, knowing full well no one heard him. Still, it gave him confidence to say those words, and he needed confidence for what he was about to attempt.

He leaned over the low stone wall.

A small thunder of immature dragons swarmed below him, delicate, rippling, canvas shrouds spread between slim bones holding themselves aloft against the wind. Most of them possessed only a single set of wings. It was a dragon such as this that the gods had driven into Nephim's path as she tumbled toward the canyon floor. She'd survived the fall, but being bonded to such an immature dragon was an embarrassment, a source of shame. No one chose a child to do the work of an adult. No one purposely bonded with an immature dragon.

But Nephim had.

Perhaps her blessings in life didn't translate to those of a rider.

He would not be so foolish.

Nor so arrogant.

Karzul's gaze dropped to the flurry of dragons below. The one he selected would define his future in ways nothing else ever had. He must choose wisely. Amid the kaleidoscope of colors, a brick-red dragon caught his eye. A noble dragon with two sets of wings struggled to fit through the narrow canyon. The two pairs of wings stretched out like leather canopies rippling in the wind as each set rose and fell in time with the bobbing of the lizard body. A stout tail, half a dozen spans long, trailed behind the creature. The spade that decorated its tip and gave stability to the creature in flight was mesmerizing. Colors rippled like a sheen of oil on a pond. Hues of red and ochre followed the serrated edge of the great fin to form a heart shape that flicked back and forth, directing the dragon from one side of the chasm to the other.

The dragons congregated here as they exited the caves in search of prey. This was the place they emerged. This was the place where he would meet his fate.

"Jump," Nephim's words rang in his ears. "Face your fears. You wanted this, so commit to it. Jump before it's too late."

Karzul glanced at Nephim. He couldn't explain why he'd accepted her as his guide. She'd earned no respect from the elders. She'd achieved no honors in battle. She rode a steed that *might* sprout a second set of wings in her lifetime — if she lived long enough. She was on the lowest rung of a society he was about to join.

She made her way across the narrow span to where he stood. She was sure-footed and seemed not to care that the bridge straddled a chasm so deep the rocks below appeared as pebbles. Was it because of her dragon? Was she confident that once again, it would catch her should she slip and fall?

"I'm waiting for just the right moment," Karzul said. "I want that one." He pointed at the brick-red dragon he'd selected. "I don't want people whispering behind my back that I chose poorly, or that I failed to choose at all. This is important."

Nephim shrugged and pushed her single braid so it fell down the middle of her back. When she flew, it stretched out behind her in imitation of her dragon's tail. "You might be surprised at what you could get used to," she said. "If you had to."

She gestured to the thunder below. "We need riders. The Daresh are slaughtering us."

Karzul wrapped his cloak tightly around him, trying to protect himself from the biting wind that threatened to cast him from the bridge. His fear of falling fought with his fear of being deemed a coward, one who put his own personal safety before his duty. Every dragon rider mattered, even one as green as he. "I'm not sure a single rider can make a difference."

"Are you a coward then, Karzul?" demanded Nephim.

"No. I said I'll do this, and I will. For my mother, if nothing else."

Nephim placed a hand on his shoulder. Her fingers were short and stout, but lacked the strength of one raised on the land. When it came to the riders, there was no class. No separation of the wealthy from the poor. No division by skin tone. No male or female. Those who had the ability to call and bond with a dragon were kindred spirits, part of a family that excluded all those who could not. Or so it was said, but Karzul knew that was not the case. Nephim was a dragon rider, but she was not as respected as some.

"Choose another rather than wait," she said. "That one." Nephim jabbed a finger at a dragon headed their way. It was large. Larger than the one Karzul had his eye on. An older adult. The buds, where its third set of wings would emerge, were already pronounced. Scales along its lizard body shimmered in varying shades of green.

It banked, snapping its tail hard to the left, throwing its body into a steep roll. It careened toward the edge of the chasm, then snapped back, heading straight for the bridge, only a man-height below the rocky edge.

"Get ready." Nephim squeezed his shoulder. "Aim for the neck. Lock your legs. Don't let it buck you off. Call up the images I taught you. That will bind it to you. You won't have long. You must capture its interest quickly, or this will be over before it begins."

Karzul took a deep breath. He hoped that fate would smile upon him.

He locked his gaze on the great dragon as it sped toward the span.

It was now or never.

He bent his knees.

Any moment.

Nephim applied pressure to his shoulder, urging him forward.

He took a step, glancing down.

Too far.

The dragon she'd chosen for him was too far below. To fail was death. His knees threatened to give out even as he flexed them in preparation for the leap that would forever seal his fate.

The pressure of Nephim's hand on his shoulder increased.

He wanted to cast it off, to tell her he wasn't ready. But it was now or never. He had to do this. Failure would seal his fate forever.

"Jump." Her hand pushed against his shoulder, tilting him toward the edge.

Suddenly, the world turned inside out.

Karzul stepped back and dropped to his knees. His stomach roiled as he looked out at the swarming of colors that were the dragons.

The sight was dizzying.

Bile rose up in him.

He tried to hold it back, but his stomach turned traitor. He wretched and disgorged its contents over the edge, the foul liquid splashing precisely where he'd hoped to land — on the dragon.

The dragon screeched.

Snapping its great wings, it pivoted to rise above the height of the span. Amber wings flapped angrily as it turned its head toward him and spat fire.

Nephim leapt between Karzul and the oncoming flame, spreading her cloak to cover them both, even as the heat and stench overwhelmed him. The scent of rotten eggs was unbearable. Searing heat crackled over Karzul, carrying with it the stink of sulfur and rotting vegetation, but almost as quickly as it had come, the stench faded.

Frigid air swept away the dragon's breath as the majestic creature tucked its wings close to its body and dove for the canyon floor.

The arms wrapping Karzul shook.

Was Nephim weeping?

Had the dragon's breath harmed her?

Karzul rolled onto his back to look at her.

Tears streaked her soot-stained face.

"I'm all right," he said. "There's no need to weep."

Nephim punched him in the arm. "I'm not weeping, you dolt. I'm laughing."

"Laughing? We were nearly killed, and you're laughing?"

She nodded.

"Why?"

"Because I will no longer be the laughingstock of the whole country."

2

———

BENEATH A CRIMSON SKY

Karzul made his way down the mountain in silence, his face red from the wash of the dragon's flame, his hair stiff and matted from his own vomit. He hurried his pace to stay ahead of Nephim and her consoling words. He was miserable enough without them. The sun was out, but the light drizzle made it cold, and the wind drove that cold through his clothes and into his skin. He tucked his hands into his sleeves, trying to stay warm, but it did little to erase the numbness in his extremities or his soul.

He'd failed.

Not just failed. He'd backed out. That was worse. If he *had* failed, he wouldn't have been around to face the jeers and snide remarks that would surely follow him for the rest of his days. Had he failed, he would have been counted as a hero. Not as one who fell in battle, but as one who fell to his death trying to claim a dragon and protect his people. His name would still have been called each spring when the departed souls were summoned to bless the planting.

But it would not.

How could he face his family?

He wanted to run away, but where would he head? Deeper into Theren territory? Everyone talked. There was no place his shame would not precede him. Home? With the Daresh army approaching, it was no longer safe.

No one spoke of it, but everyone knew.

The war was going badly. Not even the riders could change that. They slowed the enemy advance, but they could not stop it.

He should, at this very moment, be astride the back of a dragon, traversing the path laid out by so many before him. Follow the river south until it forks. Take the right fork into the mountains.

That was the advice his mother had whispered in his ear before he left the fire the previous night.

The whole town of Chayak had celebrated his imminent ascension to flame rider.

They had roasted a pig.

Boiled corn.

Drizzled maple syrup over apples.

The whole town had come out to wish him well. The elders gathered around him, dressed in their ceremonial robes. They waved branches cut from the ancient live oak tree, whose canopy granted shade to the market in the center of the town. They chanted their blessings, words so ancient that their meaning was lost.

The young men claimed their own prowess by hanging close to him as if they were fast friends, even though he barely knew most of them. And the maidens. Rilyle had pecked his cheek almost timidly but whispered words in his ear that left little to the imagination. Shaiway had actually kissed him on the lips, though she had rushed away immediately thereafter. Even the shy Dyana had made it known that she was open to his advances, should he choose her upon his return as a newly created rider.

He blushed.

No one truly expected him to return.

Few did.

The riders were too busy fighting the war. Those who survived never truly returned home. They were scarred. Damaged. Unrecognizable.

No one came back from Dragonfall. Not as they'd left. Their bodies might return, but not their souls. No one returned from their date with destiny, save failures like him.

There would be no kisses for him this day. No flock of hopeful maidens swarming around. No elders offering sage advice. Karzul had been only a child when Oratia had come back from his Dragonfall without a dragon. Oratia had walked the streets as if invisible. The townsfolk had turned their backs and scoffed as he walked by. The young man had lasted almost a hand of days before he was found hanging from the rafters in the barn loft he had taken for his home after being expelled by his own family.

So why was he returning home?

He let his steps slow.

No, he would not return home. There had to be somewhere they wouldn't recognize him. Grow a beard. Hide his face. He could take on a new name. Call himself Zerule. Claim to be a wandering minstrel.

"Karzul?" Nephim had caught up with him.

At least she was not ignoring him.

She pointed toward the eastern sky. "Do you see that?"

Karzul squinted.

It was midday. The sun's position made it difficult to search the cloudless sky. High above the Theren foothills, a handful of black specks circled.

A beat of fear changed the rhythm of his heart. Chayak, his village, lay in those foothills, and the dragons were headed straight for it.

As Karzul watched, a brilliant blue-white beam lanced from one of the creatures to strike the ground below. The rumble of thunder split the air a few heartbeats later.

"Fire lance." He'd heard of the weapon, but never expected to see one in action. In his imagination, the fire lance would stab its target with a beam of light, and the target would vanish. In reality, it was so much more. From one of the attacking dragons, the fire lance stabbed the ground with a brilliant beam of light, almost too bright to look at. It sizzled like frying bacon, only loud enough to hurt his ears, and wherever the beam touched, flames erupted immediately. Five to ten man-heights, the organ flames leaped, emitting a foul black smoke.

"What should we do?" Karzul turned to Nephim, but she was already in motion.

She traced a spell in the air before her.

It was similar to the spell she'd taught Karzul to entrance his dragon.

"Dara'tia. To me!" she screamed, the spell carrying her words to her dragon.

Karzul stood transfixed.

Fire lance.

The Daresh were attacking. How had they penetrated this deep into Theren territory? He knew this day would come, but not so soon. Not today.

"Come on," he said. "We have to try to save them."

"I am trying to save them, you dolt." She nodded to a solitary black dot rushing their way, low on the horizon. She was a rider after all. Of course, she would engage the enemy in the air.

"Do what you can." Karzul's heart raced. "I have to see to the towns-folk. My mother is there. I can't wait around here while you join the battle."

"Karzul, it's too dangerous."

"You'd have me stand here while my family burns?"

Karzul took a step, but stopped as Nephim's dragon dropped from the sky like a stone. Immature, it was, but it was still the largest dragon Karzul had ever encountered. Dara'tia was easily twelve spans long, her wings twice that. She was dark mahogany with blotches of currant spread across her flesh. Scales slid across one another as she raised a horned head and let out a jet of flame.

"Go if you must, but it's not just about you. I expect you back at Dragonfall to try again if we survive this day. We need you as a rider, not some hero running into a burning town." Nephim leaped onto the back of the dragon and wrapped her legs around its neck.

"I can't leave my mother to that." Karzul pointed at the bright slash that extended from the dragon high overhead to stab the town.

"Try to keep yourself alive if you can," Nephim called as the dragon rose to its feet and spread its wings.

A blast of air swept over him as the majestic creature flapped its wings, canopies of leather snapping with each wingbeat. The dragon lifted from the earth with ease and climbed into the sky, dwindling as it rose.

"Luck to you," Karzul called out. He wished he could be up there with her, that he had not lost his nerve and missed his chance. What if he had chosen a dragon that could take down the Daresh flame rider? One that could defeat the fire lance? Had he doomed the town and his mother to death because he was a coward? If he survived, he'd make the trek back up the mountain, even if he had to do it alone. He would choose his dragon, and he would avenge his home.

He stood transfixed as Nephim and her dragon vanished into the sky. He had seen only one fire lance in the fray. Was there only one then? But going up against even one was a huge risk, especially for an immature dragon like Dara'tia. It was said that the larger dragons could survive a strike from a fire lance. Karzul doubted that. What could stand against such force?

Karzul heard the sizzle as the fire lance struck again. He turned and ran, the breeze on his face stinging with the hot wind carrying the burning of his home his way.

He was less than half a league from the town. The surrounding fields had already been harvested, the hay cut short, leaving Karzul free to run even as the wind brought more and more smoke his way. The town had grown up over many summers as a collection of houses and shops with little order to them. The main road ran through the center, granting access to the market square. It was to this road he headed. The smoke seemed thinner there, and the few buildings beside the road that had caught fire were yet to be fully engulfed.

As he ran three more times, the fire lance struck. There were five dragons overhead, but only one appeared to possess a fire lance. He gave thanks for that. How much worse would it be if all of them possessed such a weapon?

A mahogany streak flashed toward the enemy dragons. Nephim had joined the fray and was taking them on directly. She was outnumbered and facing seasoned riders. How could she expect to win such an engagement, or even survive it?

Karzul wished he had not lost his stomach and his nerve. He might even now be winging his way into the battle, and perhaps, with a bit of luck, he might succeed in preventing the death and destruction he was witnessing.

The fire lance flashed into the sky this time.

If nothing else, Nephim was diverting the fire lance from the town.

One of the enemy dragons, a brilliant phosphorescent green, turned and wheeled, banking almost horizontally as it pulled up and sped toward Nephim.

A blue-white light stabbed from the enemy dragon.

Nephim banked hard, barely avoiding the searing beam.

Again, the beam lanced from the enemy.

Nephim banked again, the searing light striking the wing of her dragon, setting it spinning toward the ground before recovering. The roar her dragon let out echoed off the hills, full of anger and frustration. Nephim had bought Karzul some time. He might be able to save his mother if nothing else, but he'd have to hurry. There was no way Nephim was going to survive this.

Karzul rushed toward the town, shoving past a stream of refugees snaking their way through the narrow streets, pouring from the roads in a multi-colored flood.

"Mother," he called out, heedless of the screams that filled the air. "Where are you?"

Amidst the chaos of swirling flames and choking smoke, Karzul fought his way through the press of refugees fleeing the city. The air was thick with a cloying, acrid smoke that stung his eyes, making it hard to see. He feared he had already become disoriented. He was not heading to his home and his mother but was already lost in the bowels of an inferno. Beneath his feet, the cobblestones were coated in soot and ash. Above, the cloud of smoke grew thicker, black coils winding their way into the afternoon sky to dissipate into a cloud that hung over the town. At least it offered some respite from the dragons.

With a whoosh, the building behind him burst into flames.

"Mother," he cried out like a lost child.

"Karzul?" Through the choke of smoke, the feeble call came.

Karzul spun, recognizing the shops that lined the street where he and his mother lived. Fear for her safety washed over him, fighting with the relief of discovering that she still lived.

"Mother. I'm here," he shouted.

A rush of burning hot wind washed over him as flames licked at the house. The door he had repaired the past spring burst into flames, not from a fire lance, but from dragon's fire. The downdraft from the creature's wings fanned the flames, fueling their fury like a blacksmith's bellows.

The roar of the flames grew deafening.

"Mother!" He pressed forward, but it was like stepping up to the forge that had just been aerated. The flames surged, shedding heat he could not withstand.

From inside, a scream split the air. A scream that would haunt him for as long as he lived. A scream he could not ignore, even if it meant the rest of his life lasted only moments.

He pressed toward the fire. The heat on his face exacerbated the burns he'd received earlier from his folly at the Dragonfall. Not that it mattered. In a few moments, he'd save his mother, or he would be dead.

He took another halting step.

The flames licked over him, singeing the hair from his arms, leaving behind a searing pain he could not ignore.

He screamed.

There was no answer.

"Mother!" he called.

Again, no answer.

He placed his arm over his face and rushed forward heedless of the pain. Stepping into his house felt like being enveloped in a fiery furnace. The stench was overwhelming. The heat was oppressive. He was blinded by the smoke. He wasn't certain which way was which. How was he going to find his mother?

He panicked.

Smoke burned his throat. Coughing wracked his frame. The pain on his face grew in intensity.

"Mother?" he called out.

He glanced up to see her small frame standing doubled over in the doorway. Her dress was ablaze as she stumbled forward.

"Mother!" He rushed to her, but a loud crash sounded as a beam broke from the ceiling overhead, crushing the woman beneath a burning heap, shattering the wardrobe where she kept her clothes and valuables.

"Mother." Karzul rushed to her, kicking aside burning debris.

He knelt beside her.

Her face was pale; her eyes, glassy and unfocused.

"Mother?" He reached for her, but she was not there.

She was gone.

Karzul looked for something to lift the beam. If nothing else, he could provide his mother a decent burial, but the flames roared around him, threatening to cut off his retreat.

Another beam crashed from the ceiling, smashing through the furnishings to bar Karzul's path.

He panicked.

What use was dragging his mother's corpse out of the flames, only to be burned alive?

He stepped back, smoke filling his eyes as he whispered a quick prayer for her soul.

He turned and took a deep breath.

This was going to hurt.

He rushed at the burning beam and leaped over it, catching his foot on it as he crossed through the flames.

He sprawled face first onto the floor.

The pain of the impact almost overwhelmed the pain of his burns.

He shook himself. He had to get out, or die trying.

He noticed that the smoke was thinner near the floor. The air beneath his face felt slightly cleaner, less choking.

He crawled toward the front door, over the floor he had cleaned and waxed more times that he could count, the polished boards, now covered in ash, soot, and bits of burning wood.

After what felt like glasses, Karzul emerged from the doorway, only to find the street ablaze nearly as heavily as the house had been.

He turned toward the street, crouching down to give himself breathing room. It was not much, but it was enough.

The road to the edge of town ahead was not clear, but littered with abandoned possessions as if the residents had tried to save their belongings, but realized, too late, that they would only be weighed down, putting themselves at risk.

Karzul had nothing to save.

Only his own skin.

He made his way along the street until he came to a raging wall of flames. The livery had caught fire; the upper loft was filled with straw. The wall had fallen and crashed to the street, completely barring his path.

This was not the way out.

He turned and followed the street back to the closest intersection and turned. Perhaps he could avoid the flames a street down.

But there too, a building had collapsed and barred his way.

He turned again, now completely lost.

But it hardly mattered which direction he went, only as long as he could escape the flames.

He coughed and dropped to his knees as he made his way along the street; the smoke growing thicker and thicker.

He pushed on, finally emerging from the thick smoke.

He rolled onto his back, coughing and breathing deeply, trying to clear the smoke from his lungs.

Overhead, the dragons reeled, their fire setting flame to anything in the town that had yet to be consumed.

The fire lance occasionally flared to life, but no longer aimed at the ground. Its brilliant beam stabbed into the sky where an ebony streak swerved, dove and soared, but the fire lance seemed to be losing its power with each pass. He prayed it would soon fall silent, but his prayers were not answered soon enough.

He watched in horror as the lance flame contacted the ebony dot, and it ceased its dodging. A roar of pain and anguish echoed from the Nephim's ebony dragon. Twisting toward the brilliant green, it tucked its wings close to its body and fell, faster and faster.

Nephim had been hit.

"No," Karzul cried out. Not Nephim. Was that the last time he would see her? Had he just witnessed her death?

He plopped down in the dirt.

He'd failed.

Nephim had failed.

She had bought him a bit of time, but it had been too late. The town had already been destroyed.

She told him the Daresh were coming, but she was wrong. They were not coming; they were already here. Sooner than anyone would have expected. She told him he had time to train, time to master his dragon, but in truth, it was much more desperate than that.

Where were the riders? Were their numbers so low that they could not protect one small border town? Was it truly that desperate? Was there any hope? Would he have been able to make a difference if he had not lost his nerve?

For the longest time, Karzul sat there wallowing in his pain, wondering what the future held for him, but there was no future. Not any longer.

There would be no dragon for him. But even if he *had* managed to bond with a dragon, what could he have done? What could anyone have done? The thought echoed through his mind, a haunting reminder of all that he had lost. There was no hope. The Daresh outnumbered the Theren troops, and they had a fire lance that the Theren riders did not possess. It was a losing proposition. There were no bright days ahead. Only death and destruction.

"Come, son."

Karzul looked up.

An old man in a brown robe offered a hand. Karzul recognized him. Rodan. An outcast. Villagers told stories behind his back. Stories of some shame hidden far in his past.

They had something in common now.

Karzul took his hand and stood. "Do you know who I am?" Karzul asked.

"I do," said the old man. "You may be our only hope."

"Hope?" Karzul shook his head. "I'm a failure."

"Not until you give up."

Karzul inhaled. He expected to breathe in smoke and ashes, but the air he took in was fresh and clear. Maybe a gust of wind from the mountain had carried it here.

Rodan's words were like a slap in the face. "We need every rider we can get, but we need more." He looked deeply into Karzul's eyes. "We need you."

3

SHADOWS OF SURVIVAL

Karzul woke with a chill. He pulled his cloak tight, but it did little to drive away the cold. The morning should have been silent, but it was not. Buzzing swarmed around Karzul, torturing him, making returning to sleep improbable despite the earliness of the morning. The sun had yet to rise; the moon, yet to set. The usual stars were absent from the sky overhead; the moon shone blood red through the pall of smoke that lingered in the air. The field he'd slept in smelled musty. Last year's chaff decomposing beneath the clover. He sneezed twice and sat up, joints complaining from sleeping on the cold ground.

The urge to make water was nearly intolerable.

He stood, walked a short distance and began relieving himself against a rock. After a few heartbeats, a second stream joined his.

"When you get to be my age, you'll be up three, four times a night." Rodan stood beside him. "That's the secret to a long life. Drink plenty of water before you retire. You'll wake up so often that you won't get a chance to die in your sleep. Except on some days, you may wish you had. My eyesight is not what it used to be, and my hands shake. I envy you. You have your whole life ahead of you, and if you are what I think you are, it will be some life."

Karzul squinted at him. He recalled the rumors. Rodan was almost as infamous as Nephim.

"Did you lose your dragon?" Karzul asked.

"I did."

"Why not get another?"

"None accepted me." Rodan buttoned his trousers and turned to Karzul. "They knew."

In the pre-dawn darkness, it was hard to make out more than the outline of the man. He was old, with his beard neatly trimmed, and his clothes tailored to fit. Not the sort of thing Karzul expected of an outcast.

"Knew what?" Karzul asked.

"They knew I wasn't a real rider. That I didn't take care of my dragon when it came down to it. They can sense much about us. That's why you failed yesterday, is it not?"

"I was afraid."

"Are you certain that was it? Or was there something else, perhaps? Something about the dragon you selected?"

"It wasn't the one I chose for myself."

Rodan shook his head as if Karzul had confirmed his suspicions. "You let someone else choose for you? No wonder you panicked. Imagine what would have happened if you had jumped."

Karzul recalled the terror he felt standing on that span, how far down the dragons appeared, and how much farther down the bottom of the chasm. He knew in his head that leaping from the span was the only way to summon the dragon that was meant for him, but the one Nephim urged him to try for, just seemed wrong. There was no way to explain why it felt wrong; it just had, and his stomach had reacted to that feeling even before his mind had.

"Why do you think some fall and others bond?" Rodan asked. "When you choose your dragon, it chooses you. Choose incorrectly, and it rebuffs your efforts. If you had jumped, you most certainly would have fallen."

Karzul thought of Nephim and how she had fallen from her chosen steed, only to be caught by another. "That's not always what happens."

"That's right. You were friends with the girl," Rodan said.

"She was my guide, and my friend." Despite all her annoying characteristics, Nephim had been his friend. Possibly his only friend after he'd accepted her invitation to become a rider.

"Was that why you were calling out her name in your sleep?" Rodan asked.

Karzul paused. Calling out her name? As if that simple question brought it all back to him, he recalled the terrible nightmares. He'd been plagued by dream terrors. Visions of his mother in flames. His home was in flames. A fire lance pierced everyone he knew. Worse than all that was the image of Nephim's fall. Karzul had no idea what it was like to fly, but in his nightmares, he'd been there with Nephim. Sitting astride Dara'tia as they glided through the sky. The wind of their passage swept Nephim's hair out behind her, the single braid whipping in the wind.

Then the fire lance struck.

A blinding beam of blue-white light sliced through the air toward them. He'd imagined it would be like an arrow, stabbing forth to pierce them, but it was not. It was a solid beam of searing light that cut straight through the dragon's wing, slicing off half a span of the tip.

The dragon veered to the left as it lost wind, suddenly toppling, and spinning as it fell.

Nephim clamped her legs tight about the dragon's neck.

The next time the beam passed, it sliced off Dara'tia's horns. The smoldering stumps stank like burned hair as the tips turned black and fell away.

Nephim ducked before the beam struck, almost as if she'd seen it coming.

Was this a dream, or was he seeing what had happened? Why did he have such a vivid recollection of this nightmare? Was it because he wished things had gone otherwise? That he'd prevented Nephim from charging into a battle she couldn't win? Why had he dreamed this? Was it even real? Or just his mind trying to make sense of what little he did see?

The final image he saw was of Nephim releasing her grasp on the dragon and pushing herself away from it moments before the fire lance sliced through her faithful steed's neck. He would have expected more blood, but the severed head of the dragon simply parted from its body as the fire lance sliced through it. It went spinning toward the ground beside the body of the dragon, wings rippling in the air as it fell, the leather snapping as it slowed the fall of the lifeless dragon.

That was the worst scenario for any rider — losing your dragon in the sky — and it was nearly always fatal. Yet Rodan had lost his dragon. In flight, if the stories could be believed. How had he survived?

"She fell," Karzul said.

"That happens."

"Did you?"

"I did."

"How did you survive?"

"Some things are better not spoken of."

Rodan was searching the ground, collecting small sticks and cradling them in his arms.

"So if Nephim had done things differently, she could have survived as you did," Karzul said.

Rodan shrugged. "It's a possibility, but if I were a betting man, I'd not bet on it."

He had not seen Nephim fall. Perhaps there was some trick that the riders knew. Maybe she had used the dragon's wings to slow her own descent. Rodan had survived, so why not Nephim? "I choose to believe she did," he said.

"Choosing to believe something does not make it so."

"Only when proof exists to the contrary," Karzul said. "I don't know that Nephim was killed, so until I do, I choose to believe she lives."

"And what will you do about your belief?"

Karzul felt his face go flush. What would he do about it? What had he done about it? He'd thought Nephim dead. How could anyone have survived that? If he'd for one heartbeat, thought she survived that fall, he would have gone after her, but after a dream like that, was it a sending, or an accusation because he didn't immediately go look for her?

He should have rushed to find her, but he had chosen his home and his mother ahead of her. He felt shame at the thought, and a little anger. He had done what was required of a diligent son, but what if Nephim had survived?

"I'll find her," he said.

Rodan jutted his chin toward the town. "You truly think so?"

A hazy line of smoke hung over it. None of the building remained standing. Nothing but a few charred beams jutted from the smoldering gray ashes. If she fell over the town, there was no way Nephim survived. But if not, there might still be hope. He felt shame at the thought, and a little anger. He had done what was required of a diligent son, but what if Nephim had survived?

"I should have gone sooner." Karzul threw Rodan a look that demanded the old man argue with him, but Rodan only shrugged.

"Don't chastise yourself; you were busy with your home and family, were you not?"

Karzul shuddered. He had been, but that was no excuse to abandon his guide and mentor. He headed off in search of Nephim.

The once-thriving town lay in ruins, its main road trampled by fleeing survivors, with evidence of many feet and marks where heavier possessions had been dragged. It was clear that some fled with more than most, as evidenced by abandoned wealth along the way. A trunk had been broken open, and some of the clothes taken, while some of the more ornate and stylish had been left in the mud, abandoned as useless. The trunk itself was cracked as if dropped. A young woman, not much older than Karzul, wandered in the field near the path.

"Have you seen my baby?" She cried to no-one in particular. "I only left him alone for a moment. Please help me find him."

Not much farther along, Karzul almost tripped over the burned body of a child, abandoned and alone. He wondered if this was the child the woman sought, or another. The sight of it made him retch. He covered his face and continued. Entering the town proper would yield only more of the devastation he was already witnessing. He knew what was there, and he didn't want to see it.

Nephim.

This was about finding Nephim.

He'd seen her fall across town. Normally, he would have taken the main road through town, but he feared it was still blocked with the remains of beams and buildings, and the putrid stench of death was more than he could take.

He cut across the hayfield to the south of the town proper, following a little-used cattle track. The sun lit his back as the orange orb rose above the horizon. It was chilly, but the day promised to be tolerably warm later.

He soon cornered the last of the town's structures, the sun now casting a long shadow into the field to the west. This is where he'd seen the dragon fall. This was where he'd find Nephim, if she was to be found.

He shuddered. What would it be like to come across her dead body? Would her eyes be open and accusing? If only he'd had the nerve to jump. He might have influenced the fight, even if only in the slightest.

"Nephim!" he called out to her, but there was no answer.

He was beginning to think there never would be.

He shielded his face from the biting odor of death and pressed on.

By midday, he'd scoured the field. There was no dragon corpse there, just a burned circle of hay surrounding dirt that had been dug up, as if the dragon had crashed there, claws digging into the soil, then bursting into flames to be completely consumed.

Was that what happened to Nephim?

Had she been consumed by her dragon's demise?

He searched the field until the sun sank low on the horizon. He'd need to do something about food and shelter soon, or risk another night sleeping in the open.

And then what?

Strike out into the mountains?

Bring down a goat or perhaps an unwary fowl?

He would not be the only one to think of that.

He would have company.

No.

He needed a better plan than that.

As he neared the rock outcropping where he'd spent the previous night, Karzul noticed a thin line of cook-smoke snaking its way into the still afternoon air. He hoped it was Rodan. The old man was a strange one, but he had a charm about him that Karzul found comforting. Nothing seemed to bother him. Not his status as an outcast, not even the attack on the town. Rodan had shrugged when Karzul asked him if he'd lost everything in the attack. It was as if the old man knew it didn't matter, as if he had a plan, and that was precisely what Karzul needed.

Rodan bent over the fire, turning a spit. The sizzle of fat as it dripped onto the coals combined with the aroma of meat roasting to make Karzul's mouth water. Rodan must have been cooking since well before midday.

Before Karzul could say a word, Rodan asked, "Find her?" The old man did not look up from the fire, so Karzul addressed the back of his head. It made speaking about Nephim easier. "No sign of her."

Rodan shrugged. "Did you come up with a plan while you were away?"

Karzul plopped onto the ground beside Rodan. "I don't know what I'm going to do. I can't stay here. There's nothing back in town. I could head into the mountains and hunt, but I won't be the only one trying to survive on the slopes. And winter's nearly here. I could look for work in a nearby town like Untawo, but so will everyone else. Labor will be cheap. It will be hard to earn a meal every day, much less any sort of living."

Rodan nodded as if he'd already thought of these things.

"I have a plan," he said. "But you're not going to like it."

4

THE CRUCIBLE OF ASCENT

Karzul slept on and off for most of the afternoon, only to be rudely awakened by a foot in his side just as the sun was setting. The moon had only just risen, and mist already hung over the field, spreading its chill. The air reeked of burned wood, smoldering hay, and something else he didn't want to think about.

Nothing was as it should have been.

"Best we get started," Rodan said. "It's a long climb." He brushed at his neatly trimmed beard. Was it personal preference or a custom among the riders that he still followed?

Karzul rubbed his own chin. The fuzz that grew there was barely in need of attention. It would be summers before it needed regular trimming.

"Why do we have to be there at first light?" he grumbled. "Why not sleep through the night and climb in the morning, when it's safe?"

The old man threw Karzul a look that made him feel foolish for even asking. Dragons swarmed at first-light. They woke famished. That was then they left their caves for the open fields where game was plentiful. That was when every dragon, in every thunder, would pass beneath the single stone bridge. If a potential rider were to find his steed, daybreak would be the time. Later in the day, only dragons that were aged, immature, or infirm would be about, and no one wanted to bond with one of those.

The climb would be more difficult this time. The light was fading, and they would have to navigate the path with only the pale moonlight to guide their footsteps. The first time, Karzul had no real concept of what would be required of him. Now he knew. It frightened him. What if no dragon wanted him? What if he froze once more? Or worse yet, what if he fell? There was nothing he could do about any of that. He'd fill his water skin from one of the mountain streams that were so plentiful, but for food, he was dependent on Rodan, a debt he swore he would one day repay. For now, he had no choice but to accept charity.

Yet, he was uncertain about Rodan's plan. Was it the proper course of action for him?

He recalled how Nephim had stepped into the firelight as Karzul and a small group of his friends were enjoying the evening. She wore her cape and boots, polished to a shine in the firelight.

She's swept into the circle, turned to look directly at him, and said, "Karzul, you have been chosen."

A chill had gone up his spine at her words, not because of what she said, but as if her words had power over him. He peered at her; perhaps it was because of the way she carried herself, or the streak of white in her hair. Whatever it was, it was both unsettling and alluring. He wanted to tell her he was not interested, but instead he found himself drawn to her. "Chosen for what?" was all he could think to say.

"To be a dragon rider."

He'd laughed at her along with his friends. Dragon riders were not chosen; they were born. Everyone knew that. Either you had what it took to call a dragon and bond with it, or you didn't. Karzul was a nobody. A nothing. He didn't even know his father.

"The dragons have spoken," she'd said sternly.

Hatid, the more adventurous of Karzul's friends, stood up to her. "What are you playing at? It was barely a few summers ago when you used to come to the market with your fancy clothes and your silver coins to lord it over your betters. You have no business with us. Stick to the manor house. We don't take kindly to yours."

Nephim had lifted her hands to her face and called out in a tongue that was both strange and beautiful. High overhead, the screech of a dragon echoed in the distance. Flame appeared in the night, falling toward Karzul and his friends.

Hatid backed away, hands in the air as if to ward off an attack from Nephim, but his eyes turned to the sky.

Nephim had paused, her eyes piercing Hatid for a hand of heartbeats, then turned to Karzul. "Come, boy. You've been chosen. The gods know why, but you have, and I've been charged with educating you before your trial."

"What trial?" Karzul had asked, but she had not explained it that night; indeed, it was several nights or more before she let him in on what was required of him. He was to be her charge, to learn from her, and she was to be his mentor and guide, to escort him to Dragonfall, and help him secure his own dragon. She had been reluctant to speak of what to expect, where the dragon riders lived, or what they did beyond fighting the Daresh. Did she have so little faith in Karzul that she kept the secrets of the riders to herself?

He wondered if changing his mentor to Rodan would make any difference. On his first trip, he had made the journey because he wanted to prove he had what it took to become a rider, but this time, something else drove him. Was he doing this because of what had happened to Nephim? Did he feel that he was somehow taking her place, continuing her legacy? Was this his way of keeping her memory alive when she most assuredly was dead? He thought all this over and remained silent as they ascended the mountain through the twilight and into the depths of night.

The path seemed more precarious this night than it had before, the streams louder in their babbling and the sound of animals more distant, as if they had fled the mountain in fear of the carnage below. Karzul pondered his reasons for doing this again and strengthened his resolve to succeed this time. He had to. For Nephim if nothing else.

He felt no need to speak his thoughts aloud, and neither did Rodan.

Nephim had maintained a steady stream of conversation throughout their climb. Whether to remind him of his responsibilities, or to improve his odds of actually bonding with a dragon, Karzul wasn't certain. Nephim had forced him to practice the spell that would enhance his chances of bonding with his chosen dragon. He was to trace his fingers in the air in a very specific manner. She explained that the lines of the spell were critical to its success. He would need to clearly imagine the figure he drew even as he fell through the sky. That was the challenge, she'd said. To retain his presence of mind while falling.

Forgetting the spell would result in his demise.

She'd been quite clear about that.

But Rodan must have had more confidence in him. The old man remained silent throughout most of the ascent as the air grew thinner and colder. The wind whipped around the mountain and whistled down the path, kicking dust into Karzul's eyes.

The moon was high overhead when Rodan finally paused for rest. He said there was a spring nearby. Not far from the path, a small burble of water splashed from a crack in the stone that was quickly swallowed up again. After taking a heavy draught from his cupped hand, Rodan refilled his water skin, reached into his pack, withdrew a slice of jerked meat, and handed it to Karzul. The meat was heavily spiced and thoroughly dried. It was tough and busied Karzul's mouth, masticating it into something edible, preventing him from beginning any conversation. While he chewed, he considered his predicament. The old man had told Karzul that Nephim's interference could have cost him his life. Was Rodan not afraid his own interference would do likewise?

"Show me your spell," Rodan said almost offhandedly.

"Are you to be my guide, then? My mentor, as Nephim was? But you have no dragon," Karzul said.

Rodan shook his head. "I'm just here to keep you company and to make certain no one interferes with your choice. You will make a great rider, and we need all the riders we can get."

Karzul snorted. "I wish I shared your confidence."

Rodan snapped a dead branch from a nearby bush and handed it to Karzul. "Draw me your spell."

Karzul scratched a circle in the dirt beside the path. Then, there are the major divisions. He drew each of the six lines, careful to make sure they met at the proper intersection. Then he added the four small circles that Nephim had told him were the true magic of the spell, the thing that would draw the dragon's attention and hold it long enough for Karzul's mind to enter the dragon's. That was how he would begin to form the bond, and it was the bond that would be used to call and influence the dragon. After its formation, Karzul and his dragon would be close, closer even than siblings. It was a closeness Karzul had never experienced, being an only child. How would it feel to be bonded to such an ancient being?

"More like an egg." Rodan jabbed a finger at the circles in Karzul's drawing. "The egg shape reminds the dragon of the time before it hatched. It makes the creature susceptible to your thoughts. Too round, and it won't be sympathetic enough for your thoughts to sneak in."

Karzul felt like a schoolchild who'd forgotten his lessons. Nephim had never explained how the spell worked. She simply insisted that he must perfect it, or fall to his death. She had made him trace the lines over and over again, first in the dirt, then in the air, telling him he would have little time to cast the spell under very difficult circumstances. Perhaps Rodan was a better guide than she was. The old man had experience Nephim lacked after all. She'd only been a rider for half a hand of summers before she fell.

Karzul felt guilty for thinking such a thing, but he pushed the matter from his mind. They were running late. Rodan was nowhere near as agile as Nephim. They would need to keep moving to reach the bridge by sunup. If they missed their opportunity, they would have to wait another day. Karzul was not certain he would be up to the task. As it was, he was tired and distracted. He probably should have rested at the foot of the mountain for another day. Why had he let Rodan talk him into this foolishness?

"Come," Rodan said.

"What do I need to do differently this time?" Karzul asked.

Rodan just shook his head.

Despite Karzul's insistence, Rodan refused to answer questions that were not specifically aimed at how to select and bond with a dragon.

Otherwise, he remained silent all the way to the narrow span that crossed the gulf where the dragons would soon appear.

The bridge was shaped by wind over aeons past, leaving the rock formation to stretch across a canyon a hundred spans wide. The bridge curved up, reaching a man-height above the canyon walls at its center. Not that it mattered, the floor of the canyon was so far down that no estimate could be made about its distance.

The wind whistled through the gorge, threatening to send Karzul tumbling. According to legend, the wind helped the dragons take flight in the narrow chasm and aided in their return, but to Karzul, all it did was make it more precarious.

Rocks of various sizes littered the bridge. Small ones, large ones, flat shards of rock that looked as if they had been sliced from the surrounding mountains.

Karzul carefully navigated the treacherous terrain, lest he catch his foot on one of these rocks, letting the wind take him.

Soon enough, he found himself once again standing on that narrow sliver of rock looking down into the chasm. The wind was no less strong this time. His footing, no less precarious.

The last time he'd stood here, the idea of becoming a dragon rider had seemed like a glamorous prospect. Now he knew better. He'd lost everything and everyone to the Daresh. His contribution might be minor, but it might be enough. He would bond with a dragon, join the fray, and avenge his mother and Nephim. He would not back down. But why were his knees shaking then? Should he turn back now, while he still had a chance?

Karzul stood there, his gaze drawn to the dark opening where the dragons emerged. One after another, they crowded to the edge of the cave, grasped the lip with claws as large as Karzul's torso, and shoved themselves into the air. Each dragon arced from the ledge, plummeting toward the chasm below. It gave Karzul a queasy feeling in his stomach.

As they fell, the dragons spread their wings.

With a snap, the multicolored leather caught the rushing air of their fall and the wind that whistled through the canyon.

With a few beats, each dragon rose above the level of the cave as they approached the span where Karzul stood.

They were magnificent, regal, mesmerizing.

The sun had just crested the horizon and shone upon the dragons, accentuating their colors as they departed their nest in search of food.

Karzul scoured the sky for one that called to him as he'd been instructed.

But none did.

Was that the way of it? Had Nephim been wrong? Rodan? Was he not one to bond with a dragon? Would he stand here all morning without so much as a single dragon calling to him?

"Give it time," Rodan said. "The one destined to be your partner may well be a late riser."

His words did little to calm Karzul. Would he be forced to leave in shame, unsuited after all?

He let his gaze wander until an itch called to him.

There.

Far below him flew a medium-size dragon with two well-formed pairs of wings. It was a bit smaller than the one he'd selected the time before, or the one that Nephim had selected for him, but it had an appeal to him. The way it snapped its wings in time to Karzul's rapid heartbeat, the width of its tail, the way the light caught the great crenelated fan that drove it side to side. Everything about this dragon called to Karzul. It had two pairs of wings, and a deep purple color to it that shimmered in the sun.

This was it.

The one.

He was confident that the dragon for him was right below.

He called up the image of the spell and leaped into the air just as the dragon he'd chosen soared beneath the span.

For a moment, he panicked.

He was falling.

All thoughts of dragons and spells were driven out by sheer terror.

Man was not meant to fall.

Falling meant death.

But not this time.

He aimed for the dragon, spreading his arms and legs to guide his fall. The air rushed past him, and he wobbled, but he managed to stabilize himself just before impact. The dragon scales were like landing on rock covered in ice, except the dragon gave way under the impact, dropping at least a man-height before recovering. Karzul wrapped his arms and legs around its neck.

So far, so good.

He called up the image of the spell. He was to use it to begin the attachment to his dragon, to form the bond. He'd traced the path of the spell as he fell and again once he'd landed on the dragon's back. He reinforced the spell with a shimmering golden light. Nephim had explained that the light made the spell more vivid and more attractive to the dragon. The dragon would sense his thoughts and join him in imagining it. That's what would open its mind to him. After that, things were unclear. No one had ever been able to explain what came next.

The magnificent creature settled beneath him. For the briefest of moments, Karzul felt a thought begin to form. It was a nest. Not the sort of nest a bird made, but one crafted from whole uprooted trees and stone. Three eggs rested within the nest. Each day, the mother dragon visited the nest and brushed the eggs with flame until they were ready to hatch.

Karzul recognized the thought. It paralleled the spell he'd memorized. The lines represented the flame from the mother dragon; the small circles, the eggs; and the enclosing circle, the nest. This was the thought that would capture the dragon's interest and leave it open to the bond.

But how did the bond come about?

Karzul tried to overlay the image of his spell onto the faint thoughts of the dragon, but they didn't match. This dragon had emerged from a nest of three eggs. His spell had four.

Did it matter?

The dragon banked.

Hard.

Wings on one side folded tight against the creature's body as the dragon rolled. Karzul struggled to remain seated, intertwining his feet to hold on as the dragon banked violently, first one way, then the other.

The dragon had rejected him.

He felt it push his thoughts out of its mind.

It did not want him there.

It bucked wildly, and Karzul's legs came free. As if this were a signal, the dragon folded both sets of wings and nosedived. It dropped from beneath Karzul like a stone.

Once again, Karzul was falling.

He windmilled his arms and legs in the air as he tumbled. It did little to slow his fall. The rush of air past his face bit into the flesh where the previous dragon had burned him. His stomach lurched as his weight vanished. As he rotated in the air, the bottom of the canyon came into view to be rapidly replaced by the walls of rock. Would he splash into the river deep below, or be dashed to death on the rocks? Not that it mattered. At least he would be reunited with his mother.

He managed to stabilize himself so that he was no longer spinning. He wondered whether he should retain this position all the way to the ground, or perhaps make a spectacular dive. Surely Rodan would witness his demise and report back. A perfectly executed dive might earn him some honor. At least now, his spirit would be invited back to bless the planting.

A streak of vermillion rushed toward him. It was a monster dragon. Three pairs of wings. The size of a small house. Its jaws were wide open. Fire shot from between two rows of needle-sharp teeth.

Did it intend to make a meal of him? Was that why no remains had ever been found on the floor of the crevasse? Did a failed rider become a meal for one of the larger creatures?

As it approached, the image of a nest flashed in Karzul's mind once more. This time, the image perfectly paralleled his own. As if the spell had been drawn from the vermillion dragon's memory.

The dragon snapped all six wings in one fluid motion and slid beneath Karzul.

Startled, Karzul clamped his legs about a neck so stout he could barely reach around it. The image of a nest wavered, replaced by one of a young dragon. Wingless, it stumbled along the ground seeking sustenance, frightened, head swiveling to watch for predators from above.

Karzul responded with his own memories as a small child, pulling himself up on his mother's leg, eager for attention.

The dragon replied with the image of a dragon sprouting its first set of wings and taking flight.

Karzul called up the memory of a toddler struggling to maintain his balance as he took his first halting steps.

The dragon replied with another image from its past. Karzul responded in kind. On and on they went, summers passing in an instant, until the dragon delivered the image of Karzul falling.

Karzul pressed a wave of gratitude onto the creature.

The dragon screeched and soared toward the bridge.

As they rose above it, Karzul spotted Rodan standing dead center, arms spread wide. Was this how a failed rider ended up? One final leap? Was this why Rodan had accompanied him? To end his life?

Just before the mist swallowed his image, Rodan leaped from the span, arms and legs wide.

5

LEGACY OF THE FORBEARERS

Karzul felt his stomach lurch as the dragon rolled into a descent headed for the forest below. As it came into view, he noticed a vast clearing in the woods. The trees had been cut down, exposing the sand-colored earth. In the clearing was a large square of deep blue. A pond or lake, but man-made, not natural. It was half a league on a side and perfectly formed. He'd heard of this place; everyone had. It was a place where the forbearers had once lived, but now, was death to enter. The square was laced with dust-colored stripes in perfect array, separating the great pond into strips of deep azure. Square corners were the work of man.

Nestled near the square lake were a handful of buildings. Two we long and low, little more than walls that remained from ages past. The stones crumbled, the mortar shattered, the wooden roofs decayed almost to dust. The ages had not been kind to them. Beside those ruins, ran a road. Wide enough for two wagons to pass abreast. They divided the clearing in two.

Across the road from the ruins were three perfectly preserved building, surely the work of the forbearers. Two were square, standing side by side between the river and the road. The third was long and wide, with doors that could have accommodated a pair of dragons side by side. They were built of stone, the sort often left behind by the forbearers. From one building came the sound of wind, a great rushing of air that reminded Karzul of a winter storm. From the other came an insistent thrumming, a beating of a great muffled drum, consistent as a heartbeat, another relic of the forbearers, who had such power that their artifacts not only lasted through the ages, but continued to function.

The square pond fed a stream that vanished into the woods with its banks coated in white. The trees nestled along the river downstream of the site were stunted and twisted as if they were somehow sick or deformed. This too was a sign of man. It was said that the forbearers had disrespected the earth, and the earth had in turn disrespected them. Most of the wonders they created were long overgrown and torn to shreds by the earth, as if the ground itself was trying to eradicate the last memory of those who came before.

The dragon banked, and Karzul's stomach lurched.

It was headed for the clearing.

His heart raced. All across the land there were places like this. Places no one visited. Some said they were haunted by the ghosts of the forbearers, others said that the demons the earth had released to consume the forbearers that lingered, waiting for the return of the last of the dying clan.

Why would the dragon be taking him there?

The dragon stilled her wings.

The air grew silent. The wind in Karzul's face diminished as slowly, the dragon spiraled down, closer and closer to that forbidden place.

The dragon passed low over the trees. The smooth rhythm of its wingbeats was interrupted by a jerk as the dragon lowered its legs. They had been tucked up against its body for flight, but now reached for the ground. It curved its wings with a gentle snap that slowed its forward motion for half a heartbeat before settling gently on the ground. Great claws touched the dry and cracked earth. The massive vermillion canvas rippled as the dragon folded all three sets of wings, giving Karzul his first real look at them. The bones that supported the canvas were thin and light, appearing almost delicate, but Karzul had been taught that they were strong, stronger than the strongest wood, or even the iron the smiths worked to make weapons. The flesh that stretched between the bones appeared translucent, a deep network of veins spider-webbed their way from the root of the wings to their tips, where long claws stabbed from the end of those fragile-looking bones.

Karzul slid from the dragon's neck and stepped back. He had no idea what the dragon had in mind, but the idea that came to him was one of caution. His majestic companion had a mind of her own. If she was fearful, what sort of danger might they face?

Wings tucked tight, the dragon lumbered toward the edge of the pond, leaving Karzul to rush after it, hard pressed to keep pace. For such a huge creature, the dragon was limber and quick.

It paused at the edge of the pond and dipped its snout into the deep blue water.

The sound of slurping was pronounced.

Karzul knelt beside the dragon and reached for the water. If the dragon could drink it, so could he, and he was thirsty. The final trek up the mountain had yielded no water, and the dry air at altitude had left him with a powerful thirst. He was parched, and hungry, and cold. He was beginning to think that being a rider was harder than he expected, but the thrill of streaking through the sky more than made up for it. He had no idea how to control the dragon he'd bonded with. And bonded, he had. Part of his thirst was surely a reflection of the majestic creature's own desire. Whispers of thoughts that were not his own echoed in his head, almost as if he stood in a great hall listening to the far-off conversation of unseen individuals who conversed in a half-recognized language. He tried to focus on one thought or conversation, but it eluded him. All he could make out was a great thirst and a deep abiding hunger, not for flesh, but for something more, something he could not put his finger on, but was of utmost importance to his dragon.

After a bit, he abandoned his attempts to understand the dragon's thoughts and gave in to his thirst, but as he reached his cupped hands to the water, a razor sharp claw as long as Karzul's forearm reached out and nudged his arm away.

The claw was hard like iron, and curved like a raptor's, yet the way the dragon held him away from the water was gentle, but insistent, like a mother keeping a child away from danger.

The dragon continued to slurp the water noisily.

After what felt like forever, the dragon withdrew its snout and shook its massive head. Droplets of blue water struck the surface of the pond, sending a myriad of circular ripples racing across the still water. The dragon drew a deep breath and shot fire into the air, not the flames of a wood fire as Karzul had been told to expect, but a great blast of hot air that reeked of sulphur and brimstone, flames shooting forth like a fountain of water, fading into a cloud of black smoke a dozen feet from the dragon.

A feeling of intense satisfaction washed over Karzul, followed by the conviction that the dragon had finally slaked an intense thirst. So strong was it that his own thirst was quenched by the idea that permeated every bit of him. He was energized, his whole body resonating with the dragon's elation, so strong was her image in his mind. He wondered what it would be like when the dragon had other desires that it experienced or satisfied. Would he be equally influenced by those?

The dragon lowered its head, and Karzul resumed his seat. With a few quick strides, the creature spread its wings and took to the air. The clearing and pond quickly dwindled to the size of a child's toy as they climbed into the morning sky.

The mist cleared as Karzul and his dragon rose above the clouds shrouding the mountain peaks. The thrumming and rushing sound of the winds faded as they ascended to where the air was crisp and cold, and the rising sun, brilliant orange. Spread across the world below was a blanket of white streaked with amber and gray.

Karzul took it all in. Was this what Nephim experienced? Rodan?

A strange thought echoed faintly in his head. The dragon was hungry. Of course, it was. That was the whole reason the dragon had emerged from its cave at sunrise.

Not for him.

Not to create the bond.

But even as the thought crossed his mind, another one, more subdued, said that the dragon *had* been waiting for him, as if it had known he would be there.

"Hunt," Karzul whispered. He didn't feel the need to shout. Indeed, he was certain he had no need to whisper either, but he felt foolish simply thinking at the dragon. Perhaps in time, he'd grow accustomed to their bond and develop a true form of communication with her.

The dragon understood his intent. A wave of pleasure washed over him as the majestic creature folded its fore and aft wings and plummeted. Had the dragon seen something through the clouds that Karzul had not? Were they even now descending on unsuspecting prey from above?

They plunged into the fluffy white of the clouds, and the cold washed over Karzul. A cloying, damp cold that clung to him even after they sped through the thick mist.

When they emerged, the whole world had changed. The rising sun was visible only as a bright spot in the clouds that hung on the horizon. The fields below were shrouded in shadows.

The dragon banked toward a black spot in the middle of the green fields. It took a moment for Karzul to realize they were descending on Chayak, or what had once been Chayak. His heart sank. It was plain to see where the fire lance had struck. Wide swaths of the town had simply ceased to exist. In the town square, the ancient live oak was gone; generations of his forebears had sat beneath that tree. Beside it, the livery had been completely rendered to ash. Outside the livery, the charred remains of what could only be a horse lay beside a water trough, dry and scorched.

He let his gaze work its way to his own house.

Not even the outline was visible to tell him where it had been.

He shuddered.

Somewhere down there lay the remains of his mother.

The dragons must have sensed his distress. It banked sharply, taking them away from the town and over the fields and woods that

Karzul had known all his life. But soon enough, even the familiar fields were gone. The dragon lazily winged its way over woods that Karzul had heard of but never reached. They were flying low enough that he could make out the shape and color of each individual tree. Was the dragon going to land there? In the woods?

A sense of amusement came to Karzul. No. While a dragon could land in the woods, it could not take off. A dragon needed space to run before its wings became effective. Dragons leaped from the mouths of their caves into the air and gained speed that way, but on the ground, they must run. Trees made that impossible. A dragon would be vulnerable in the woods, open to whatever wished to prey upon it. And people said there were beasts that would prey upon a grounded dragon.

Karzul wondered what such beasts might be, but no image came to his mind.

As they flew, the trees thinned. A large meadow filled with wild grass lay directly ahead. A herd of deer grazed in the distance, oblivious to the danger winging its way toward them.

A thought came to Karzul that it was best to be first to the hunt, before the prey realized what was happening.

The dragon locked its wings, folding the fore and aft wings against its body, and twisting the mid pair to create a deeply curved surface. The world went silent.

Almost gently, they glided toward the herd.

A buck with large and complex antlers grazed at the edge of the herd. How any animal could support such a weight was beyond Karzul's experience. The buck stood half a dozen hands taller than the nearest animal. It grazed with its head down as it nipped at the long grass. Karzul tried to count the points on its antlers, but he had no time.

He had already experienced the dramatic dive of the dragon with its stomach-twisting weightlessness, but this was the opposite of that. His weight seemed to increase as the dragon turned from its dive to glide at treetop height straight for the buck. It was exhilarating and brought with it a familiar echo of a thought that Karzul was coming to understand emanated from the dragon. She was eager for the hunt. As if it had been too long since she'd hunted. She was hungry, but that was not all. She needed the thrill of the kill. All this came to Karzul as a rapid stream of images.

Karzul held on for fear of falling from his perch even as the dragon radiated a surge of satisfaction. A jerk nearly threw him from his seat as the dragon's claws grasped the buck and drove it into the ground, coming to an abrupt halt.

The buck screamed and thrashed, but it had little effect on the talons that held it fast.

The dragon reared its head, letting out a screech that was so loud Karzul had to cover his ears to keep from going deaf.

It paused and looked at Karzul.

For the life of him, he was certain the dragon was offering him the honor of the kill. It brought back memories of his first hunt, when he and Burem had managed to snare a hare by its leg. The poor creature tugged at the snare, the cord digging deep into its leg. He'd thought hares were silent, but this one screamed much as the buck had.

"It's your kill," Karzul had told Burem.

"I ... I can't," Burem had thrown down the knife and turned away. He had no stomach for killing.

Not so, Karzul.

"It's suffering." He reached for the hare, pinning down its body, the silky smooth fur beneath his grip. He grasped the hare by the back of the neck and twisted.

With a sickening snap, the hare fell still.

It had been Karzul's first kill, and that memory had never left him.

A satisfying feeling of kinship flooded Karzul, bringing him back to the present.

With a snap, the dragon's beak struck the buck's neck, breaking it easily.

The buck ceased its thrashing.

For a moment, Karzul felt guilty for taking such a prize. This was the sort of beast seasoned hunters respected too much to bring down unless they were desperate. The thought must have amused the dragon. It projected an image of a twenty-point buck being snatched up and consumed in a single bite.

With that thought, the dragon began its feast. The dragon's jaw was filled with two rows of knife-sharp teeth that tore at the buck, slicing chunks from its flesh. The dragon tossed its head back and swallowed each chunk like an oversized raptor. While Karzul could have lived off that meat for half a moon if properly dried, the dragon had nearly consumed the entire buck in the span of a handful of heartbeats.

Before it finished gorging itself, the dragon tore a slice of meat from the side of the buck and placed it on the ground. It opened its jaws and let forth a gentle stream of fire, holding it on the meat until it was evenly roasted.

It nudged the meat toward Karzul.

The flesh of the buck was tender and juicy, one of the better cuts of meat Karzul had tasted in a long time. It satisfied a hunger that Karzul had not known he possessed. Was this the way it would be from now on? Would he be sharing in the kill of the dragon? He bit at the meat, tearing chunks from it with his teeth. He wished he had brought his knife, but it was in his pack, and his pack was back at the stone bridge. For the briefest of instants, Karzul recalled Rodan falling. Without Rodan, he would not be here, not be bonded to the dragon. He wondered what had become of the man. Had he found a new dragon or fallen to his death?

When Karzul finished eating, he turned to the dragon. "Thank you for this. I think this is the beginning of a great friendship."

The dragon snorted, but the thought it pushed his way was one of collegiality and comradeship.

It had accepted him.

But why?

In the wild, dragons fed, and mated, and kept to themselves. Most folks hated them. While they generally kept away from populated areas, they occasionally raided farms, and that led to conflict between man and dragon.

Karzul recalled a time when a dragon had raided a prosperous farm not far from Chayak. The farmer had recruited several of his neighbors and set a trap for the dragon. They had tied a lamb to a stake in the field where the dragon had been spotted and waited. When the dragon arrived to consume the lamb, the men attacked.

Even though it was aged and infirm, the dragon managed to kill three of the men before one was able to work a spear beneath the iron-like scales and strike at something vital. The men had severed the head and left the carcass to rot. They carried the head through Chayak as if it were a prize won in battle.

Wild dragons were considered little more than animals, acting on instinct. It was only after forming a bond with a human that they showed not only intelligence, but a deep wisdom that most men lacked. Was that why they bonded with humans?

Karzul's admiration for the riders had been based on their bravery and their ability to ride their dragons into war against the Daresh. Yet, the Daresh possessed their own riders. Were those who rode the dragons in Daresh equally looked upon with awe and respect? They had harnessed their dragon to their will, also, had they not?

The image that the dragon pressed into his mind was one of laughter. The bond was not one of control or influence, but merely a shared thought. If the dragon wished it, it could break the bond at any moment and return to its former life. It accepted the bond and cooperated simply because it wished to. No more, no less. Even so, Karzul thought there was more to it than that. Something the dragon was not sharing.

He worried.

What if this dragon decided to return to its natural state in the middle of battle? Would it dump Karzul into the air and flee? How could he ever trust it?

He pushed the thought at the dragon, but the only response he received was one of exhaustion. The dragon was tired. Even though it was still morning, it had already been a long day for both of them. His concerns could wait for now. He realized that he too was tired, so very tired. He needed to sleep, and the sun was poking through the clouds, and the breeze was starting to grow warm, and the grass was soft, and the dragon beside him was already sound asleep.

He laid his head on the dragon's neck and drifted off to sleep.

When Karzul woke, it was nearly midday.

The dragon roused itself, raised its head and glanced around. It stood and shook its body; the scales clanking together like iron plates. It stretched and dug its front claws into the ground before glancing at Karzul and lowering its head to the ground.

Karzul mounted, and they were off, but where?

The dragon lumbered along, slowly at first, but gaining speed. Karzul worried that there might not be enough room for the dragon to gain the velocity it needed to become airborne. The jerking intensified until Karzul felt he was about to be thrown off when the dragon spread her wings wide, pushed off with her hind legs and lifted from the ground.

It was not the leap into the air that a bird makes, but a lumbering slow climb as the dragon transitioned from earthbound to airborne. She spread all three sets of wings and flapped rhythmically. As soon as they were properly airborne, the dragon alternated between pairs of wings. The ride became smooth, and the ground fell away; the trees melding into a lush carpet of green that covered the low rolling hills.

As they climbed higher and higher, Karzul took in the countryside. He half expected to see smoke rising from Chayak, but there was none, only a swath of ash where the town lay, but that soon vanished behind them. The dragon had a destination in mind, but where that was, was a mystery. Nephim had been closed-lipped about such things, focusing on dragon lore, and how to read star signs and constellations, as if something like that would ever be needed. Karzul probed for answers, but received none.

He pushed a thought to his dragon, wondering where she was headed. He half expected no answer, but what did happen took him completely by surprise. For a moment, he was high above the clouds, looking down on mountain peaks covered in snow. One peak stood out, flattened on top with a great citadel sprawling across the plateau. The colors were all wrong. Instead of the gray of stone, the structure radiated with a faint green glow, showing him that it shed its warmth into the frigid air. The image shifted into the normal visage and back so rapidly Karzul became dizzy.

His vision zoomed in to see a number of stone carvings in the likeness of men and dragons. He had no idea where such a place might be, but apparently that was where the dragon was headed.

The vision faded to reveal the land below. Rivers snaked across fields and into woods as the landscape undulated into rolling hills. The mountains where the stone bridge was located lay to the south, but the dragon was taking him north. The land grew unfamiliar. Ponds and lakes flashed beneath them as they sped through the clear sky.

Karzul spotted a body of water that stretched so far into the horizon he could not see its northern shore. He wondered whether he was looking at a lake or a sea. A pang of fear shot through him. He had never learned to swim. What if something happened, and he was unceremoniously dropped into that water? Was its water fresh or salty? How wide would a body of water need to be if he could not see the far side?

Karzul felt a sharp ache in his lower jaw. Saliva poured across his tongue. Salt. He tasted the salt. An inland sea. He'd heard rumors of the salty sea, but never expected to see it firsthand. Karzul spat in disgust.

The dragon angled its head to look at him. Was that amusement showing in her huge yellow eye?

Karzul spat again.

The dragon was in his head.

Would his thoughts ever be his own again?

6

BEYOND THE STORMY SKIES

he dragon flapped its wings, carrying Karzul across the vast inland sea and into the strange mountains. The peaks were covered in white, not with clouds, but with snow that was constantly being torn from the jagged rocks in the wind. The air was clear, but breathing became difficult. With the approach of evening, it was cold. Bone chilling cold. Yet, the scene remained peaceful and silent, save for the rhythmic flapping of the dragon's wings. The dragon radiated a warmth that took away the worst of the chill. Karzul realized how unprepared he'd been. He'd worn warm clothes to Dragonfall, but he had not been prepared for this. Thankfully, the dragon provided some measure of protection.

"Where are we headed?" He asked, not really expecting an answer.

In response, an image came to mind, but not just an image, an overwhelming sensory vision that filled his mind to overloading. He felt as if his head were about to burst.

"Not so much," he cried out.

The vision faded to one his human mind could comprehend. The mountain with a plateau cut into the top. He'd seen this before. As he expected, the location matched what the dragon had hinted at, but this time there was more detail. A large orange sun set behind the plateau, casting long shadows on the twin monoliths that guarded the doorway at the top of a long stairway leading from the edge of the plateau. The structure appeared to have been carved from the mountain itself, gray granite that had been trimmed square with a flat roof. Along the face of the structure was a portcullis, a roof supported by dozens of pillars, easily twice the height of his dragon. They stood in perfect lines on either side of the entrance.

The entrance was flanked by a pair of statues. On the left was a dragon, wings folded back, mouth open, a foreleg extended, claws open as if prepared to grasp anyone who dared enter. It was nearly the size of Karzul's dragon, but not as mature, with only two pairs of wings.

On the other side stood a statue of a man. It was larger than life, as if to compete with the statue of the dragon. The figure stood straight and tall, his hair and beard neatly trimmed. He was clothed in uniform. A thick jacket, adorned with straps and numerous pockets, dropped well below his waist. Heavy trousers were tucked into thigh-length boots with thick heels. The man reminded Karzul of Rodan somehow. Why?

The vision faded as the dragon plunged into a bank of fast-moving clouds. The clouds were cold, dark, and foreboding.

Storm clouds.

Thunder rolled, echoing off the mountains.

Lightning lit up the sky.

Chills raced down Karzul's spine.

The lightning was so close he could smell it.

Thunder rumbled as the lightning flashed.

A blast of snow blinded Karzul.

Air currents caught the dragon from below, sending it lurching upwards, leaving Karzul with a sickening feeling. The sense of peril gnawed at him. His dragon was struggling.

A downdraft caught the dragon, sending her plunging.

The dragon folded her fore and aft wings, leaving just the larger mid wings stroking against the streaking white that obscured everything.

Again and again, lightning blinded Karzul.

Gusts of unseen wind shears knocked the dragon about.

He held on for dear life.

But as Karzul feared the worst, the dragon emerged from the clouds. The air stilled, and the thunder rumbling behind them diminished. Ahead lay the exact scene she had pressed upon his mind. Everything was as the dragon had portrayed it, the long stairs even more impressive in real life than in his vision. The setting sun was wondrous to behold, a great orange globe resting atop the distant mountain peak, casting long dark shadows onto the great stone portcullis.

The dragon settled onto the plateau and lumbered up the steps, stopping before the statue of the glaring dragon. It lowered its head and deposited Karzul on the great slab of granite that lay before the huge main doors to the structure. Beside the statue of the dragon, a large pit of sand had been meticulously carved from the raw rock. For what purpose? The sand steamed with heat in the chill air. Karzul wrapped his light cloak around himself and shivered. He hoped the doors were unlocked. He needed to seek shelter, and soon.

Without preamble, the dragon curled up in the sand, lowered its head, and was soon snoring loudly.

Karzul stood there, taking it all in. He was a rider. This was the place he had so longed to see, even if he had only just now come to know of its existence.

But what now?

There was nothing to do but enter.

If he could.

The doors were tall. Tall enough to admit even his dragon with ease. Towering oak beams braced with beaten iron hung from hinges of brass. A large ring adorned the door at about the height it would need to be to be grasped by a dragon. Below, at man-height, was another ring more suited to his hands.

He pulled at it, but nothing happened.

Were the doors locked?

He hoped not. The temperature was falling, and he was shivering. His teeth chattered as he bent to examine the door.

The ring hung from a stud placed in the middle of a large brass circle. The circle was engraved with designs representing the major constellations. The outer ring rotated freely, bearing symbols of the planets. Vague recollections of one of Nephim's lectures on the night sky came edging into his awareness. He tried lining the figures up as she had indicated they would be in the sky. At this time of the season, the Wanderer was high overhead in the sky, as was the constellation of Oterat, the hunter. He tried arranging the figures and pulled at the ring once more.

Nothing.

He looked to the sky.

Clouds obscured the stars.

He bent to examine the images more closely.

Tiny lines radiated from the center circle that almost matched the outer ring.

He shifted the outer ring to carefully line up the radial lines and was rewarded with a clicking sound even as a gust of wind blew his cloak open, sending shivers up his back. He yanked the ring, and the towering oak door swung slowly open.

A rush of warm air greeted him.

It was a relief from the frigid air at these heights.

Behind the doors stretched a hall a dozen spans wide. Polished granite had been laid on a perfectly flat and nearly seamless floor. The tiles reflected the ceiling and the great pillars that supported it. Dusty footprints bore evidence of recent use.

As he stepped inside, the interior of the building burst into light.

There were no torches and no lamps.

The light appeared to emanate from the junction of the walls and the ceiling high overhead. It was a steady light, like the light of the sun, and not that from a lantern or candle.

Was it magic?

The light revealed images painted on the pillars and walls.

He approached one wall.

Not paintings.

Mosaics.

Karzul ran his fingers along the likeness of a dragon's tail. Tiny green tiles had been carefully cut and set to create the image. The colors were vivid and brilliant, almost as if they provided light and not reflected it.

He stepped back to view the entire dragon.

Each tile was a slightly different shade of green.

They glittered in the strange light.

He leaned in again.

Dragon scales.

A painting made of dragon scales.

The artist had worked in a medium that provided an array of colors and sizes ranging from as small as a fish scale, to plates the size of Karzul's head.

Every mosaic depicted a dragon and its rider. Many of them showed a man or woman standing by a dragon, as if posing for a crowd. Others showed dragons in flight. In these images, the rider held a lance that could only be one of the famed fire lances. The sort of weapon that the Daresh had used against Chayak.

From what little Karzul knew about the fire lances, they had been created by the forbearers who had long since disappeared. Fire lances were rare. Nephim said that only a few had been found, and none of them worked. How the Daresh had found one, much less gotten it to work, was a concern to the riders. It was a weapon so powerful that it had changed the balance of power between the two warring nations.

A chill breeze brushed past Karzul. He needed to find a place to sleep. His dragon was already sound asleep. Who knew when it would wake? He had to find shelter somewhere. While the great hall was warmer than the outdoors, it was not a place he would welcome spending the night.

His footsteps echoed as he made his way deeper into the structure. The light shifted as he walked, illuminating his footsteps. Anticipating his future path? Or determining it? Karzul didn't know.

Eventually he reached a raised dais. Behind the dais, a wall rose all the way to the ceiling of the structure, decorated with a mosaic of a single dragon. One with four sets of wings! On the dais sat a pair of chairs, thrones, for what else could they be? Each chair was intricately carved from a dark red wood, depicting vines intertwined with leaves and acorns. The seat and back were upholstered with a red velvet that showed no signs of wear or even use. The back of each chair was a head taller than Karzul and topped with a dragon perched above, wings stretched wide as if protecting the one seated beneath.

Beside the thrones, a short ornate wall formed an octagon easily large enough for Karzul's dragon to curl up within. Inside the octagon was a fine, smooth, manicured layer of sand. The sand was warm and drove the chill from his bones. More space for a dragon to warm itself? This place had certainly been built for man and dragon both.

Karzul stepped onto the sand. It was warm, almost hot. He dug his feet into it. Pure white, as fine as sugar or salt. He felt bad disturbing the perfectly flattened surface. Certainly, someone had worked diligently to smooth it out.

He traced a line in the sand with his foot, then another. Before he knew it, he had the spell he'd used to attract his dragon. It seemed to come alive, and a thought entered his head. He recognized it as the thoughts of his dragon, but much weaker than they had been before.

Had he inadvertently summoned her?

He scraped the lines away with his foot and sat for a while, letting the heat soak into him and drive away the cold.

He was not sure how long he remained seated, but the sand warmed him up to the point that the growling in his stomach became apparent. He was hungry. He hadn't eaten since early in the morning when the dragon had offered him the roast meat.

"Is there anyone here?" he called out, his cries echoing from the distant walls. While the place had the feel of emptiness, he sensed that it was not abandoned. Perhaps everyone was busy elsewhere. The war?

He made his way to a hallway that led south, away from the grand hall. The hallway was wide enough for two dragons to walk abreast.

Karzul passed by doorways tall enough to admit a dragon, and some built low, only for men.

He opened a man-high door at random, hoping to find a kitchen, or a privy, for he was going to need both of those soon.

As the door swung open, a dim red light appeared along the

perimeter of the room not far from the ceiling. It grew in intensity until he was able to make out the contents of the room. The interior was long and narrow, packed with beds, three to a stack. The chamber and its row of beds was so long it disappeared into the shadows.

Karzul tried to calculate how many people could sleep here. A hundred? Maybe more. Who had slept here? Was it possible dragon riders had once rested in these bunks? He stepped into the room and ran a hand over the nearest bed frame.

Not a hint of dust.

The place had recently been cleaned.

Every bed was made perfectly, the blankets stretched tight and the sheets perfectly folded.

Karzul wondered why his dragon had brought him here if the riders were elsewhere. It gave Karzul pause. Did all those beds belong to dragon riders? How many were there, or were they for troops or servants? Were there once a host of riders and now no longer? Was there a lack of dragons or riders? Surely not dragons, for the thunders that Karzul had witnessed when he bonded with his own dragon had certainly been plentiful. Even so, there were at least a handful of riders. If this was their base of operations, where were they?

But he had more pressing matters to worry about.

If there were beds, most certainly, there would be a privy.

There was.

Relieved, Karzul continued his search for a kitchen.

He walked along a hallway intended for human use. Every few yards, there were doors on either side. Each one had a slate mounted on it. Some of them had names scrawled in a heavy hand, but most did not.

Did that mean that there were only a handful of riders? From what he knew, that was the case, but the number of doors spoke to a time when there had been many more.

He paused at one of the doors with a clean slate.

Was this room free? Would he be assigned to one of these, or to a bunk in the larger room?

He opened the door to find the room clean, but empty. A desk and chair sat along one wall, one door at the far end of the room opening into a bedchamber, the other opening onto a water closet.

A personal water closet.

He'd never imagines such luxury.

He wondered who would be assigned to a place like this, then felt a twinge of guilt for intruding.

His stomach rumbled, reminding him that he was in search of sustenance.

The dining hall, when he located it, was near the rooms with the slates. Apparently, those rooms were for the more privileged riders who would not want to waste their time traversing the hallways for meals. The dining hall was long and narrow, with rows of tables arranged end to end. A low bench stood beside each table to accommodate at least a dozen diners. Most of the benches had been turned upside down and rested on the tables. Only two tables gave the appearance of recent use. Chairs had been hastily shoved beneath the table, which bore crumbs as if abandoned in a hurry.

With a dining hall like this, the kitchen must surely be nearby.

His hunger was growing.

Before he could locate the kitchen, a faint screech reached his ears.

It sounded like a dragon.

Outside.

Was it his dragon calling for him?

No.

The sound seemed to be coming from far away.

Karzul rushed from the kitchen back into the narrow hallway, the echoes of his footsteps reverberating off walls too far away to see. He raced across the grand hall and yanked the tall door open, emerging onto the granite stoop just as the sound of a dragon pierced the air.

He squinted into the sky, trying to make out what it was behind the driving snow, pulling his cloak tighter around himself as the wind tore at it.

There.

Amidst the swirling flurries, a lone dragon materialized in Karzul's line of sight.

Did that mean the riders were returning? But he saw only one. A single dragon positioned itself for the descending glide. Wings spread wide. Ebony. One set.

Nephim's dragon had only one set of wings, but he'd seen her fall. Could there be more than one immature dragon bonded to a rider?

His heart beat fast as he stood transfixed.

Beside the door, his own dragon lifted her head and gazed into the sky. She let out a screech and then, as if disinterested, laid her head back down, closing her eyes.

Was he about to meet someone in authority or an enemy? Was this where the Daresh riders made their home?

What would he do if it was? He had no weapon and no training, but his dragon seemed unfazed by the newcomer. Did that mean there was no threat to Karzul, or just not to his dragon? She had so far demonstrated a willingness to protect him. He could not believe she would lay down and sleep if there was any danger.

He did not have long to wait.

The dragon stilled its wings and floated onto the plateau, skipping the ascent of the steps that his own steed had made. Rather, it flared to a stop at the head of the steps, a single pair of wings snapping as they brought the dragon to a halt.

It settled to the ground and lowered its head.

The rider nimbly dismounted and turned to him. He could not tell if it was a man or a woman, for the face was covered with a thin cloth. To protect against the chill air?

The voice that spoke was female and familiar. "I hope you found your way to the kitchen. I'm starving."

The rider reached up and unfastened her face covering.

It was Nephim.

7

A GLIMMER OF TRUTH

Karzul pushed the plate away and belched into his hand to stifle it. Nephim had shown him the kitchen, and together they'd prepared a dish of seared meat and spicy noodles. Small cubes of lamb dipped in spiced flour were cooked in oil and added to a mushroom sauce that, to Karzul's surprise, contained wine. The same wine that Nephim had served with dinner. He'd never tasted wine. Mead occasionally, but never wine. It was strong on his palate, but tasty. He could get used to it.

After the meal, Nephim insisted that they wash and re-stock whatever utensils and cutlery they had used.

"Didn't you have servants for this?" he asked.

"Do you see any servants?" she replied. "Besides, doing what needs doing is part of the discipline of a rider. Did it not give you satisfaction to restore order and cleanliness to this place?" She wiped a finger along the edge of the counter and held it up for examination.

It was spotless indeed.

"When you rise in the morning," she continued. "You make your bed. You perform your morning ritual. You wash your face and put on your uniform. Then you come to the morning meal." She raised an eyebrow at him. "Not before."

Karzul felt like a child who'd been reprimanded, but who was he to argue? "I understand."

"Good," she said. "Let's find a place for you to sleep. It's getting late."

"I already found the sleeping area," he said. "The large room with all the beds."

"Not there. You're an officer. You have private quarters."

"An officer?" Karzul had no idea how the riders were organized.

"We are officers. We ride our dragons into battle."

"But I saw you fall," Karzul blurted. "Your dragon was killed. Rodan said the dragons rejected him because he lost his dragon. Why not you? How did you survive?"

"I didn't lose my dragon. She was blasted out from under me. But I didn't fall. Not all the way. Dara'tia was hit. Tore a rip in her wing. We both fell, but in the end, she managed to save me. I thought I was dead. I was so close to the ground. But at the last moment, she swooped underneath me. She ended up tumbling along the ground instead of landing. We were so close to the town that the smoke was overwhelming, but we made it. She was nearly killed, but as you can see, she survived. I sewed up her wing. She will heal in time. Dragons are resilient like that. They heal faster than we do."

"But I saw you fall. I saw your dragon beheaded by the fire lance."

"Whatever you saw, or thought you saw. It wasn't me. After Dara'tia was able to fly again, I tried to find you. We need you. Look at this place. It's empty. I was desperate to find you. I circled the town for half the night. You weren't there."

Karzul nodded slowly. "I was asleep in a field, then climbing the mountain with Rodan."

Nephim raised an eyebrow at Karzul as if skeptical about his story. She clicked her tongue. "How did you get that dragon outside to bring you here?"

"I didn't get her to do anything. She just brought me."

Nephim glanced at his dragon, then looked at him curiously. "What's her name?"

"Name? How would I know?"

"Did you ask her?"

"No. They can speak? All I got was images."

"She should have told you by now," Nephim said. "How do you address her? How did you bond with her and not know her name?"

How indeed.

Karzul shrugged.

"Ask her when she wakes." Nephim waved her hand in dismissal. "Let's get you settled. We can worry about the dragons in the morning. I'm exhausted, and the sooner I get you settled, the sooner I can get settled."

Nephim led him along a human-size hallway and stopped by the second door. The door bore a chalkboard, on which she marked his name. "So you can find it back. I'll see you at first light."

Karzul watched as she vanished down the hall before opening the door. The room was larger than the modest house he'd shared with his mother. There were no windows. The room was lit from above by the glowing strips that seemed to be in every room. The light had come on when he entered and gone off when he exited. The bedchamber light worked the same way. He wondered how one turned it off when one wished to sleep.

The bedchamber contained a bed, a dresser, and a wardrobe. The dresser contained small clothes, socks, and a supply of washcloths and towels. It contained half a dozen uniforms, much like the one that adorned the statue up front. Karzul fingered the cloth. Heavy but not coarse. He'd imagined himself in this uniform ever since Nephim had called him out. It saddened him that his mother would never see him in it. He held it up and looked at himself in the mirror. It looked to be tailored for him. Had Nephim prepared it? How had she known he would be here, or had she prepared the way for him before his failure that day? He would make up for that. He would make her proud.

He closed the wardrobe door and examined the rest of the bedchamber. There was a small door that led to a privy. His own privy, with a pump, a sink, and a porcelain chamber pot that was fastened to the floor. How odd.

A second door led to a sitting room, with a pair of comfortable chairs and a low table. A writing desk was set against the far wall, with a simple upholstered chair nestled against it. To the left of the writing desk was a long, thin door, taller than he was, and about three hand spans wide. It was carved out of the same stone as the wall, and he almost missed it. In the center of the door, was a slight impression.

He ran his hand over it.

It was palm-shaped.

Barely a fingernail's thickness in depth, with a pronounced ridge.

He placed his palm within the impression.

A perfect fit.

He pressed.

Nothing.

Of course not. Why had he thought it would open for him? Surely there was a key, or a spell that would open it.

He sat down at the writing desk.

A recessed ring bore a hole large enough to place his finger in. It tilted up, and a drawer popped open.

"Let's see what you left for me, shall we?" he asked no one in particular.

The drawer contained one item. It was a rectangle of glass set in a thin silver frame, much like a fancy mirror, but it was not a mirror. The glass was clear.

He lifted it out and held it up.

It came alive. The glass shimmered as if lit from behind. Running along the frame were a series of what looked to be engraved images, a digit on each side. Each one was different. They were all strange and unfathomable, save one. The artisan had taken great care to create an image that, while small and indistinct, clearly portrayed a sword.

He touched it.

The glass flickered, and words appeared along the upper edge. At least he thought they were words. Strange symbols were grouped together into clumps that scrolled across the top of the glass. After a few heartbeats, the outline of a hand appeared on the glass.

He placed his palm within it.

Was it another lock like the one on the wall?

As his palm touched the glass, light flared. A brilliant bar of green light appeared along the left side of the glass. It swiped quickly to the right and back again, then fell dark once more.

He lifted his palm from the glass.

A glowing palm print remained where his hand had rested.

It looked familiar.

In the middle of the palm, lay a scar. The wound had bled profusely and taken a full moon to heal, and he would carry that scar as a reminder of his carelessness for the rest of his life.

What did that mean?

Had the glass recognized his hand?

Was that what the green light was all about?

Had it recorded the image of his palm?

Why?

Was it somehow tied to the narrow locked door?

He placed the glass back in the drawer, pushed the chair beneath the table, and stepped up to the narrow door. It appeared to be some sort of storage locker.

For more equipment?

He placed his palm on the impression.

There was a slight warmth as his flesh contacted the surface.

He pressed.

With a click, the door popped open.

The cupboard was narrow, only a few hands deep. Inside, a long silver metal staff was clipped to the wall. The shaft was almost as long as was tall; a metal rod the size of his wrist ended in a barrel that was bound in rope. But the rope was made of metal. Not the silver metal of the shaft, but braided copper. The ends of the rope vanished into the shaft. Around the shaft, about midway, was a wooden grip that sported a few small studs. For some reason, when he looked at the lance, he got the same feeling he did when he'd first met Nephim. Were they somehow connected?

He reached for the lance but pulled back, hesitating. The lance gave him the same feeling he had experienced when he had met Nephim for the first time. A tingling warmth in his blood, as if his heart had grown warmer and that warmth was spreading through his body.

He glanced back at the strange device.

Who had this belonged to? The same person who owned the glass?

Why had the door opened the second time he tried it and not the first?

Had the glass unlocked a spell?

Nephim had chosen this room seemingly at random. Had he taken command of it by placing his hand on the glass?

He looked at the shaft. What possible use could it be? The picture on the glass indicated a sword, but this was not a sword. He reached for it, drawing it from its clips. It was light, much lighter than he expected. The metal felt almost warm in his grip.

He leveled it at the door, checking its balance, letting his fingers wrap the wood at the middle of the staff. It felt natural to hold it there.

His fingers touched the studs, but he refrained from pushing them. There was no way of knowing what might happen. If it was a weapon, he'd best wait until he was outside to investigate, lest he discharge it in his room.

He tested the fit and balance of the thing.

It was perfect.

His fingers rested on the small studs.

They fit his hand as if had been made for him.

He placed the staff back in the locker and closed the door.

It clicked shut and blended almost perfectly back into the wall.

So much for that.

He would investigate further in the morning.

But for now, he needed to rest.

He was exhausted.

He could learn more about the staff later.

When he woke in the morning, he knew what it was.

8

A FLICKER OF DESPAIR

The next morning, Karzul rose to a light brighter than the dawn. Where was he? He glanced around the room. Bed, wardrobe, and a door that opened into a privy. The room was chilly. It had a faint, musty smell that he could not place. It was silent. No roosters crowed nearby, nor even off in the distance. No wind whistled through cracks in boards, for there were no boards. Nothing intruded except the sound of his own breathing.

He threw back the blanket and slid to the edge of the bed. His feet touched the cold tile. Colder than he'd expected.

He palmed the door open to check that the fire lance was still there. It rested in the holder, just where he'd placed it. He thought of taking the lance with him. But no. Not yet. He wasn't ready to share what he had discovered. Not until he knew more. He felt bad hiding something from Nephim, but he hadn't yet come to terms with what he'd found. A fire lance could change the course of the war if he could figure out how to use it and survive an encounter with the Daresh fire lance wielder. Nephim had told him a fire lance had once been found, but no one was able to operate it. He wondered if this one was also useless, or perhaps it was just what was needed. So much had happened in such a short period. His head was spinning.

He made his way to the kitchen.

Nephim was already at work, breaking eggs. "Hard time getting dressed?" She inclined her head toward the slab of pork belly on the cutting board. "Cut that, would you?" Karzul was impressed. "Meat and eggs. Never had both of them in one meal before. We couldn't afford it."

"Thin slices," she said. "You're going to fry them up while I cook the eggs." She grabbed the knife and shifted it from hand to hand, twirling it in the air, with a familiarity Karzul envied. She caught it with her left hand and deftly sliced a thin strip from the meat. She switched the knife to her right hand and deftly cut away another thin slice. "Like that," she said.

"Sorry. I woke when the light came on. I wasn't sure how quickly I needed to be here."

"With just the two of us, take your time. When everyone else is here, the rules are a bit less strictly interpreted."

"How many riders are there?" Karzul asked.

"Only a handful remain. At last count, there were thirty of us."

Karzul sliced half a dozen thin slices of salt pork and placed them in the pan.

He glanced over at Nephim. Was that a tear in her eye?

"But this place was built for hundreds," he said.

Nephim didn't look at him. She sniffed and violently attacked the pan in front of her. "It's been a long war," she finally said.

She stirred the pan once more, slid the cooked eggs onto a plate, and then turned to him.

"We've lost our best and brightest. The way things are going, within a moon, there'll be nobody left, and the Daresh will overrun Thera, and there will be no one to stop them."

She paused as if composing her thoughts. "If I had been more advanced in my training, I might have been able to take out the Daresh Flame Rider, that would have turned the tide of the war."

"How many fire lances do they have?" Karzul asked.

According to our spies, only one. The gods know where they found that one, or how they got it to work. Everyone thought they were lost to the depths of time, or no longer functional."

She took a deep breath and continued as if unprepared to pursue the current line of thought. "While in training, one of our duties is to tend the injured."

"My mother taught me a little about healing," Karzul said. "She used to make medicine for the locals, before..." Karzul paused. Talking about his mother brought back the memories of a burning Chayak.

Nephim laid a hand on his shoulder. "We've all lost someone. That's why we fight. And why we train as medics. Not just broken bones, minor cuts, that sort of thing, but wounds of war. Sometimes we have to remove a limb to save a life. Sometimes we can't do anything. If a fire lance severs an artery, that dragon rider..."

"Is dead." Karzul finished the sentence for her, supplying the words she didn't want to say. "Are they in battle right now?"

"Heading into it. They're flying to the border. This is our last-ditch effort. If we can't stop them now, there is no stopping them. They'll burn every town and village in Thera."

They continued to eat in silence. They cleaned the kitchen in silence. A hundred leagues to the south, the dragon riders were preparing to engage the Daresh in battle. Karzul could not imagine what it must be like for them, facing the fire lance as Nephim had. They were his kin now, even though they had not met. It was all the family he had left.

"Ready for your first lesson?" Nephim interrupted his reverie.

Karzul nodded and followed her through a set of tall double doors that opened into a wide hall filled with beds for the injured. The sheer number of beds was mind-boggling. Were there so many injured in battle? Karzul remembered the burn victims left to suffer after the Daresh had destroyed his town.

He shuddered.

"When they're brought in," Nephim explained. "They all start here. We look them over and decide which ones can be saved and which ones are too far gone."

Karzul tried to imagine what she was telling him. The idea of death seemed somehow honorable, but injury on this scale was something else.

"Karzul?" Nephim turned to him, her face in a scowl. "Are you listening?"

Karzul simply stared at her.

"I know it's a shock, Karzul, but that's what war is."

"Why do we have to fight? Is there no other way? Why not let them have the land? How can they be any worse than our own lords?"

"You mean my family?" she asked. "Those the Daresh would execute to take their lands?"

"No. Not them, but..." Karzul paused. He hadn't thought it through. But why had the war started in the first place? It had been going on for summers, generations. "Why do they want our land?"

"They hate us. They hate our society. They want to abolish the lords and nobles and make everyone equal, or so they say. They will take our land and kill our people if we don't stop them. Giving in would mean the end of my family. The Daresh are known for their cruelty. They don't care one whit for the folk who live on their lands, only that they're in control."

"It's all so horrible," Karzul shuddered.

"Our job for now is to find the injured and bring them back here. We tend to them. Patch them up. So they can return to battle."

"Return?"

"Yes. That's their lot. We patch them up, and if they're able, and most who survive are able, they return to the front."

Nephim brushed away imaginary crumbs from her uniform. When she spoke, she didn't look up. "Most don't survive a second injury."

"Is that why there are so few riders left?" He shuddered. He imagined being a rider was all about the glory, not risking injury and death.

"How can we possibly win this war?" Karzul asked.

"We can't win. We can only stall. Some days, I wake and think that we're doing nothing but slowing them down. But what's the alternative? Let them burn our villages? Burn my family alive? I can't allow that. I have to fight."

Karzul didn't know what to say to that. He simply watched as her face fell. The passion had run its course. He could tell she was as exhausted and frightened as he was.

"I found something," he said. "I should have told you earlier."

He rose, led her to his room, and walked over to the slim door that concealed the fire lance. "Here." He placed his hand into the palm print and pressed.

The door popped open soundlessly.

He reached inside and retrieved the fire lance. It was warm to the touch. "I found this," he muttered, holding it out for her inspection.

Nephim grabbed it from his hand.

"You son of a whore," she screamed. "Why didn't you tell me about this?"

She shook the fire lance at him.

"This changes everything."

9

ECHOES OF FIRE

Karzul stepped back as Nephim shook the fire lance. He had never seen her so angry.

"Do you know what we could do with this?" she demanded.

"I'm sorry. I..."

"Sh." Nephim held up a finger to her lips.

"Someone's coming. Dara'tia hears a dragon. Put this away and meet me at the main entrance. And hurry up. Your real training is about to begin."

Karzul took the fire lance, replaced it in its locker, and closed the door, running to keep up with Nephim as she rushed down the hall to the area she had designated for receipt of the injured, the infirmary. She opened a cabinet and withdrew a pile of freshly laundered white garments, handed one to Karzul and began disrobing.

"What are these for?" he asked.

"To keep your clothes clean. To keep the patient clean."

He blushed. She had disrobed to her small clothes and was already stepping into the fresh whites. Did she expect him to do the same?

"No time for modesty," she said. "But since you are modest, change and meet me out front. And don't dawdle."

Karzul donned the white garments and hurried to catch up with

Nephim just as she burst through the great doors. Karzul's dragon crouched on the left side of the door, Nephim's on the right. They both squatted on their hind legs, with their wings tucked tight. They sat up, forelegs straight. They were alert, as if listening to something Karzul could not hear.

The air was clear and crisp, and the storm from the previous night was gone. The morning air was thin and carried no scent. A faint dragon call came from the empty sky.

"There," Nephim pointed. "Only the one."

Karzul peered into the sky. He saw nothing. He opened his mouth to speak, but Nephim silenced him.

"Wait for it," Nephim said. "The dragons know who approaches. We're needed."

She stood staring off into the sky.

He followed her gaze. He could just make out a dark dot bobbing up and down off in the distance. The dot grew larger, took on a bright purple color, and then sprouted wings. It was indeed a dragon. The rider was dressed in the standard uniform, his face covered with a cloth as Nephim's had been. As it approached, the dragon spread two sets of wings wide and halted almost at Karzul's feet. In its forelegs, it cradled a wounded man. The dragon deposited the man on the marble tile and stepped back. The rider waved at Nephim and Karzul but did not dismount.

Nephim rushed to the injured rider. She knelt beside him and quickly examined his leg. The man's uniform had been sliced along one leg from his toe to his thigh. The edges had not been cut, but rather burned. The flesh beneath the gash was charred black and stank like meat that had been accidentally dropped into the fire.

Nephim slid a hand beneath his head and lifted it. "You're safe now, Lorest," she said. "We have you."

She turned to Karzul. "With the escalation in fighting, everyone is on the front lines. Usually I have help, but not today. Today, you're my help. Pick him up. Carry him. We don't have much time."

Karzul knelt down and slid one arm beneath the wounded man's legs. The other went behind the man's back. He bent his knees and lifted.

The man screamed.

Karzul quickly lowered him.

"Don't stop," Nephim shouted. "I know he's in pain, but if we don't tend to him right now, he'll die. Pick him up."

With that, Nephim fled into the hallway, rushing to the infirmary.

Karzul hefted the injured man and rushed after her.

Nephim ushered him into the infirmary. She gestured to the table. "Put him here."

Karzul laid the injured man on the table.

Lorest groaned and shifted as if trying to get comfortable.

Nephim put a hand on his forehead. "Try to stay still. I'll give you something to take away the pain in a moment."

Nephim handed Karzul a dark glass bottle with a stopper in it. "Take this. Put some on that cloth, and put the cloth over his mouth and nose. Just a dash. And don't breathe it yourself, or you'll be no good to me."

Karzul tipped a drop of clear fluid onto the cloth. The fluid smelled sweet and made his head swim.

He held the cloth over the mouth and nose of the dragon rider.

In a few heartbeats, the man's breathing slowed.

Karzul withdrew the cloth.

The man was breathing deeply, as if asleep. Karzul pushed his jet-black hair away from his face. "Who is he?"

"Lorest is one of our best riders. He'll be out for a while. Now cut away his trousers so we can see what we're up against."

Nephim handed him a pair of shears.

Steel and sharp.

He placed the blade beneath the man's trousers and cut. The fabric was stuck to the charred edges of the wound, so he cut around it. He wasn't about to cause any more pain by tearing the fabric from the man's already damaged leg.

Nephim placed her hand on the man's thigh where the wound was deepest.

"We can't amputate this high. He would not survive. It may not matter what we do, but we have to try. For his parents. Their daughter died last moon. She was a rider too. They have only Lorest left."

She reached for a cord and tied it around Lorest's thigh. "We'll amputate here."

She looked up at Karzul as if asking for his confirmation.

He nodded softly. Or did he shake his head?

Nephim picked up a gleaming blade and made the first cut. Blood welled up behind the blade as it sliced through flesh. She wiped the blood away with a clean cloth and tossed it into a basket, continuing to part the flesh and the muscle beneath. It made Karzul's stomach turn. He'd butchered plenty of animals, but this was somehow different. This was a man. A thinking, feeling man.

Nephim was determined and focused. Karzul doubted whether she knew he was even in the room. She cut through the man's leg, peeling back flesh and muscle. When she was ready, she sawed through his thigh bone, making quick, short strokes with a saw.

When the bone was severed, she worked quickly, layering the flesh back over it and stitching it together with what she said was catgut — thin strips of dried flesh threaded through a large needle. She quickly but gently pinched the flesh together, trimmed the edges, and sewed them flush. She made a neat set of cuts and folded the edges of the man's skin together, just like a seamstress does when making a dress, or a pair of trousers. Only her stitches were large and imprecise.

When she tied off the last stitch, she tossed the implements onto the tray and let out a sigh. "I did my best. The rest is out of my hands."

Karzul stood back in fascination. He'd known Nephim only a few moons as she trained him on what was necessary to find and bond with his dragon. Never in that time had he suspected she possessed such bravery and determination. He'd assumed that, because she was born to the manor, she had grown up shielded from the vagaries of war. He could not have been more wrong. She was capable. Determined. Brave.

Nephim frowned at him. "What are you looking at?"

"You were amazing," Karzul said. "Where did you learn to do this?"

"Right here. I told you. This is my job. Our job."

"I'm not sure I can do it."

The artificial light made her eyes appear otherworldly blue. "You can, and you will."

"Do you think he'll live?" A deep voice came from behind Karzul.

He started.

He was so wrapped up in the surgery and the gruesomeness of the ordeal that he'd forgotten it was a rider who'd brought the man, not just the dragon.

He turned to see who it was.

It was Rodan.

Nephim wiped her hands on her whites and turned to look at Rodan. "Let's pray you arrived in time. He's blessed you were able to bring him. Too many will not be this fortunate."

"He was indeed fortunate." Rodan shook his head. "The war is not going well. It was a bit rough getting him out of the heat of battle and back here."

Karzul stood frozen, unsure what to say. He'd seen Rodan jump, assumed he had died at Dragonfall. After what he'd witnessed in the operating room, it was hard to find the right words. "I saw you jump. I thought you were..."

"Dead." Rodan supplied the word Karzul was unwilling to say. "I'm sorry for shocking you, lad. I watched you jump. Saw you find your dragon. It was beautiful. *She* is beautiful. One of the finest dragons I've ever seen.

"I was set to leave the bridge when a dragon called to me. Me? Can you imagine?

"I thought my days as a dragon rider were in the past.

"After you and your dragon bonded, the other dragons sensed that I was there to help. The dragon who rejected you previously called out to me. It chose me. I was accepted back into their good graces. I bonded with O'hinar and we headed straight for the battle. In the heat of the battle, Lorest got sliced up by the fire lance. He was fortunate. We caught him as he fell. At first, O'hinar was reluctant to leave Lorest's dragon behind, but I convinced her that she was already dead."

Rodan reached out and tussled Karzul's hair. "You made it. What do you think?"

"Your young man has been quite busy," Nephim said. "One day as a rider and he's already outshined any expectations I had for him. You were right to select him. He's no more a commoner than I am. He's already found a fire lance."

"Where?" Rodan asked.

"In my room," Karzul said.

"Fully charged?"

"I don't know."

"Fetch it."

Karzul stripped out of the bloodied whites, scrubbing the last of the blood from himself before donning his uniform. Was he in trouble for concealing what he'd found, or was he to be praised for finding it? Rodan seemed excited, but Nephim seemed upset by the whole incident. He hoped he'd done well by finding it.

When he reached his room, the lance was right where he'd left it. As he drew it from the clips, it seemed to come alive. A slight vibration shook beneath his hand, and it seemed to grow warmer.

Outside the great hall, he found Rodan and Nephim standing at the head of the stairs that led down the mountain, talking in low voices. He stepped out of the shadows and handed the fire lance to Rodan.

The old man hefted it and turned it over, examining it. He placed his hands in the indentation that Karzul had found and aimed it at a pile of stones not far off. Nothing happened.

Rodan handed the fire lance back to Karzul. "You try."

The fire lance fit perfectly in Karzul's hand, his fingers grasping it firmly, the tip of his finger resting lightly on the studs.

He aimed the lance out into the air and fingered the stud. The strange warmth erupted in his blood that he'd felt before, but this time it was different. His heartbeat quickened as if he were struggling to climb the mountain where he'd met his dragon. He had little time to ponder what he felt. A brilliant flash of blue-white light shot from the lance, accompanied by a loud sizzling sound. The light that emanated from the staff was so bright, it left a trace in Karzul's vision that took a while to fade. His palms grew warm, and he almost dropped the staff.

He fired again, this time moving the stud only a tiny bit. This time, he was able to follow the path of the blue-white light, see its course and length, and see how far it traveled. The beam didn't burn a track in his vision.

"Where'd you get the lance?" Rodin asked.

"In my room. In the locker where the lance was stored."

"How did you get into the locker?"

"With my palm."

Rodan turned to Nephim. "Did you have any idea?"

She shook her head.

"Anything else I should know?" Rodan asked.

"I found this strange glass in the desk drawer. It came alive when I picked it up. There was the outline of a hand. I placed my palm on it, and a green light passed beneath it. After that, the locker opened to my palm."

"A glass, you say?"

"Yes."

"Clear? Framed in shiny metal?"

"Yes."

Rodan leaned closer to Karzul. He appeared to be searching for something. He glanced at Nephim, then back to Karzul. Finally, he straightened up.

"Do you know who your father was? His lineage?" Rodan asked.

"No," Karzul stated. "What does that have to do with anything?"

"Everything," Rodan said. "Positively everything."

10

A SPARK OF POTENTIAL

Karzul spent the remainder of the morning cleaning the surgery. That's what Nephim called the place, the surgery. Everything needed to be thoroughly cleaned between patients, washed with alcohol if it was metal, glass, or wood, soaked in bleach if it was fabric. He grumbled and asked why they did so much work when the place was clearly already clean. She told him it was written in the ancient texts, and as a good soldier he would learn to do as he was told.

After a while, Nephim proclaimed it sufficient, inspected his work, and pronounced it acceptable.

"I've just checked in on our patient," she added. "He's still alive and in pain. He seems to be healing nicely, but he is very distressed. He's probably never going to ride again. With only one leg and after losing his dragon, the chances are slim he'll be rejoining us, and his prospects as a farmer are even worse. Who ever heard of a one-legged farmer? Attitude is a big part of healing, and he is not eager to live."

She led Karzul from the surgery and closed the door. "Let's go eat, shall we?"

Karzul hadn't realized how hungry he was. It had been a long day. It felt like two days had passed since the morning meal. It was hard to believe it was just midday.

He wasn't sure he was going to be able to keep anything down after witnessing a man lose his leg. His stomach was still somewhat unsettled, but when he arrived in the kitchen, the aroma set his mouth watering. Roasted meat of some sort, probably beef, vegetables, bread, mushrooms? He wasn't certain he'd ever eaten a meal with so much variety. Had Nephim cooked it, or Rodan? He would have to ask. No doubt soon it would be his turn to cook. That bothered him more than it should have. He had a few things he could cook, but nothing like this fare.

Rodan was seated at one of the dining room tables.

Nephim joined him and shoved a chair out with her foot. "Sit. Enjoy. You've earned it."

Karzul sat and scooted up to the table. The meal was the most generous he'd ever seen. Were they to eat like this at every meal?

"Why did you want to know who my father was?" he asked Rodan.

Rodan responded with his own question. "You never knew your father then?"

"No. My mother said he was a soldier. A miscreant. A young stranger who took advantage of her. She never saw him again. He didn't care that he'd fathered a son. Never knew." Karzul paused. He'd grown accustomed to being without a father. It stung. When he was young, he had been taunted for it, but he'd grown to accept it. It was just the way things were. "Why does my father matter? I don't know him. Never did."

"I expect you didn't," Rodan said. "The royal family and the nobles are much more aware of it than the common folk. Perhaps your father was a nobleman searching for trouble, or someone in your line was of noble birth, even if born outside of proper circumstances. That's the only way you could have gotten the blood."

"Not just nobility," Nephim interrupted. "Royal blood. On both sides."

Rodan raised an eyebrow at her.

"No one in my family could command a dragon like his," she said. "Did you see that dragon? She's huge. More powerful than the ones the royal guards ride. That's not just noble blood. Karzul must have royal blood."

Rodan waved his hand in the air. "Where he got it, is a discussion for another day. He possesses it. That means he might just be the key to winning this war. If we can keep him alive."

Nephim bristled, glancing at Karzul as if checking for signs of whatever he possessed that Rodan believed was so critical. "I felt a bit of the pull when I first saw him. That's why I recruited him. I figured he'd make a decent rider, but that's about all."

"Test him then." Rodin stood. "See if I'm right."

Karzul watched Rodin walk toward the door. "Test what?"

"Your fate," Rodan said as he left.

Nephim stood. "Shall we go?"

"Can't say I'm not a bit baffled by all this, and nervous. What are you testing me for?"

"This won't hurt," she said."I just want to see if you truly are what we think you are. Trust me?"

"Do I have a choice?"

"Not since you became a rider. You gave up the right to argue when you leaped for that dragon. You knew that. I advised you beforehand. You were fine with it then. Not so sure you made the right decision?"

"It's just so much." Karzul glanced in the direction of the surgery. "So fast."

Nephim followed his gaze. When she spoke, her voice was soft. "That's why we have to move fast, Karzul. People will die if we don't. Come. Let's get going."

Karzul pushed his chair against the table and followed her.

She led him to the living quarters, to a door with her name scrawled on the chalkboard, opened it, and entered.

Her room was exactly the same as his — desk, chair, bed — but every surface had been decorated with trinkets. Stones painted to look like animals. Tiny paintings of flowers and lakes. Crocheted dolls. It gave Karzul the impression of someone who had lived in the fortress for a long time. As if she'd grown up here. He knew she hadn't.

"Here." Nephim tugged at the drawer on her desk. "See if you can open the drawer. I can't. I've never been able to, but you might. If the fates have blessed us the way Rodan seems to think." She yanked at the drawer once more. It made a metallic sound but remained firmly closed.

Karzul placed his hand on the drawer. His own had offered no resistance. He expected the metal to be cold to the touch, but it was warm, body temperature.

He hesitated. What if it didn't open? What if it did? Would he find another fire lance that Nephim or another rider could wield in battle? It seemed the fate of the war rested in his hands.

He gently pulled at the drawer.

It slid open with ease.

He let out a sigh and glanced at Nephim.

"Rodan was right," she said.

"Right about what?"

Nephim reached past him and picked up the single item in the drawer. A clear glass framed in silver.

It was just glass in her hand.

She touched it, examined it, ran her finger around the edge, turned it over, tapped on it, then set it on the desk.

"Now, you."

Karzul took the glass in his hand.

It was cold and dead.

Perhaps he was not the man Rodan thought he was.

He turned the glass over, examining it. The back was silver, some sort of metal. The front was glass over something black that gave it a mirror look. Along one edge, there was a small button.

He touched it.

It felt warm in his hand.

The glass came to life; the edges glowing blue.

Nephim gasped.

He ignored her, peering more closely at the tiny graven images that appeared around the edges of the glass. They must indicate things the glass could do. He had not had the time to investigate his own glass, and he was curious, but Nephim was impatient, her breathing heavy beside him.

He found the tiny drawing of the sword and touched it.

The outline of a hand appeared on the face of the glass.

He moved his free hand toward it. He had placed his hand on the glass, and after that, his own locker had opened. Would he be able to do the same here?

Nephim grabbed his wrist. "No. These are my quarters. It should be my hand."

She took the glass from him and gently placed her palm on the mirror's surface.

A brilliant line of green light appeared. It rushed back and forth beneath her palm, just as it had done for his. When it dimmed, the palm print on the glass had lines in it, just like the lines in her hand.

A soft click sounded from behind them.

Karzul turned. On the wall, right where his locker had been, a palm print flashed. Had he just granted her access to her own locker? Would there be a fire lance in there for her?

Nephim placed the glass back on her desk.

The magic had already faded.

She glanced at Karzul and stepped up to the wall.

He drew a breath and held it. The air had an odd flavor to it, one of dust and ancient decay that tried unsuccessfully to hide beneath the scent of cleaning potions.

Nephim faced the wall.

She glanced over at Karzul.

He motioned for her to place her hand near the wall.

Perhaps she needed to be closer.

She raised her hand, palm toward the wall.

The handprint appeared.

She placed her palm against it.

For half a heartbeat, nothing happened, then, with a pronounced click, the tall, narrow door swung open.

Inside was another fire lance.

Nephim reached for it, tugging it free of the clips that held it.

She drew it to her, running her hand over the gleaming silver shaft, carefully examining the copper basket at the end, fingers tracing the braided cable that wove its way in and out of the staff.

She placed her thumb against the trigger.

Karzul gasped.

Surely she was not going to try it here.

She lowered the staff to her side and turned to Karzul.

"I'll be dipped in pig dropping," she said. "I can't wait to try it out." She tucked the staff under her arm and headed out the door at a brisk walk. Karzul was hard-pressed to keep up as she made her way to the kitchen, where Rodan was cleaning up from the midday meal.

"He did it," Nephim said.

Rodan snapped his head around, his eyes going wide. He looked Karzul up and down as if seeing him for the first time.

He extended his hand to Nephim.

She handed over the fire lance.

Rodan examined it just as Nephim had, the smile on his face growing as he gently passed his fingers over the intricacies of the device.

He handed it back to Nephim.

"Shall we go see just what Karzul has done for us?" He turned and headed off without waiting for a reply.

When they reached the great entry doors, Rodan turned to Karzul. "Fire yours over there." He pointed to a stand of rocks a few yards from the stairway. "Aim for the top. Just a heartbeat. No more."

Karzul raised his lance and fingered the stud. It sizzled and popped. The blue-white light shot forth and struck the stone. Whether from the sight or sound, Karzul was not certain, but his head felt light, as if he had stood up from the bed too quickly.

He pushed the thought out of his mind. They had more important things to worry about.

"Now you," Rodan nodded to Nephim.

Nephim mimicked Karzul's actions.

The blue-white light from her staff was nowhere near as strong as Karzul's had been, but the stone sizzled and split where she struck it. As Nephim fired, a tingle erupted in Karzul's stomach. He felt as if he had dropped suddenly, only he was standing on solid ground. Why, then, did he feel this odd sensation? Was it the lance firing?

Rodan nodded, as if satisfied with what he'd seen.

"Step away." He jutted his chin at Karzul, then at the pillars that held up the great entryway. "Not too far. Just a bit. I want to see how close you need to be."

Karzul did as asked. He wasn't sure what Rodan was testing, but he was curious.

"Again," Rodan instructed Nephim.

Once more, Nephim fingered her lance. This time, the light was weaker. The stone barely budged, and the twisting in Karzul's gut was much less pronounced.

Rodan nodded at Karzul. "Further away, if you don't mind?"

Karzul took half a dozen steps away from Nephim.

"Again."

This time, Nephim's staff shone with a light that was barely discernible.

She had power only when close to Karzul.

"This is going to make things interesting," Rodan pronounced.

11

A TASTE OF POWER

*T*he next morning, Karzul woke with a start. The lights were on full-bright in his room, brighter than usual. Was this because he'd overslept?

He rushed through his morning duties, splashing water on his face before putting on his uniform. He grabbed his fire lance and rushed down the hall, arriving at the dining hall just as Nephim and Rodan finished up.

"Rough day yesterday?" Rodan asked.

"Sorry," Karzul said. "I don't usually oversleep."

Rodan laughed. "You spent quite a bit of time with your fire lance yesterday. You also demonstrated that you were the one powering Nephim's lance. Where did you think that power came from?"

"I felt it draw from me. We proved that with my backing away from her, but I never stopped to consider just what that meant."

"Not only that, but your own fire lance is powered by your body's energy. It's why only the strongest bloodline can drive a fire lance. Your body possesses a way to store up the energy that the fire lance converts to the blue-white light."

Rodan gestured to the fire lance. "Do you mind?"

"Go ahead." Karzul handed it over.

Rodan stood. The fire lance came up to his forehead. The shaft, as thick as his wrist, rested firmly on the ground, its gleaming silver surface reflecting the lights in the room with a strange distortion. A grip of thick wood wrapped the shaft midway along the shining metal. It was shaped in such a way as to allow the user to grip it with one hand while he tucked the shaft beneath an arm. At the forward end of the grip, was a stud that could be slid forward and sideways. This was the control Karzul had used to widen or narrow the beam and to determine how much of the blue-white light was created.

At about chin height on Rodan, was the basket. It appeared as if someone had woven a basket, not of wicker, but of thick copper strips. A set of thick braided copper ropes emerged from the basket to join a ring that surrounded the staff halfway down the shaft. The ring was dark green and looked much like jade. The braided copper ropes disappeared into it.

The open end of the basket supported the clearest blue gemstone Karzul had ever seen. It captured the light and threw it back onto the walls in a dizzying array of colors. The gemstone had been crafted by a master crafter, the face was polished to a mirror finish; the facets falling away to be captured by a thick black ring just inside the basket.

While Karzul rushed through his morning meal, Rodan and Nephim took turns examining the fire lance. Rodan poked at it with the tip of his knife until at one point it cracked and emitted a spark of lightning that startled the old man so much, he nearly dropped the lance.

"I wish I had the blood to power one of these," he said. "If so, I might never have lost my original dragon, and we would not be in such dire straits. We could have defeated the Daresh fire lance the day it appeared." He shook his head. "We just don't know enough about the fire lances to craft the winning strategy just yet, but with more than one, we should be able to prevail."

"I wish I had more of the blood," Nephim said. "Without Karzul, I can barely toast this bread." She gestured to the loaf sitting on the table. "What if he falls? What then? We're right back where we started."

"Not completely," Rodan said. "There seems to be some connection to the dragons as well. Perhaps your dragon will provide a source of power just as Karzul does."

"Even so, it's still a matter of the blood. Have you seen my dragon? Not the most majestic creature around."

"We can but try."

"Try what?" Karzul stuffed the last of his meal into his mouth and gathered his plate and utensils.

"Test what effect your dragon has on the fire lance's power," Rodan explained. "I think there might be a connection there; why else would the fire lances be associated with the dragons?"

"Dara'tia is awake, so we can try right now," Nephim said.

"Why so eager?" Karzul had barely had time to let his morning meal settle. He would have preferred to spend time examining the fire lance and planning strategy, but Nephim seemed in a rush. Was she upset about her need to have him near when she used her fire lance? Was she embarrassed about that?

"People are dying," Nephim said.

12

BONDS OF THE SKY

Karzul and Nephim practiced with the fire lances, testing what effect the distance between them had on the power and accuracy of each weapon. When in Karzul's hand, the fire lance always fired brightly and right where he aimed, the smell of ozone tickling his senses, the sound of crackling rising in his ears and the brilliant flash nearly blinding him. He was getting better with practice. He was even able to hit the targets Rodan tossed into the air with reasonable certainty.

Nephim, on the other hand, was not doing as well. A lance in her hands only worked properly when Karzul or her dragon, Dara'tia, were within a dozen yards. Even then, it was nowhere near as powerful as his. She did have an accuracy that Karzul envied, though. She seemed to be able to hit anything, no matter how far away, or quickly moving, so long as he was close to her. When they separated, her lance seemed to lose most of its power. With just her dragon nearby, her lance was nowhere near as powerful as Karzul's was. That would certainly limit her effectiveness.

The sun was low on the horizon before Rodan seemed satisfied. "Let's begin before it gets dark. The fire lances were made to be a weapon for a dragon rider, and Dara'tia is definitely going to be critical to any plans we make."

Karzul was eager to learn anything about dragons, and practicing with the lance was exhilarating.

"What about you? Aren't you going to look for a lance?" Karzul asked.

Rodan shook his head. "Had I access to a fire lance, and I do not, I would no more be able to use it on my own than Nephim. I know my lineage, and it's nowhere near nobility, much less royalty."

Karzul stood there, head hung low. Of course, Rodan didn't have a fire lance. If he had, he never would have lost his first dragon. He would have been a decorated hero, an invincible warrior. It was foolish of Karzul to ask such a thing, and he knew it.

"I see you understand," Rodan said. "Or at least you begin to."

Karzul relaxed a bit, but he was still uncomfortable. Rodan had been just another old man with a story when they first met. He assumed the old man had accompanied him up the mountain and encouraged him to choose his dragon because he wished to strengthen the forces fighting the war, but he was seeing a new side to him. Buried inside the dusty, limping, aged frame was the core of a fighter, a commander who was used to giving orders that were carried out without question.

"I believe I do, sir," Karzul said.

"I believe you do," Rodan said. "Let's call the dragons and see about some flying lessons before the sun sets."

Rodan stretched out his hand. His lips moved, but no sound came out. Was this how he called the dragons? Could Karzul summon his own steed in this manner? He was eager to ask, but he didn't want to intrude on what Rodan was doing. One reprimand for the day was more than enough.

Soon enough, three dots appeared in the distance.

They became dragons and landed side by side on the great steps.

"Come. Let's try this." Rodan waved to Nephim. "Before we begin. I want you to understand what we are about to do." He looked at Karzul.

"First. Know your dragon. Learn what she can and can not do when it comes to turns and dives and what you can and can not tolerate. I assure you, your dragon can take a turn much harder than you can. Let her know when you're in distress, and she can lend you strength.

"Second. Asses the situation. Observe your enemy. How many are there? Where are they? Determine as best you can what their flight patterns are. What are the weak points in their strategy? And most importantly, stay alert to changes that affect your strategy.

"Third. Establish and maintain communication with the other riders. When you are close, you can shout to them. When you are far away, you will need to relay information through your dragons. This can be frustrating at times as their communication is not like speaking and it may be difficult or impossible to convey what you want.

"Fourth. Don't be too eager to engage. Begin with evasive maneuvers. Let the enemy think you are helpless or timid. It will cause them to make mistakes you can take advantage of.

"Fifth. When you do take offensive action. Commit. Utilize your dragon's capabilities and your fire lance in whatever way you can. Try to coordinate your moves with the other riders. Keep moving. Keep your eyes open.

"Your strategy for this exercise is to isolate the enemy if you can. Engage more than one Daresh rider, and you'll lose track of their positions. One of them could drop onto your tail and attack. Isolate one target. If you're flying in tandem with another rider, you can do the same to them — one distracts while the other attacks. The more experienced riders on both sides know this. So it becomes a matter of who is the superior flyer, whose dragon is more nimble or more powerful, and who has the strongest nerves. Without the fire lance, it's swords or staves, but with the lance, things are different. You can take down an enemy flyer at a distance. It improves the odds, but not if you're surprised from behind while you're focusing on your target."

Rodan paused and held Karzul in his gaze. "You understand any of this?"

It all sounded reasonable, but there was so much to remember.

"I'm expecting you to forget, boy," he said. "There's only one way to ensure you don't. Know what that is?"

"Practice?"

Rodan nodded. "That's it. We practice over and over again until it becomes second nature." He glanced at Nephim. "Feel like taking the enemy position on this? You're familiar enough with one-on-one combat."

Nephim nodded. "You had best be careful with the lance, Karzul."

Karzul swallowed. Was he supposed to practice with the fire lance and learn to fly at the same time?

"Maybe no lances. Not yet," Rodan said. "This is the battle practice. Carry them. Get used to the weight, the balance, but no firing. There'll be plenty of time for that later."

Nephim tapped the end of her fire lance on the ground, acknowledging the order, and leaped onto the back of her dragon.

She was off.

Within half a hand of heartbeats she had disappeared into the vast blue of the afternoon sky.

"Karzul," Rodan said. "She's the enemy. The enemy does not advertise their position. That's the first lesson. What I'm going to show you is how you can take down an overconfident enemy. The tactic is this. I'll let her think she's isolated me. She'll follow close on my tail, hoping to overtake me. I want you up above. Not too far, but far enough. She won't see you as a threat. As the chase develops, you come lower and lower. When the time is right, I'll bank hard to the left to separate from her. That's when you strike."

"I thought you said no lance."

"Correct, no lance. You drop down on her and steal her wind. Fly right above her, and the downdraft from your dragon will cause hers to falter. That's how you destabilize an enemy and create an opportunity to attack. In real combat, you'll use your lance to take your opponent down from above. That's the reason for turning sharply. I don't want to be anywhere near her when you unleash the lightning."

Karzul nodded, but he wasn't sure he understood everything. He wasn't even sure he could control his dragon.

Rodan frowned at him. "Something wrong?"

"I don't know how to direct my dragon," he said. "Sir."

"How did you get here, then?"

"She carried me. I had no idea where I was going."

"What's your dragon's name?"

"Name?"

"Don't tell me you never asked? How could you..." He shook his head. "Sorry. I forgot you were so green. Come with me."

Rodan stepped up to Karzul's dragon. He spread his arms wide and bowed, sweeping his hands forward and clasping them together before straightening up.

The massive head lowered to stare straight into the old man's eyes.

"Apologies, mighty queen. This one is but a sapling. He understands little. Would you do me the kindness of offering him your name?"

The dragon snorted. Wisps of smoke rose from her nostrils. When she spoke, the mountain rumbled. "Kin'tara."

"Thank you, oh gracious queen." Rodan paused as if in thought. "I have heard tales of your mighty deeds. It is an honor to receive your name."

He turned to Karzul. "You're more fortunate than you can imagine. Kin'tara is old. Older than our oldest records. She has bonded more times than you can count, outlived hundreds of riders. And she has chosen you, and you have awakened her."

"Awakened her?"

"When a dragon is bonded to a human, it gains the power of speech and thought. When they hatch, they are wild creatures with no interest in the world of men. They hunt, they mate, they exist, but not as thinking beings. They are little more than animals in their wild state, acting on instinct. But when they bond with a human, they take on the characteristics of their mate. They become aware. They think. They plan. They feel emotions that normal dragons do not. They become like us." Rodan paused. "And we, like them."

Karzul looked at the dragon with fresh eyes. Kin'tara. Somehow the name felt right, as if it were perfect for her, and perfect for him.

"Do you not feel it?" Rodan asked. "Without the dragon bond, you wouldn't have been able to open the lockers or wield the fire lance. She has given some of her power to you, and her soul, and you have given part of your soul to her."

Karzul paused. He'd never really thought it through. The bond with a dragon was a short-lived affair for the majestic creatures, but for him, it was a lifetime commitment, unless his dragon died. Was that why so few of the riders he'd ever met had a bond-mate? Was the bond with the dragon closer than with any human? What did that mean for him? He imagined himself growing old, bonded to Kin'tara. As if she had read his thoughts, she pushed an image at him of an ancient man with white hair, a long beard, and wrinkled leather-like skin sitting astride her back."

Karzul brought himself back to the business at hand.

Rodan was saying, "That's the way it works. When you need her, simply call her name. In your thoughts. Reach out to her, and she will come. It also helps if you trace the spell you used to summon her at times of great need. She will recognize it and come quickly."

Karzul blinked.

"It's that easy. When you're in flight, simply imagine what it is you wish to do. She will do know what you want, but do not force her. Sometimes she will see things you do not. Heed her. You don't get to be a thousand years old unless you know what it takes to survive."

Karzul swallowed.

Rodan gave Karzul a shove. "Off you go before we lose the sun."

Kin'tara lowered her head, allowing Karzul to mount.

The suggestion that he slid between her first pair of wings was suddenly there in his mind. When he did so, scales rose from Kin'tara's back and formed a saddle that was quite comfortable. Another set of scales clamped around his legs, holding him firmly but gently in place. His feet reached another set of scales that protruded from her side. All in all, he felt very comfortable and safe, not that he was in any hurry to test out the limits of his perch. He had no idea what it was like to ride a dragon in battle, but Kin'tara did.

Amusement flooded through him. A deep voice rumbled in his mind. "Ready?"

He nodded his assent.

The dragon whirled, took three lumbering steps down the wide stairs, extended all three sets of wings, and leaped into the updraft that rushed across the mountain, catching the wind. Karzul's stomach sank as the wings beat furiously and the dragon sped upwards. The cold air slapped his face, even as the mountain fell away below. Karzul wondered if he would ever grow bored with seeing the land below him shrink as the dragon soared ever higher.

It wasn't long before Rodan caught up with him. The elder rider sat astride his dragon, legs wrapped around the body and hooked beneath the aft wings. He seemed comfortable there, as if he had been born to it. Rodan caught his gaze scanning the sky, even turning almost backwards to scour the sky behind him. "Found Nephim yet?" Rodan asked.

Karzul shook his head.

"Then get to it."

Karzul searched the sky. Nephim should be easy to spot. There were no clouds. The air was still. She would stand out starkly against the ground if she were below him, but she was nowhere to be seen.

The air was clear.

The sun was setting.

The great orange-red globe hung low in the sky, not far from the horizon.

It hurt Karzul's eyes to look at it.

He blinked back tears as he searched the sky near the sun.

Suddenly, a dark blotch appeared directly ahead of him.

Before Karzul could react, he felt a sharp rap on his arm, and almost lost his grip on his fire lance.

"Got you," Nephim sped past on her dragon, fire lance in hand. She'd been hiding in the blinding light of the setting sun. He hadn't seen her until it was too late.

"Lesson learned," Rodan shouted at him. "Let's head back."

Karzul rubbed his arm.

Nephim had not been gentle.

The lesson hurt.

13

THE WEIGHT OF WINGS

The following day, Karzul woke to the lights coming on in his room. He washed, dressed and raced to the kitchen, expecting to help prepare the morning meal. But when he arrived, the aroma of baking bread and frying pork belly already filled the room. The air was chilly. He had come to expect that. This high in the mountains, summer never really came, and winter was much worse than it was on the plains below. It was always cold. Not as cold as it was when the dragons flew at altitude, but chilly all the same.

The table was already laid with plates and utensils. How had Nephim and Rodan made it to the kitchen so much earlier than him? He worried they'd think he was trying to avoid helping with breakfast.

"I'll get down earlier tomorrow," he told Nephim.

"Don't worry," Nephim said. "I like to cook. Gives me something to focus on first thing in the morning. Succeeding in the kitchen sets the tone for my day."

Karzul leaned over, lifted a strip of salt pork from the cooling plate and bit on it. "Eating a good breakfast sets the tone for my day."

Laughing, Nephim shooed him away.

"What are we up to today?" Karzul took his seat, poured himself a steaming cup of the dark bitter brew he'd never known of before, but was becoming quite fond of, and filled his plate. He was beginning to enjoy living here. The good food. The comfortable bed. He worried that, should anything ever happen, he would find it difficult to adjust to his old life. But, no. His old life was gone. His home was gone. His family, even if only his mother, was gone. There would be no going back. He was a rider, and he'd die as a rider.

"We'll be observing a battle today," Rodan explained. "I've received word that the Daresh fire lance has gone east. It won't be deployed here in battle today, so we should be safe to observe from a distance. I want you both to see some real-life tactics. You need to understand just how little all of our plans mean in the heat of battle. We practice to give you the ability to adapt instantly to every change in the battle, but when you're up there." Rodan pointed to the sky. "You're changing tactics constantly, hoping that you're faster to notice something than your enemy. If not, you may not come back. That's what we're going to watch today. To give you a chance to see a battle firsthand. Understanding what you are up against. It may save your life."

"We're just supposed to watch?" Nephim asked. "Is this punishment? Will I never be allowed to redeem my past failure?"

"Your last engagement didn't go so well, did it?"

"They had a fire lance."

"Nevertheless, we will watch," Rodan said. "There will be time enough to demonstrate your bravery in the coming moons. To join a battle, you must be ready for battle. The only thing you're ready for right now is to learn how to control the fire lance. We're not ready to let the Daresh know that we have one, let alone more."

Rodan left Nephim and Karzul to clean up the kitchen and joined him outside.

The chill air hit Karzul as they stepped out the great doors and onto the long steps. He suppressed a shiver and pulled his cloak around himself as he pushed a call out to Kin'tara. She appeared almost as soon as he finished the thought, lowering herself down to allow him to board.

He cradled his fire lance in his left arm as he settled into the saddle she created for him, glad of her grip as she raced down the steps and launched herself into the updraft that buffeted the face of the cliff.

The sinking feeling lasted only a heartbeat before all three pairs of wings caught the air and Kin'tara rose into the cloudless morning sky.

The mountains became hills, then woods, then pasture. Karzul wished he had traveled at least a bit before becoming a rider. He knew the names of the towns and their general direction in relation to Chayak, but had no idea which was which from the air.

When a mid-sized town appeared on the horizon, Rodan signaled for them to descend. Beside the town was an array of identical tents. Rodan explained that the Theren riders were attached to the ground troops, and today, they would be accompanying the troops into battle.

At Rodan's signal, all three dragons dropped earthward. They landed in a field near the array of tents and dismounted. The dragons immediately took off in search of prey, while Rodan led his team to a tent pitched not far from their landing site.

A middle-aged man approached, dressed in Theren Black, but instead of the blue piping that Karzul and the rest of the riders wore, his was trimmed in red. On his shoulder instead of the stylized dragon, he bore a sword and quill. On the tip of his collar, a single gold star had been embroidered. His face was weathered, like a piece of driftwood, his beard neatly trimmed, hair short.

He smiled when he saw Rodan. "How's Lorest?" he asked.

Rodan shook his head, but remained silent.

"He's resting," Nephim said. "He lost the leg. If he survives the next few days, he'll live. A burn like that is hard to recover from."

The man paused for half a hand of heartbeats, then extended a hand to Rodan. "Glad to see you back in the black. Are you ready to assume command?"

Rodan released the proffered hand and turned to Karzul without answering. "Commander Alchua, this is the one I told you about."

The commander extended a hand to Karzul.

Karzul gripped his forearm as firmly as he could and released it, wondering what words the two men had exchanged about him in his absence. "I'm afraid I'm untrained and a bit green."

"Everyone starts that way," Alchua said. "Soon, you'll be a grizzled old veteran like Rodan here."

The commander turned to Nephim. "Good to see you mounted again. We were worried we might have lost you. Heard you took on an entire raiding party? The one with the fire lance."

"Not that it did any good," she said.

"You were brave," he said. "That's always good."

Alchua turned. Ahead was a large tent, twice the size of the rest. It was green and mottled to match the grass. The center pole poked out of the canvas. It too was painted a drab green. Light gray smoke seeped out of the top of the tent but disappeared in the morning air almost as soon as it appeared. In front of the tent was a canopy, a man-height and a half tall. The grass below it was covered with a drab brown carpet that led to an open flap. Inside the tent, several men moved purposefully around a low table.

Alchua, Rodan and Nephim stepped inside without a word.

Karzul followed close on their heels.

Once inside, Alchua rolled out a map on the table and gestured to a few symbols. He explained that over the last several days there had only been a few minor skirmishes. The Daresh troops had been harassing the Theren troops to hold the ground they'd gained in the last battle while the fire lance was away. That meant some other troop would be taking the brunt of the attack for a few days, giving Commander Alchua and his troops a bit of a respite.

Alchua explained that over the last several days, a single Daresh rider came shortly after sunrise. Each day, the rider had been intercepted by the Theren riders and driven back, only to return again the next day. He said that single Daresh riders would engage anyone they thought was isolated, but generally refrained from entering a full-on battle. They were cautious and would probably hold off anything grander until the fire lance returned before making any sort of stand.

While Alchua was speaking, the sound of a horn split the air. The call was one Karzul secretly dreaded. A short blast, a few quick notes and then silence. The silence of expectation.

"That's it," Alchua said. "They've been spotted."

"This will be your first look at a real battle," Rodan said. "Watch. What you learn today may very well save your life, and no fire lances. That's a carefully guarded secret for now."

The words barely registered with Karzul. It was all becoming real now. He might be held back from the battle, but this was war. The lone Daresh might even be one of the riders who attacked Chayak and killed his mother. He wished, if only for a moment, he could join the fray, unleash the fire lance on the Daresh and end the war. Or at least pay them back for the damage they'd done to him and his family. But Rodan said they were to watch, nothing more.

He exited the tent to find four dragons ready for their riders.

Each Theren rider stood beside their dragon, looking at Karzul with a look he'd never seen before. They respected him. Was that because of Kin'tara?

He pushed a thought at Kin'tara and almost immediately she dropped from the sky, snapped open all three pairs of wings and touched down gently before him.

He hopped on and turned to Rodan, waiting for instructions.

Rodan made a gesture toward the horizon, and the dragons rose, Kin'tara taking the lead as they formed a V in the sky.

Alchua had prepared him for a lone Daresh rider, but off on the horizon were half a dozen dots, bobbing up and down as they made their way toward the encampment.

Karzul leaned into the wind as Kin'tara raced toward the Daresh. Was she eager to join the battle? Did Rodan still wish him to hold off and wait? How could he? The Theren riders would be outnumbered. Surely they needed every dragon they could muster.

As one, the Theren riders broke formation, streaking past Karzul, startling him. Kin'tara's laughter in his mind was good-natured. He hadn't seen them come, but she had.

Follow them. Karzul projected a thought to Kin'tara.

Kin'tara spread all three sets of wings and flapped. Her wings caught the air like oars catch water. The mighty creature shot forward like an arrow from a bow. Kin'tara took up position behind the line of riders, who formed a new V shape without her.

They raced toward the oncoming Daresh.

As they approached the enemy, the Theren riders broke formation. The ends of the V peeled away and raced upwards, quickly vanishing from Karzul's sight. Another group dropped low and fell back, revealing a diamond formation headed straight for the enemy.

The enemy line broke. At first, it seemed completely random where they were heading. Karzul lost track of most of them. That worried him. Even held back, they were a threat.

He was glad there was no fire lance in play today. He fingered his fire lance. For a moment, and entertained the idea of leveling it at one of the invaders, but Rodan had been quite firm. The time for the Daresh to learn of the Theren fire lances was later, at the last possible moment when a fire lance could determine the outcome of the battle, and not a heartbeat sooner.

Rodan returned and pulled abreast Karzul, gesturing in the sky off to his right and just above the horizon. "Do you see?"

Karzul peered into the distance. It was hard to make out, but the Daresh dragons were heading their way. Two of the Theren dragons raced past on his left to engage an oncoming Daresh dragon pair. The Theren dragons were brick red and black; the Daresh blue and gold.

Karzul's gaze followed the two pairs of Theren riders as they engaged the enemy. The brick-red dragon broke formation and rolled hard to the left. The black dragon rose quickly, stilled her wings, tucked them close to her body, and started to drop. While she was doing this, the trailing pair closed the gap with the brick-red dragon. They were almost upon her when a black streak came diving from the sky.

Karzul inhaled. It looked as if the black dragon was going to collide with one of the two Daresh pursuers. As they drew close, the black Theren dragon snapped its wings, extended its legs, and drove its claws deep into the back of the gold Daresh dragon. The two tumbled, no longer flying, but locked together in free fall.

"They're both going to die," Karzul shouted.

"Wait," Rodin said. "This is what you're here for."

Karakul signaled to Kin'tara to give him a better look.

She pulled in her mid pair of wings and banked hard, rolling into a tight spiral that drove Karzul's stomach toward his feet.

The two dragons spiraled toward the earth, a cacophony of black and gold, swirling as they fell. Perilously close to the ground, they broke, each heading in a different direction. Karzul exhaled. His heart raced. Who had called off the death grip, the riders or the dragons? Would the creatures have fought to the death of both of them and their riders, or could they be counted on to save their riders? He posed the question to Kin'tara, but before she could answer, a loud scream raced past him.

It was Nephim.

Her dragon flew so close he could feel the wind of its passage.

Where was she headed?

Karzul tracked her path.

She was heading toward three Daresh riders circling above a solitary Theren rider.

Karzul wondered who the sole rider was. Was that what Nephim was up to? Was she going to even the odds a bit? Rodan had told them to hold off, but was he expected to accompany her against orders?

Nephim and her dragon raced straight for one of the unaccompanied Daresh riders, passing by the enemy dragon by less than an arm's length. A glint of silver flashed in her hand as Nephim passed.

Nephim pulled her dragon into a vertical climb, the dragon's momentum carrying it straight up, the dark mahogany with vermillion splashes brilliant in the clear sky. She made a sharp turn and headed back down. Beneath her, one of the Theren riders was darting and turning, unable to shake the mottled green Daresh dragon on her tail.

Nephim dropped onto the tail of the mottled green, but was unable to catch it. Dara'tia was no match for the mottled green. In moments, the Daresh would catch its prey.

Karzul wanted to turn away, but he could not. He was here to witness the battle and learn tactics, even if they failed.

A glint of copper flashed as Nephim plucked her fire lance from its holder and aimed. A weak blue-white light arced out, licking the opposing rider. The mottled green dragon folded its wings and dropped like a stone.

A blur of red rushed by Karzul.

Kin'tara let out a screech.

It was headed straight for Nephim.

Too close.

A flash of silver flickered at the closest point.

Nephim spun out of control, clutching her fire lance to her chest as she clung to the dragon, her bloodied arm dripped red onto the gleaming chrome shaft.

Karzul screamed.

"Stay here." Rodan urged O'hinar forward, streaking towards the spinning Nephim. Her dragon was stunned or dead, spinning like a leaf toward the ground.

Rodan maneuvered close to Nephim and steadied her dragon. He reached for her, plucked her from the back of her dragon, and turned for the horizon.

Karzul was stunned, but Kin'tara knew what to do. She stretched all three sets of wings wide and launched herself after Rodan, carrying the still form of Nephim before him, just as he'd carried the wounded rider the prior day.

Karzul hoped he was equally successful today.

But he feared the worst.

14

WOUNDED WARRIOR

Karzul landed immediately behind Rodan on the grand stairs that led into the citadel. He leaped from Kin'tara's back and rushed to help carry the stunned Nephim into the surgery. Her right arm had a large gash on it that extended from her shoulder to her elbow. Blood seeped from her uniform onto the polished stone floor. In her left hand, she still clutched her fire lance. Good thing she hadn't lost hold of that.

The wound on her arm smelled of copper and oozed blood. Rodan wrapped it in a cloth to slow the bleeding, but the cloth quickly turned red.

Karzul searched for the tray of implements Nephim had used to stitch up the injured rider. He found them on a shelf by the door, selected a knife and extended it to Rodan. "Do you know what to do?"

"You're the surgeon," Rodan said. "My hands shake and my eyes are weak. It's up to you."

"Me?" Karzul was no healer. He'd witnessed Nephim at work, but he was in no way prepared to do what she had.

"She's bleeding. She doesn't have much time," Rodan said.

"What do I do?"

"Cut away her sleeve. Clean the wound. Trim away any ragged edges. Sew the muscles together, then the flesh. Keep everything clean."

As he picked up the shears, and began. He carefully cut away the arm of her sleeve and the bandage.

As the bandage came away, the blood flowed freely.

Rodan gestured to her upper arm. "Bind it up here before you start."

Karzul took a roll of white gauze and wrapped it around her upper arm, each layers tighter than the one before until the blood slowed.

"Now, stitch her up. You've cut off the blood to her lower arm. That means you're fighting necrosis. Move swiftly or she'll lose the hand."

Rodan placed the rag over Nephim's mouth and nose, as Karzul had done for Lorest.

Her breathing grew shallow.

Karzul picked up one of the needles that he and Nephim had threaded with catgut, never realizing it was going to be used on her. He probed her upper arm where the wound was deepest. The muscle was cut nearly to the bone.

"Stitch from the bottom. Work your way up."

Karzul pierced Nephim's muscle with the needle. It resisted, puckering beneath the point until it finally slipped through. He pulled the catgut through the hole, leaving two digits worth sticking out, then picked another point on the opposing side of the cut. He pushed the needle through, pulled on the cord and watched as the gap in the muscle drew together. He tied the knot he'd been instructed to use and stood, stretching to relieve the tension in his shoulders. "It's working."

"Quickly," Rodan urged. "It must be done quickly."

Karzul stitched the muscles together, then the flesh, working his way along her arm until the wound was completely closed.

Karzul pulled the last stitch together and tied off the thread. "Done."

Rodan released the bandage binding her arm. "Now rub her fingers. We need to get the circulation going."

Karzul massaged Nephim's fingers. They were cold and blue, but began to warm as he worked on them. "The color's coming back."

"Good. Her breathing's nice and steady. Now dress the wound with this."

Rodan handed Karzul a jar of brown paste that smelled like tar.

He applied it to Nephim's closed wound.

"Now bandage it, but not so tight as last time."

Karzul did as instructed and stepped back. He hoped he'd done it correctly, that Nephim would regain the use of her arm, that she would live. He hated to think she would die because of his ineptitude.

"You did a good job," Rodan said. "Now we have to hope that she didn't lose too much blood, that the wound heals clean, that she didn't sever a nerve and pray that she regains control of her hand."

Karzul just blinked.

"Just because you stitch someone up doesn't mean they're out of the woods. What did you think war is? Play acting? We rush at each other with wooden sticks and scream 'go you'? People get maimed, killed. People lose their lives, their homes, their families. What did you expect?"

"I never imagined it would be like this. I thought being a rider was a glamorous occupation, with dragons and uniforms and camaraderie. Not this." He pointed to the sleeping form of Nephim. "It's." He hesitated, trying to think of a word to describe it. "It's all so dark."

"Except for the blood, it is everything you imagined it to be. The blood — you never get used to it. Now help me get her into the bed and let's check on Lorest."

Karzul helped roll the table into the room where Lorest lay sleeping and lifted Nephim onto a bed beside his.

Lorest was awake, but just barely. He moaned softly, rustling as if trying to get comfortable.

"How are you feeling?" Rodan placed his hand on Lorest's forehead, and he ceased his rustling.

"My mother. Make sure she's taken care of," he whispered.

"You'll take care of her. When you're rested." Rodan turned to Karzul. "Check his bandage while I get Nephim settled."

Karzul did as instructed. Lorest's bandage was wet with blood and stained ochre liquid that was seeping from the wound. It smelled foul.

"Is this normal?" Karzul asked.

"Can be. If it smells bad, it can be a sign of gangrene setting in.

That's what we have to watch for. Once that gets into you, you're done for."

Karzul unwound the bandage, dropping it into a bucket beside the bed. The stump was angry red, with lines of darker red spreading up Lorest's leg. It didn't look like it was healing.

Rodan bent to examine the stump.

He took a whiff and grimaced. "I was afraid of that. The corruption is set in. Not much we can do now but keep him comfortable. He'll be gone in a day or so."

Karzul stiffened. How could that be? He'd been injured, to be sure, but Nephim had done a fine job with his surgery. How could he have taken such a dire turn in just a day?

"Surely there's something we can do?" Karzul asked. "Amputate higher. Cut away the gangrene. We can't just let him die."

Rodan lifted the blanket, tracing the path of angry red lines radiating from the injured man's leg and up his side. They branched out and invaded much of his rib cage. "See that?" Rodan asked. "That's how far it's gone. We can't cut that away. Not and have him live."

Rodan carefully re-draped the blanket over the man's legs. "The only way we can help now is to ease his pain. Gangrene hurts like fire. It's a horrible way to die. See that bottle on the top shelf, the one marked with an X? It contains milk of the poppy. Give him a thimbleful every few hours and he'll sleep like an infant. Give him two and he'll never wake up."

Karzul glanced at the bottle.

"It's your choice," Rodan said.

Karzul paced the room. In one bed, Nephim slept quietly; in the other, Lorest. The missing leg was glaringly obvious. Even if he lived, he would never be the same. What sort of life would that be? For the first time, Karzul realized that his life, too, was on the line. One day, it could be him lying on one of these beds. If it was, who would be charged with administering the merciful release?

He walked over to the shelf and peered at the bottle. It was brown glass with a stopper wired to the neck. The liquid inside was thick, like syrup.

He reached out and gently lifted it from the shelf.

15

WHISPERS OF BETRAYAL

Karzul settled in beside Nephim. Her breathing was heavy. Long, slow, indrawn breaths were followed by even slower exhales. At times, he thought she had stopped breathing. His heart raced, but by the time he'd decided to check, she'd invariably resumed breathing. Was that why Rodan had asked him to watch her? What would he do if she stopped breathing? He had no idea. There must be something, but what that was, was beyond him.

As time went on, Lorest began to groan in pain. Karzul offered him a thimbleful of the poppy milk, and he fell back into a deep sleep. His breathing was no less labored than Nephim's.

"You sure did it this time," Karzul told the still form of Nephim. "What were you thinking? Rodan says now they know we have a fire lance. It changes all our plans. No more training. No more waiting. They will surely summon their own fire lance back to the front, and we'll be part of the battle whether we wish it or not. And with you injured, that means me, and I have no idea what I'm doing, and I just sewed up your arm, and why did you leave this all to fall on my shoulders?"

Nephim whispered something Karzul could not hear.

"Nephim. You're awake. What did you say?"

"Come closer," she whispered. Her words were barely discernible.

Karzul leaned closer. "What do you have to tell me?"

"Karzul?" Her whispers were weak and came with a struggle to breathe.

"I'm here," he said.

"Please stop whining!" Her voice faded on her final words, but the look on her face told him she meant it.

"Stop whining? Do you know what you've done?"

Nephim blinked both eyes.

Slowly.

Twice.

"I know." She squeezed out. "Now let me sleep."

Karzul fell silent. Nephim was in pain. She didn't mean anything by her outburst. She would be back to her old self in the morning, or maybe after a few days. There was nothing for her to be upset with him about. He would be there for her when she woke in the morning. She would be embarrassed about her outburst if she even remembered it.

As she slept, Karzul sat between the two patients, often dozing off to come awake when one or the other moaned in pain. Each time she woke, he offered Nephim a half thimbleful of the poppy milk, but she made him cut that in half. Said he was ignorant and didn't realize how much smaller she was than Lorest. Was he trying to kill her?

Karzul pushed her rudeness out of his mind. When morning came, he would fetch her a tray of eggs and bread. Perhaps some fruit. He'd seen some fruit. Apples and something he didn't recognize.

She would eat, and then she would be better.

Sometime in the night, Lorest gasped for breath. It sounded like something heavy was on his chest. Every breath was a struggle. He cried out in pain. Karzul was certain he was witnessing the man's death. This was what Rodan had described, and the moment when mercy was the only gift left to give the man.

That bothered him. He had seen animals die. He'd killed animals for meat. But he'd never seen a person expire before. Was it different? Would there be something to see when the spirit left the man? Karzul had never been religious. He only half believed in spirits. He was confident that everyone made their own lot in life and that luck was nothing more than being prepared or failing to prepare. Still, there was something to be said for those who believed life continued after death. That would be nice, but many of the folks who believed in that sort of thing spent little time on anything else. They seemed consumed by the idea. Still, he believed those who summoned the spirits of their ancestors to bless the planting and indeed hoped to be so summoned himself one day. Far in the future, with any luck.

At the moment, Karzul had other things to worry about, like keeping both of his patients alive throughout the night.

Karzul glanced at the brown bottle on the shelf. It was almost empty.

The rider's breath caught.

He coughed.

"Lad," he said, gesturing for Karzul to come close.

"What is it?" Karzul asked.

"See that my mother is cared for," he whispered.

"I'll try."

Lorest blinked slowly. "I have a message for you. From Un'tor, my dragon. She told me to warn you. Kin'tara is not the only queen. You can not trust her in matters of family."

His chest rose, then fell.

He gasped.

Karzul listened, but no breath was drawn. He placed his hand on the man's chest. It was still. He felt his neck where Nephim had told him to check for a heartbeat.

There was none.

He was gone.

"Cover him up," came the whisper from Nephim. "Do you think I want to look at him?"

Karzul turned to her. She was awake. Not the drowsy sort of awake she'd been before, but wide awake, as if the medication that they used in the surgery had worn off.

"Are you listening?" she demanded. "Cover him up, then get over here. I want to see what you've done to me."

Karzul pulled the sheet over the man's face and tucked it beneath him.

"Now," Nephim demanded. "Remove this bandage. I want to see your handiwork."

"How do you know it was me?"

"Because Rodan can't see anything close up. Or did you not notice that? If it's less than an arm's length from his face, he can barely make it out. He has spectacles, but he hates to wear them. Says they make him look old. My guess is that he made you do the surgery, and I want to see what a mess you've made of it."

Karzul sat beside Nephim and carefully unwrapped her arm. He fetched a bowl of clear hot water and washed away the worst of the blood. The wound was angry, red and swollen, but there was no blood and no pus. He was proud of his handiwork. Not too bad for his first time.

Nephim examined her arm, wincing as she moved it, careful not to flex her elbow. When she had finished her review, she lay back and heaved a great sigh.

She turned her gaze to Karzul and motioned for him to come closer.

He bent an ear to her.

She grabbed his ear and pulled him close. "Who on this great green earth taught you to sew?"

16

FRACTURED RESOLVE

arzul helped Rodan carry Lorest's body outside. There was a cave cut into the hill not far from the main entrance to the citadel. Rodan said it was specially made to honor the fallen. When he opened the doors, Karzul could only stand and stare.

They stood in a hallway wide enough to accommodate three men standing side by side, and twice as tall as Karzul. The floor of the hallway was polished granite. Rodan touched the wall, and light sprang from the joint where the wall met the ceiling. A soft yellowish light, not the harsh light of the kitchen.

The walls had been tiled, but not with images as in the great hall; here they bore an intricate design that held rows upon row of nooks. The shadows partially concealed what was inside the nooks until Karzul drew closer. Most of them were empty.

Rodan led him along the hallway to an ornate brass door. It was decorated with images of the sun, the moon, and dragons. The sun was at the center of the image, radiating power, illuminating a pair of dragons who stood respectfully beside the moon, gazing at it in sorrow.

He grasped the handle and drew open the doors.

Inside was a small room with a raised pedestal. In its center was a deep indentation. At the foot of the pedestal, was a large glassless window. The chill wind blew through the window and the open door as they placed Lorest's body in the indentation.

Karzul approached the window. It opened onto a view of the mountains that took his breath away. Not far away, a towering peak poked into the sunrise, snow blowing from its crest, sending streaks of brilliant rose into the sky to fade away against the backdrop of the azure sky.

"Come. Let's honor the fallen." Rodan carefully arranged the man's hands over his heart.

Karzul noticed his uniform was not straight where the leg was missing. He gently folded it under the stump and smoothed it out. Rodan did the same for his hair and the rest of his uniform. When he was satisfied, he stood and glanced at Karzul.

"He fought valiantly, but his dragon died in battle. She will not be here to honor him. That will be your responsibility. I will say the words; you repeat them."

Rodan led Karzul back into the hallway and closed the brass doors. He paused for a moment, then started whispering.

"To the great dragon who sleeps at the heart of the earth, the one who first breathed fire into the sun to spread its life giving warmth on the earth, we call on you to send your daughter to honor this fallen soul and welcome him into your thunder."

Karzul repeated the words aloud as Rodan said them. It had never occurred to him that the dragons had their own gods.

Deep within the mountain, something rumbled. The chamber shook. A brilliant orange glow erupted from the cracks between the great doors. Karzul felt the presence of Kin'tara, but no words or images were shared with him. Was it she who provided the fire to consume Lorest?

The doors grew hot, so hot that Karzul and Rodan had to step back.

The orange light lingered for another hand of heartbeats, then subsided.

Rodan drew a breath. "It's done," he said. "Let's prepare the urn."

Rodan swept his cape from behind him and wrapped his hand in it before reaching for the door handle. When he opened the doors,

Lorest's body was gone. A layer of fine white ash covered the pedestal.

The chamber stank of sulfur.

Smoke lingered in the corners of the room.

Dragon fire. Kin'tara had answered his call and used her fire to cremate the fallen rider's remains. She had indeed honored the man.

"Select an urn," Rodan said. "It is your right, as you were there when he passed."

Karzul stepped up to the wall. Each nook contained a different style of urn. Some were plain, simple brass with no decorations, not even a graven pattern. Others were ornately decorated. Jewels and precious stones adorned one urn that appeared to be inlaid with gold.

What sort of urn would he end up in?

He chose one that caught his eye. It was brass, spun on some sort of spindle, and embossed with a complex design that was hard to follow with the eye.

Rodan indicated an iron scoop, and brush nestled in another nook near the door.

Karzul used them to scoop the ashes from the still-hot pedestal. When all the ashes had been placed in the urn, Rodan sealed it by dripping hot wax onto it. Karzul tucked the urn under his arm and followed as Rodan led him deep into the mountainside.

About a hundred yards into the main tunnel, they came to a branch. Above the entrance were carved words in a language Karzul was not able to read.

Rodan translated. "Take the soul of our fallen comrade and fly him to the sun."

Karzul raised a hand to touch the carving.

It seemed important to acknowledge the words.

Rodan chose the tunnels right branch.

Karzul had to move quickly to catch up.

"Why are there so many tunnels?" he asked.

"Because there are always wars. There are always those who die in war. It never ends."

Karzul took in the enormity of the dead. Row upon row of urns sat in their alcoves. Simple and ornate. How many had died in the war? Who was he to think his own ashes would not be stored here in the near future?

Rodan directed Karzul to place the urn in the first vacant alcove.

"He asked me to see that his mother is taken care of," Karzul said.

"She will be."

"Do we need to say any words? Like the prayer that called the dragon?" Karzul asked.

"I thought you weren't devout. Was I wrong?"

"No. Not a devout. I just thought..." Karzul stammered. "I've never buried anyone before. Don't they usually say some words when they bury someone?"

"Those words are for the family and friends of the deceased, which neither of us is. There's no reason for any words."

"I understand. It still makes me feel like we left something undone."

"We have, but this is not it. We have shown our hand to the enemy. From now on, Nephim will be hunted. They know we have at least one fire lance. If we are fortunate, they'll think we have just one, but that doesn't really help the cause much. From now on, they will keep their own fire lance close to the front where they saw Nephim. They will employ any tactic they can to find and defeat our fire lance wielder. Nephim has made herself a target. They'll be watching for her dragon and the fire lance from now on."

"Is it really that serious?"

"I had hoped to give you a bit more training, but now we're up against it. There's no time left. Let's hope you're up to the task."

Karzul prepared the midday meal on his own. Rodan was off setting up targets that he said would teach Karzul how to aim and control his fire lance. Nephim was still asleep under the influence of the poppy milk. Later, he would bring her broth and bread and watered ale. Rodan said that the watered ale helped replenish blood lost to injury and provided much-needed sustenance while the patient recovered.

He ate in silence and then prepared the meal for her, all the while debating what he would say.

She was injured. She was embarrassed. She was usually quick with her tongue, but it felt like there was more. She was quite upset with him, and he didn't know why.

When he finished preparing her meal, he placed everything on a tray and took it into the dispensary.

"Good to see you're awake," he said.

"No thanks to you. No more of that poppy milk. I can tolerate the pain, at least during the day. That stuff makes me sleepy and keeps me from thinking straight."

"But Rodan said..."

Nephim cut him off. "I'm the healer. I said no more. I don't need it. If I do, I'll ask."

"Suit yourself." Karzul set the tray beside her. She tried to reach it with her injured arm, then threw him an angry look.

"Sorry." Karzul moved the tray to her other side. "Do you need help?"

"Only if you put it on my injured side," she snapped.

Karzul bit his tongue, but then decided he was not going to be her whipping boy. It wasn't his fault that she was injured. She'd been told to stay out of the fray, and she hadn't listened. "I think I've had enough of your snapping at me. You were ordered to stay out of the battle. I didn't break the rules and engage. You did. Don't take it out on me."

"You should have followed me. If you had, my lance would have fried that rider, but you abandoned me when I needed you the most. You're useless. I should never have agreed to train you."

"Useless?" Karzul was angry now. "Who found the fire lance? Who has the heritage to operate it? If you hadn't trained me, you would never have had that fire lance in the first place. You might have died out there in that battle. As it is, you've compromised our plans and left us vulnerable. It wasn't me who did that. I was just following orders, something you decided not to do."

Nephim opened her mouth to speak, but Karzul cut her off. "Because of what you did, they know we have at least one fire lance.

They'll bring their own fire lance wherever they think you are, and if they don't see you, they'll kill as many of our troops as they can. Are you and I to be in every battle from now on? Or will we let the Daresh massacre our forces? You wanted to be a hero? You wanted to demonstrate your worth? Well, you did. You showed everyone you don't care about them, just yourself."

With that, he whirled and stormed out. Let her stew for a while. She was already insufferable.

"Didn't go so well?" Rodan asked when Karzul emerged from the citadel to get a breath of fresh air.

"Not really. She blames me for not following her into battle to power her lance. I was doing as I was told. She was the one who disregarded her orders."

"Have you considered that she expected you to violate orders to protect her? That's how she sees it."

"You want me to disobey orders just because she does?"

"No, but you need to understand why she feels the way she does."

"Is there anything I can do about it?"

"No," Rodan said. "Let's get some practice in before dark."

He'd set up a series of stone piles, each one about waist high. The stones at the base of each were large. As the piles grew higher, the stones became smaller. Some were topped with stones the size of cantaloupes, others with stones the size of apples.

"Stand over there." Rodan pointed at a pillar at the edge of the citadel. "And fire at these. Start off by trying to control how much power you release. It's important that you learn how to conserve power. The lance runs on energy it absorbs while it's in the locker and what it draws from you. Once it runs dry, you must return it to the locker or it will suck you dry and become useless."

Karzul nodded. How did Rodan know that? There was much about dragon riding and magic he had to learn.

"Begin," Rodan commanded.

Karzul hefted his lance and aimed it at the largest of the stone piles. He gently applied pressure to the stud.

Air sizzled as a brilliant line of blue-white light arced from the fire lance. The top stone vanished in a blinding flash.

He released the stud, and the world fell dark and silent once more.

"Little too much," Rodan said. "Don't you think?"

"How do you control it?"

Rodan shrugged. "How would I know? They never worked for me, but try pushing the tor forward and back, then from side to side. There is only one. It must control everything."

Karzul tried again, this time gently easing the stud a bit with his finger. He tried not to move it very far.

He was rewarded with a blue-white flash that washed over the stone but did not destroy it. The stone steamed in the chill air.

He'd done it.

He'd controlled the power.

"Again," Rodan said.

Karzul tried to hold back the power even more. This time the lance let forth a white light that broadened to bathe the entire area, but appeared not to do anything in the way of damage.

"That will come in handy," Rodan said. "You can light the battle or blind an opponent with that. Again. You must be able to reproduce it under pressure."

Karzul repeated the attempt. This time, the light was blinding.

"Need practice, I see," Rodan said. "Perhaps tomorrow."

Nephim emerged at the top of the citadel stairs. She was carrying her fire lance in her uninjured left arm. "Let me try."

"Do you think you should be out of bed?" Rodan asked.

"I certainly should not, but we have to win this war, or die trying."

She juggled the lance in her good arm, almost dropping it before leveling it at the stones. The light flared, then died. The stone was gone.

"Angry with it, were you?" Rodan asked.

Nephim glared at Rodan.

"Try again. Not so much power this time. Think of it as if you were trying to warm it up. Imagine it's Karzul, and he's cold. You need to warm him, not kill him."

Nephim fired. The beam sizzled as it struck the rock. It vaporized in a heartbeat.

"That's enough," Rodan said. "You don't have the fine control necessary in your left hand. You need to heal first. Let's get you back to bed."

Karzul watched as Rodan guided Nephim up the stairs. As soon as they were out of sight, he aimed the fire lance at the rock directly below the one Nephim had destroyed. It still held residual heat from her shot. Carefully, he released power from his lance, warming the rock further, raising its temperature gradually until it steamed but did not shatter.

17

WINGS OF DISCORD

Karzul stood on the great steps leading up to the citadel. It was cold and crisp in the predawn quiet. The air was still, and the mountains smelled of nothing, not cook-fires, not cattle dung, not even of ice. It was as if nothing but the citadel existed. If the sky had not lightened from inky black to silver, it would have been easy for him to believe that dawn did not exist, either.

He'd been ordered to witness the awakening of the dragons.

In the wild, they slept in caves. Once bonded, they tended to remain close to their human. Across a windswept valley, rose a peak that stood so tall its summit was constantly shrouded in the clouds. Somewhere in that cloud layer, the bonded dragons sought peace.

Just as the sun rose over the peaks, a screech echoed off the mountains. The trio of dragons emerged from the shadows with a swirl of color and flew past at a furious rate, wings beating in concert, eager to begin their day.

"Have you eaten?" Nephim asked.

Karzul started. He had not noticed her arrival. He quickly recovered, hoping for a more peaceful exchange this morning. "I have not. Are you feeling well enough to be up?" He asked.

Nephim was dressed in her uniform and stood there, fire lance in hand. Her right arm was still bound, but not as tightly as the last time he'd seen her.

"Rodan said it's time for us to test our skills on a real enemy. We're going scouting today. Looking for a straggler or a loner to take on. He was most insistent that it be a loner. He still worries that we'll get ourselves killed in a real battle."

"I worry about that too," Karzul said. "More than I should."

"Karzul. You need to have at least a taste of confidence or you will fall in your first battle. I've seen it before. The timid are the ones who die first." She paused for a bit as if in thought. "The arrogant ones are the second ones to fall. But you need to move a bit from timid toward arrogant. It will keep you alive."

"Is Rodan coming with us?"

She shook her head. "He has other tasks."

"You want me to go alone?" Did she truly expect him to go alone? He had never tasted battle, and she expected him to go alone?

"No. Not alone. I've been stuck in this sickbed for what feels like ages. It's time to get out and get back in the action. Especially now. We need to find a way to destroy their fire lance, or at least its weirder. They seem to have only one. If we can defeat him, then victory is ours."

Karzul rubbed his arm. "You seem confident. Are you certain you aren't one of those who will fall quickly?"

She winced. "I suppose I deserved that," Nephim said. "I was a bit overconfident."

When the dragons returned, Karzul and Nephim took to the air and headed east.

"There." Nephim rolled her dragon to spill its altitude and dropped like a stone.

Karzul visualized what he had in mind, and how he would support Nephim in her efforts. He hoped Kin'tara would understand. When they found the Daresh rider, they would drop behind and take up position on his tail. Give him a bit of time to realize he was in a fight. The idea was to learn tactics, not make a quick kill. It was more important to discover how to use the fire lance to safely defeat an unsuspecting lone rider than it was to actually kill one.

He shook off the thought. Now was not the time to get lost in the morality of what he was doing. Nephim was already engaging the enemy. She pulled out of her dive directly in his path. Her task was to distract the Daresh rider while Karzul targeted him. Was Karzul worried about Nephim's exposure to the enemy? Of course. She was a comrade-in-arms. It was his job to worry about her.

He glanced down to see her bank hard to the left. The rider followed, just as they had hoped. The Daresh rider was now broadside to Karzul's lance.

He set his finger on the trigger. He'd intended to wash the rider in the light, but he pressed too hard. The beam of blue-white light stabbed from the end of his lance; it sizzled deafeningly.

He swept the beam towards the Daresh rider.

The beam of light touched the rider and flared with a brilliance that was almost too bright. For half a heartbeat, he thought he saw the rider's bones, just before the rider vanished completely. Not flared to brilliance. Not burst into flame. Simply vanished.

The dragon, suddenly riderless, let out a mournful screech as she craned her neck looking for her missing rider. Finding herself riderless, the dragon turned and accelerated toward Nephim, drawing closer with every wingbeat.

"Nephim. Behind you." Karzul called out, but his words were lost in the distance between them.

"To her. Take me closer," Karzul shouted to Kin'tara. "That dragon is going to attack her."

Nephim must have noticed she was still being pursued. She pulled up violently, ascending close to vertical. Her dragon rolled sharply, then banked again, twisted to the right, spun and dove once more.

The pursuing dragon followed her every move, each wingbeat taking it closer.

Karzul was shocked. He had never seen dragons pursue one

another like that. Was that something they did in the wild? Or had they been trained for it?

Time to wonder about it later.

He saw an opening.

"Nephim!" Karzul screamed. "This way."

She couldn't hear him.

"Faster," Karzul urged Kin'tara.

The thought she returned to him was calming.

Have patience.

Nephim rolled and banked once more. The pursuing dragon was now directly in Karzul's path. He lowered the fire lance. Could take out the dragon? And not hit Nephim?

As his finger hovered above the trigger, an idea formed in his head. This dragon was only doing what came naturally. Now that her human was gone, she was no more than an animal. He could not kill an innocent animal. Was this his own thought, or had the idea come from Kin'tara? He wasn't certain. The dragon was now only yards behind Nephim and had a good chance of catching up. He could use the fire lance against the dragon, but he would risk missing it and hitting Nephim. He could not use the fire lance even if Kin'tara had not urged him to use restraint.

"Move," Karzul screamed. "Move."

As he touched the trigger, waiting for an open shot, Kin'tara raced forward and grasped the enemy dragon by its wings.

Together they fell.

"What are you doing?" Karzul clamped his legs tight, trying not to fall from Kin'tara's back. Was she trying to get them both killed?

Karzul's guts knotted as the dragons twisted and turned, falling from the sky. Kin'tara's wings, wrapped tightly to her body, still snapped in the wind with a popping sound that sickened him. He craned his neck trying to catch sight of the ground every time they revolved far enough. It was coming up fast.

Perilously close to the ground, Kin'tara released the other dragon and spread all three sets of wings. They caught the air with a crack, and Karzul's stomach lurched for his feet. He almost blacked out with the force as she pulled forward, translating her falling velocity to forward momentum.

The enemy dragon, free from Kin'tara's grasp, spread its wings, and raced toward the horizon, fleeing the field of combat.

Kin'tara had saved Nephim and the Daresh dragon.

Karzul glanced skyward, searching for Nephim. High above him, he spotted her mahogany dragon. She wasn't alone. Two dragons were in pursuit and closing in. Neither rider had a fire lance, but their swords were drawn. Karzul knew firsthand how much damage they could do.

He had to do something.

He lowered his fire lance and took aim at the lead rider, but as he did, the dragon pulled abreast Nephim. If he missed, even by a little, the bolt of light would strike Nephim. He was beginning to think that the fire lance wasn't a magical weapon that would win every battle. More often than not, it had been useless. He would have to out-fly the Daresh rider to gain a clear shot.

"Off to the left. Flank them," he muttered, but even before he could form the thought, Kin'tara banked hard to the left and accelerated. Within heartbeats, Karzul had a clear line of sight of the two pursuers.

He lowered the fire lance and fingered the trigger to the side, creating a wide beam as he had done with the rocks. He pushed it as far forward as he could. The light flared brilliantly, the crackling sound deafening. The rider and dragon both vanished in a puff of ash that floated toward the ground.

A wave of sadness washed over Karzul.

Kin'tara mourning the loss of a sister?

He had little time to wonder. The second rider was almost upon Nephim.

"Use your lance," Karzul shouted. He was close enough to Nephim that her lance should have worked, at least a bit. "Use your lance," Karzul shouted once more. How could they coordinate a battle if they couldn't hear each other?

Without warning, Nephim banked hard to the right, then the left.

She lowered her lance as she clung to her dragon with her legs. The sizzling bolt of blue-white light passed so close to his head that his hair stood on end. She'd missed her target and nearly hit him.

The Daresh rider was undeterred.

Karzul prepared his own lance. This time he aimed for the rider, hoping to leave the dragon unharmed. He felt a strong sense of satisfaction from Kin'tara, as if he had chosen correctly. He narrowed the beam and fingered the stud. The brilliant blue-white light flared, flicking across the rider. This time, the light struck the rider, and he screamed before bursting into flames. The fire consumed the rider in the space of a heartbeat, turning him first to a black charred mass, then crumbling into ash that caught the wind and vanished.

Karzul shuddered.

The riderless dragon screeched as had her sister, but this one immediately turned for the horizon and dove for the ground, pulling into level flight just above the treetops.

Karzul encouraged Kin'tara to take up position on Nephim's left wing and prepare to return to the citadel, but before he could move, a second flash of blue-white light flared past him.

He glanced at Nephim.

Her own lance was cradled in her left arm. She struggled to hold on, her legs wrapped tightly around the dragon.

She scowled and shrugged, but her expression turned to horror.

"Behind you." Her words were barely understandable across the distance.

Again, the light flared.

Karzul felt a surge as Kin'tara banked without being asked to. The next bolt flashed past his head.

There was at least one more Daresh rider, and he wielded a fire lance.

"Flame rider," he screamed, hoping Nephim would hear his warning.

Kin'tara banked hard once more. The beam of blue-white flashed past his head.

Another bank.

Another beam of blue-white.

This was getting old.

Karzul turned back to see a single rider behind him. Was that it, just the one?

He tried to recall the tactics Rodan had instructed him in. What was it? He could not recall. Did Kin'tara know?

He received the impression that the rider was too close for any maneuver and that the only recourse was for Karzul to fire his own lance and hope to hit the rider, or at least deter him.

Karzul readied his lance.

As he fingered the stud, the rider behind him executed a steep roll, dove for the ground, and turned inverted, hiding his body behind the belly of his dragon.

Karzul paused.

On the wide setting, he had been able to incinerate both the dragon and its rider, but Kin'tara pushed a violent no as he formed the idea.

He decided to wait and see.

Perhaps he'd deterred the enemy rider.

Now that the Daresh knew there were two fire lances at play, would he remain and fight, or flee?

Karzul didn't have long to wait. After a half a hand of heartbeats, the enemy dragon leveled off mere yards above the ground and rushed toward the rising sun.

18

THE LONE FLAME

Three days after the training exercise, Karzul stood at attention beside Nephim as Rodan paced the chamber. He was dressed in black as usual, but now his hair was cut short, his beard trimmed to half a finger's thickness in length. He reeked of smoke. Had he spent the night sitting by a campfire? It was apparent that no one had cooked. The morning meal he offered them was tough dried bread, black and bitter liquid that tasted of oil, and dried meat. The kitchen was as cold as if someone had blasted a hole in the wall.

"We lost three riders yesterday! That raid was in retaliation for the three you killed on your last raid. But with the ones you killed this time, it will certainly escalate. Our riders are not prepared to do battle with a fire lance every time they take to the sky. A few more battles like that, and we'll be without any riders, and the Daresh will dominate the skies. Our ground troops will be slaughtered. You two need to put an end to this."

"We need to develop a strategy that works against the fire lance. I really need the two of you out there, but one of you is in no shape to fly. Nephim, I'm ordering you back to surgery. That arm's not healing the way it should."

Nephim threw Karzul a glance. "Someone needs to learn to follow orders."

"And someone needs to learn to stay out of harm's way. Leave us. I'll join you at the surgery and we'll see about restitching your arm. Go."

Rodan turned back to Karzul. "You're on your own today. I trust your dragon knows how to keep you out of trouble, but I want to urge you to be careful. I want you to return to the location where we engaged the Daresh fire lance. If you find a rider, don't engage unless they attack you. Your mission is to observe and report. Try to determine what tactics you might use against another flame rider. What tactics would you use against him? What things might work, and what might not? Prepare yourself, for soon enough you'll find yourself in a situation where it is kill or be killed."

Karzul blinked. He was to go out alone? Already?

He fetched his fire lance and brushed his uniform clean before exiting the grand entry doors.

The sun had just cleared the horizon. It rested there, huge, orange, with the promise of a nice day ahead. The air was clear and crisp with just a hint of moisture that spoke of rain late in the day. A few puffy white clouds cast shadows on the land far below.

Kin'tara was already waiting. How nice would it be like to simply fly for pleasure? To experience the power of the dragon beneath him. To visit far-off lands?

He glanced down. Below was a small town, almost a village; clusters of hovels and hastily constructed houses stood in disarray.

A sense of purpose washed over Karzul. Far below, he saw a dark dot speed across the land.

A rider.

Alone.

This was what Rodan had instructed him to watch for.

He imagined various scenarios of how he would attack such a rider.

Drop behind him? How silently could Kin'tara fly? Could she sneak up on another dragon?

She snorted and stilled her wings.

The air became silent.

She folded her fore and aft wings and tucked the middle wings halfway in, leaving just the tips out.

Karzul's stomach knotted as they fell toward the rider far below.

Don't engage, he willed her. Would Kin'tara heed him, or did she have her own idea?

They were still far from the solitary rider when Kin'tara gently pulled out of the dive. Her wings rippled silently as she converted the speed of her fall into forward velocity. It was thrilling, a sensation Karzul had not felt since his first flight. Would he ever grow used to her majesty and power?

Far ahead, the lone rider banked and began circling, his attention appearing to be on the village below. A thin thread of smoke rose into the morning air as the camp personnel performed their morning duties. Did they not see the threat above?

Was the lone rider a threat?

Or a scout?

Did it matter? If the rider was a scout, he could return with reinforcements, bringing the threat with him upon his return.

How many would die if Karzul did nothing?

Closer. We need a better look.

No, we don't, came the thought.

Kin'tara spread all three sets of wings and accelerated so quickly Karzul had to grasp the great scales that flanked his perch lest he be thrown from it. Within moments, Kin'tara was closing in on the brilliant green dragon.

The Daresh dragon was a beautiful creature; the most striking thing about her was her color. Karzul had never seen its like before. Brilliant, light green, almost yellow. It seemed to glow with an inner light. The dragon was mature. Not as old as Kin'tara, but the buds of the third pair of wings were already apparent.

But it was not the dragon that caught his eye.

Perched on the back of the brilliant green dragon was the rider. She was trim and tall. Her hair was black as night, tied in a single queue that trailed behind her as she flew, bobbing slightly as the dragon slowly flapped its wings.

In her left hand, she held a fire lance. From this distance, it appears just like his own. A chrome shaft almost as tall as a man, with a wide barrel at one end encircled by braided copper.

The rider scanned the sky as if looking for something.

Had she seen him?

Could her dragon sense Kin'tara? What then? He had been warned not to let himself be drawn into an aerial battle. Not yet. He was not ready yet.

He needed to withdraw before she spotted him, but as he watched, she pointed her lance at him and fired. Kin'tara banked hard to the left, and the brilliant blue-white beam passed so close to Karzul that he was nearly deafened by the sizzle as it split the air.

Karzul leveled his own fire lance, taking careful aim at the woman, and slid his finger across the firing stud.

He fingered the stud, but something prevented him from activating the lance at full power. Just what it was, he could not say. He dialed back the power and imagined the lance throwing off a mild bolt. One that would not kill the dragon but would injure the rider. Not fatally, but perhaps he could un-mount her? Cause her to drop her own fire lance?

A blue-white light flared, but before Karzul could sweep it across the rider, the dragon reacted, spinning to present her belly to Karzul. Her wings caught the air as she turned, holding her position in midair.

Kin'tara followed suit. Both dragons hung in the air, face to face, mighty wings sweeping back and forth.

Kin'tara released a stream of fire that washed over the green dragon.

It screeched and released its own fire.

The flames engulfed Kin'tara.

Karzul tried to shield himself, but he was not fast enough. It felt as if he'd opened the door to a blast furnace and stepped inside. His face stung, and his cloak started to steam.

Kin'tara screeched.

The green dragon screeched.

Kin'tara released another stream of fire.

The green dragon responded in kind.

Was this going to be a battle between the creatures? Karzul tried to peer around Kin'tara's neck to see the opposing rider.

Then, as quickly as it had started, the battle was over.

The great green dragon was heading for the earth, to arc over and race across the ground so low that Karzul was certain she would strike anything that rose in her path.

He heaved a sigh of relief. The battle had ended. Neither of them was injured.

Karzul would like to think he'd seen the last of the flame rider, but he feared he had not.

19

MARKED BY FIRE

Karzul watched as the brilliant green dragon faded into the distance. He had not expected the battle to be over so quickly, nor to be so chaotic. He needed something to calm his nerves.

He turned and headed toward the encampment. Why had Alchua and his riders done nothing to protect the town? Why were there no dragons in the air? Did Alchua care nothing for those already so deeply affected by the war?

Karzul guided Kin'tara to the command tent, where he'd met Commander Alchua.

Kin'tara settled to the ground and lowered her head to allow Karzul to dismount, then took flight. To join the other dragons? To hunt? He wasn't sure what she did when she was away from him. He wasn't sure about anything to do with dragons.

As he approached the command tent, a soldier lifted the tent flap and gestured him inside.

"Ah, Karzul," the commander said. "I truly did not expect to see you engaged in battle so soon."

"I was sent to scout, but when I arrived, the Daresh rider was circling over the village. She fired at me. Only Kin'tara's quick actions saved me. I know I was not supposed to engage, but I had little choice."

"First real battle?" Alchua asked.

"Yes, sire," Karzul said. "I thought I was going to die. Is it always like that?"

Alchua chuckled and gestured to an empty chair. "Have a seat and let me pour you a glass to calm you down. You look like you need it."

He poured two fingers of a light brown liquid into a glass and handed it to Karzul. He poured one for himself and raised it. "To surviving your first battle. Not everyone does."

A shiver ran up Karzul's back.

"I wish you had been able to take the rider out. Could have saved us a lot of trouble."

"I've tried, but something stopped me. I just could not kill her," Karzul said. "I thought I could, but when it came time, I hesitated."

"That is a lot more common that you think. Some soldiers never fire their weapons. They usually don't last very long. You did fire though. I saw it."

"I did, but not at full power. Something was holding me back. I really didn't want to injure the rider and definitely not her dragon. I don't know what came over me."

"Sounds like your dragon had a different desire that you. I've heard of such things. It's one of the challenges of being a rider. You will need to find out what she truly wanted, and whether it will prevent you from accomplishing what you truly want."

Karzul paused. Why *had* he not fired at full power? He felt Kin'tara's presence in his mind and pushed it aside.

"The enemy knows that we have fire lances now and will be watching for their attack. That certainly will make it that much harder for us to catch them unawares. They will be watching for you from now on, and not only in the air. It's best you stay in the citadel. There are Daresh spies in Thera. We can't take the chance they catch wind of your location. Much as I'd love to have you with us, ready to spring into action at a moment's notice, the likelihood that someone recognizes you is too high. You could find yourself on the wrong end of a knife the moment you set foot outside of the camp. Stop in for a brew, get carried out in a coffin. You're famous now. You need to stay alert. Don't go anywhere alone. Not even in the sky. You're a marked man."

Karzul bristled at that. He wanted to join the fray. He wanted to defeat the Daresh rider, not sulk in some safe hiding place. The only way he was going to survive the war was to end it. "How can I help then?" he asked.

"Glad you offered, because this next plan relies on your unique abilities. I understand that you assisted Nephim in locating a fire lance and were able to augment her effectiveness in wielding the weapon."

I did. I am. But it's taxing. When I fire my own lance, I feel the power pull from me, and from the dragon. When I provide power to Nephim, I feel the power drain from me. Soon enough, she is unable to do any damage with the weapon."

"How many people could you aid in this manner?"

"I'm not sure I understand."

"I want you to recruit more lance wielders. You can sense true flame riders, can't you? Something drew you to Nephim, didn't it?"

Karzul paused. He'd never thought about it. He'd met Nephim when she'd come for him. He'd sensed something special about her, and wanted that for himself. That was why he became a rider. Rodan had been around the town all Karzul's life. It was only after the attack that Rodan had revealed his true self. Still, the commander was right. He did feel something, but that was just a fluke. How could he be expected to decide the fate of these more experienced riders?

"I'm not qualified to decide anything," he said.

"You're all we have. We need more flame riders, and you're the strongest we have ever seen. That makes you best suited to find more like yourself. You must try. This is too important." Alchua didn't give Karzul a chance to speak. He raised his voice and shouted, "Bring them in. One by one, if you would."

The first person to enter the tent was tall and muscular. He had an air of the nobility about him that was unmistakable. Karzul wondered how one such as him, someone obviously born to privilege, would fare under strict military leadership Nephim assured him was part of being a flame rider. It gave him pause to realize that he was looking down on someone by virtue of their birth and station, much as people had looked down on him his whole life. He thought he was beyond that, but perhaps it was only a matter of degree. He certainly was more comfortable among the commoners than he was around nobles. She may not have realized it, but even Nephim treated him as if he were somehow beneath her, simply by virtue of where he'd been born.

He shook off the thought and examined the man. When he'd met Nephim, there had been something about her that he recognized. Did this man possess something that had drawn him to her?

How would he know if not? What had it been like when he first met Nephim?

He reached for that feeling, the tingling that had started in his fingers and toes. When he first met Nephim. She had seemed larger than life. Crisp uniform. Standing tall despite her slight stature. She had walked into the light of the fire, and he had sensed it immediately.

He reached for the feeling. Did this man have it?

Nothing.

He shook his head.

"I didn't feel anything," he said.

"Keep trying." Alchua waved, and a second candidate was brought in.

He was a young man wearing a crisp uniform. Tall, slender but fit. Karzul let his senses focus on the candidate. He sensed a slight tingle of something that he felt whenever Nephim was near. He searched for that, but it was not present. Was this what he was to look for? Another like Nephim? Someone who could use a fire lance even if they required strength from Karzul? He tried again.

The tingle was there, but very slight. Had he not been looking for it, Karzul would have missed it all together. The candidate might be suitable, but it also seemed he would be no stronger than Nephim, if even coming close to her strength. Not what he was looking for.

He decided to take note of the candidate's name.

If he couldn't find a stronger one, he would revisit him.

The next candidate was a towheaded youth that looked to be about fourteen summers old. He had a strangely familiar shape to his face. As the lad entered the tent, Karzul's toes and fingers tingled, the sensation quickly spreading along his extremities and converging on his heart. The sensation was stronger than he'd experienced with Nephim, almost as if the lad were pushing the energy toward Karzul, and not the other way around as it did with Nephim. Surely this lad was someone worth investing more time in.

"Do we know each other?" Karzul asked. The lad, Yarak, could have been a long-lost cousin.

The lad shrugged.

"Who's your family?" Karzul asked.

"Got none. Ma died a summer back. Never knew my pa. I climbed the peak on my own and came back with a dragon. They took me in, and I've been a rider ever since."

"How old are you?"

"Sixteen."

Karzul raised an eyebrow.

"Next summer," the lad said.

Karzul nodded.

"Does that mean you're accepting me? I'm to train with a fire lance?"

"Not every candidate will be successful. We will see. Don't get your hopes up."

"I'll do you proud."

Several more candidates were presented. He rejected most of them, settling on eight people in all. Six of them were men; two were women. Nephim would be happy to see that.

For the most part, Karzul had had a good sense of the level of power each candidate carried with them. Was this because of his own natural talent, his blood, or because of Kin'tara? He had no idea why. What if he was wrong? They were depending on him. He drew a deep breath and stretched his shoulders to relieve the tension.

Alchua returned and seemed pleased. "I see you have a full complement, he said. "And you chose Yarak. He's a good lad. Much the same background as you. Maybe he has the blood. I don't expect Rodan and Nephim to take long to discover if we can turn these riders into flame riders. They all know more about aerial combat than you, but you seem to have a knack for the fire lance. If only one of them picks it up like you, we'll have an advantage. Without it, we can't hold off the Daresh forever. You think they can be ready by moon turn? We may be able to hold out that long."

"I'm not certain," Karzul said. "But I give you my word to try."

"Rodan and Nephim will train them in combat maneuvers using the fire lance," Alchua said. "Your part is to get them the fire lance, and back up any who need more power than they possess alone. Leave the flying and tactics to Nephim. She's solid. I've asked Rodan to ease up on her about the arm. She's had her fill of that. She's going to be limping along for a while, but don't take that as weakness. Let her guide the new recruits. Let her set her pace, and you try to keep up. We have little time to waste."

"I'll remember, sir." Karzul glanced at the open doorway. The day was waning. It would be sunset soon. The dragons would be eager to roost. "Best be on our way, or we're staying the night right where we are."

"The dragons are ready," Commander Alchua said. "Fly high. Fly swift. You're a hunted man now. I just hope you're up to the task I've set before you."

"So do I," Karzul replied.

But he didn't feel ready.

Did anyone?

Ever?

20

A DRAGON'S RETURN

Karzul bid Commander Alchua farewell and mounted Kin'tara. The sun was orange on the horizon, and Kin'tara's eagerness to return to her roost made itself clear, not in words, but in a general anxiety to get into the air and get going. The new recruits were behind him, a small thunder to be sure, but they had taken formation, four to a side, perfectly spaced behind him. It made him anxious to be responsible for them. He wasn't certain if that was truly his own feelings, or a residual from Kin'tara's eagerness to get home before the sun set.

They'd been airborne long enough for the forests below to turn to lakes. It wasn't much farther. They would be at the citadel well before sunset. Even so, Kin'tara was growing more and more anxious as they flew.

He pushed this thought at her, but rather than the relief he'd hoped for, there was even more apprehension.

What's wrong?

The image of a dragon winging its way high above came to him. A Daresh dragon, but he got the impression that Kin'tara knew more about this particular dragon than she was showing him. The feelings that came to him were vague. Pride, affection, concern. Why was he feeling those feelings? He glanced skyward. No matter the feelings, the last thing he needed was to be attacked so early on. He'd best go check it out and make sure his new recruits were safe.

Sensing his concerns, Kin'tara banked left. The dragon right behind Karzul belonged to Yarak.

"Take the lead." He instructed the lad. "Get to the safety of the citadel. I'll deal with the Daresh."

Yarak shook his head.

"Go. You have no weapon." Karzul shouted. He squeezed Kin'tara's neck with his knees.

She sniffed the air and started to climb, her wings beating in time as they bit into the air.

Before long, the lakes vanished into the darkness below, as did the rest of Karzul's squad. The air grew cold, sending shivers up his spine. The thinning of the air made it hard to breathe. Even Kin'tara huffed as they rose higher and higher.

Out of the corner of his eye, Karzul caught a flash of brilliant red and green.

Kin'tara banked, spread her wings wide and streaked toward the intruder. As they drew close, the red-green streak split into two. Kin'tara had sensed one of the dragons, but not the other. He wondered why that was. Rodan had explained that scouts worked alone and raiders worked in pairs, or groups of three to four. Why were they flying so high if they were not scouts? That green-gold color was unique. The Daresh rider with the fire lance. The thought sent shivers up his spine.

Karzul considered his options. Engage the enemy and die. Surely that wasn't a sane plan. Lead the raiders down where his recruits could engage? He'd just sent them onward, so that was out. What then? The Daresh rider had a fire lance. If she went after the squad members, she could pick them off one by one unless Karzul stopped her.

He had to engage. There was no other option. If he could stop her here and now, the recruits would be safe.

He had a fire lance. Perhaps he could kill the Daresh rider before she knew the battle was on.

He'd put aside his concerns about the ambush. She would kill him without so much as a warning.

He should do no less.

He cradled the fire lance in the crook of his arm, his finger resting lightly on the trigger. He pushed a thought to Kin'tara to show her what he planned. She would take him where the lance could be best used.

Be patient.

He didn't have long to wait. The rider on her brilliant red dragon banked gently and leaned over.

Karzul fingered the stud.

Zzzzt.

The lance shot its blue-white bolt of lightning straight at her.

As if she knew his mind, the Daresh rider banked half a heartbeat before Karzul's fire lance spat its fire, but not quickly enough. The red dragon faltered in the air, spinning toward the ground only to recover before striking land. The dragon leveled off and sped away.

Karzul turned his attention back to the brilliant green dragon. That was the one with the fire lance. He heaved a sigh of relief that he had not been cut down by the fire lance while taking care of the red dragon.

He leveled his fire lance at the brilliant green once more and fired.

The dragon performed the maneuver the red had earlier. Shifted all its wings wide and came to a standstill in the air. It pivoted to place itself between Karzul and the rider. Was it protecting her, or was this a tactic she had trained it in? Was the dragon not aware that Karzul could as easily roast them both, or was she counting on Kin'tara to keep Karzul from attacking her? Was there something between the two dragons that Karzul was missing?

Karzul fingered the firing stud of his lance, but before he got off a shot, Kin'tara mimicked the move of the brilliant green dragon, her wings catching the air. She came to a halt and turned her belly to the green dragon and screeched.

Karzul braced himself for the fire. He still felt the raw red on his face from the last time he'd been blasted by her fire lance. But the fire never came. Rather, there was a sharp jarring as the two dragons collided in mid-air. Kin'tara had the green dragon in her grip, mighty talons grasping all four of her legs.

The green flapped her wings wildly.

The air around Karzul turned into a raging storm.

His stomach knotted.

They were falling.

Kin'tara wrapped her front pair of wings around Karzul, halting the gale force winds even as their descent picked up speed.

Karzul screamed.

Trust me, came the thought.

He tried, but it was difficult. They were gaining speed. The air grew thicker, warmer. Breathing became easier, but soon, they would encounter the earth below.

Karzul looked down.

Water.

They were above the great salt lake.

And he couldn't swim.

No matter, the fall would probably kill him first. Was this some bizarre suicide pact between Kin'tara and the brilliant green? What was happening?

Karzul took a deep breath. Perhaps if he held his breath, he could survive.

They plummeted toward the water with its white-tipped waves.

With a mighty wrench, Kin'tara cast the green dragon away from her and spread all three pairs of wings. The sound they made as they snapped open was deafening. Karzul feared the force would rip them apart.

His gut wrenched. His head grew light. His vision closed in on him. He was going blind. He braced for impact.

Nothing.

With a splash, the green dragon crashed into the water, unable to right itself before impact.

Her rider lay face down in the water.

Dead?

Kin'tara reacted to his shock by sending an image of the dragon and its rider pulling themselves out of the water.

Stunned then.

Why let them live?

The image of an egg wavered before his dim eyes. A large egg, covered with all manner of fine gold lines, sitting in a nest of brilliant stones, all by itself. A young dragon appeared and breathed fire onto the egg. Karzul recognized the markings. Kin'tara, with a single pair of wings.

Your daughter?

A wave of warmth washed over Karzul. He felt her pride and profound relief. Her daughter was alive. Kin'tara settled to the ground, encouraging Karzul to dismount.

He watched as she took flight once more, hovering above the brilliant green dragon. She grasped the brilliant green's legs and yanked. At first, all she managed to do was to set waves rushing outwards from the dragon, but eventually, she managed to flip the brilliant green onto her stomach.

Kin'tara grabbed the dragon's tail and dragged her to the beach, settling to the ground to haul her daughter to safety.

Only then did Kin'tara go back for the Daresh rider. She grasped the prone form of the woman in her claws and deposited her on the beach beside Karzul.

Once all three were safe, Kin'tara perched on the sand. She inhaled deeply and blew fire over the brilliant green, then the rider, and finally Karzul himself.

It was not the flame he'd experienced when being attacked, but rather a warm, calming feeling, almost like his mother's embrace.

His eyes grew heavier and heavier until the darkness took him. The last thing he remembered was Kin'tara wrapping her tail protectively around him as she settled in to sleep.

21

THE PRICE OF MERCY

Karzul woke in a panic. His fire lance was gone. He glanced around. The grass bore witness to several pairs of feet and more than one person that had come and gone while he slept. The sky was just turning to the light azure that signaled the imminent appearance of the sun. Kin'tara had already risen and departed for her morning hunt. Could he call her? Would she know anything about who had raided the camp during the night?

"Looking for your dragon?" The Daresh rider seemed unafraid and unmoved by their mutual ordeal. She stood in a large circle of matted grass where, no doubt, she and her dragon had spent the night, just as Karzul and Kin'tara had. "She won't be back for quite a while. That's why you're going to lose the war. Lazy noblemen can't even be bothered to rise early and feed their dragons. We will defeat you. As soon as you return my fire lance."

"I don't have your fire lance." Karzul was beginning to regret letting Kin'tara save the woman. But what could he do? Let her drown? And why did she keep calling him a nobleman?

"You know who has my fire lance," she said. "One of your squad, no doubt. Don't worry. They won't be here for a while either. They're all lazy. Just like you. Their dragons are probably only just now rising. You're stuck where you are. All of you."

The grass stirred behind her.

She glanced back with a startled look. At least she was human. Karzul was beginning to wonder how she kept her cool in such a situation.

Out of the thick green grass rose a head, covered in brown hair that was a bit too short to hang naturally and a bit long to manage without being tied in a queue.

Yarak.

"We may be stuck here," he said. "But there are two of us, and only one of you."

"Sar'tia will kill you both," the woman said.

"Not if we kill you first." Yarak reached for the knife at his belt and drew it. The hunting knife glimmered in the red of the rising sun. It was sharp, crafted for a quick kill and for skinning even the largest animal.

"Do we kill enemy prisoners?" Karzul demanded.

"No," Yarak replied. "But she killed more of us than we can count."

"And she's a prisoner. We don't kill prisoners. Put the knife away."

The woman glared at him. "I'm no one's prisoner, and you are pigs. I'd rather die than let you take me as a slave."

"We're not what you think we are," Karzul said.

She spat. "You're dogs, animals. Without honor."

Karzul stared at her, trying to decide how to respond. It seemed that she had a very different idea of who and what they were, and wasn't going to change her mind. Was her attitude typical of the Daresh? Is that why they wanted to wipe out the Therens? Perhaps if he treated her with respect and courtesy, she might see the truth. Perhaps she would carry that truth back to Daresh.

"Come. Sit. Eat. I don't have much, but what I do have is yours." He fetched his pack. Inside were a handful of loaves of hard bread, some dry cheese, and jerked meat.

He found a flat rock and cut the bread, cheese, and meat. He layered them together to make a crude sandwich. It wasn't as appetizing as he would've liked, but it would have to do. If she didn't eat it, he would. He was hungry.

He extended the sandwich to the woman.

She pushed it away. "Why are you doing this?"

"Feeding you. Do you think we would let a prisoner starve?"

"It's what you do. Kill us."

"We don't kill prisoners, nor do we starve them."

Shrugging, he took a bite of the bread. It wasn't bad.

Before he could take a second bite, she snatched the sandwich from his hand and pushed the entire thing into her mouth. She chewed it dramatically.

It took a while.

When she was finally able to swallow it, she did so with contempt. "You're a pig."

Karzul felt the sting of the insult. He had done nothing but treat her with courtesy. Why did she keep insisting he was an animal?

He pushed the sting of that insult down and prepared a sandwich for himself. Perhaps if he acted as if he didn't care what she called him, she would stop. He steadfastly ignored her, taking a bite and chewing it slowly.

"I'm no pig. I'm Karzul."

"You're a filthy nobleman, no better than the rest of them."

Karzul laughed. "I'm far from that. I grew up in a town, one you destroyed not long ago. Now I'm an orphan."

The Daresh rider's eyes widened for half a heartbeat, then her gaze dropped toward her feet as if his words had struck her with a physical impact.

"We're not just faceless enemies, are we?" Karzul demanded.

A flush crept up her neck and bloomed across her cheeks even as she turned her head away.

"Shouldn't we tie her up?" Yarak asked.

Karzul glanced around. They were on the shore of the lake. The land stretched out, flat and marshy, as far as he could see. "Where's she going to go?"

Yarak shrugged. "I thought that's what you did with prisoners."

Before Karzul could think of a reply, Yarak turned his gaze to the sky and screamed. "Dragon."

Karzul followed his gaze just in time to see a brilliant green dragon winging its way toward them. The majestic creature was so close to the water, her wing tips nearly touching it. Tiny ripples raced away from them with each beat.

She didn't look to be preparing to roast them, at least not while the Daresh rider was with them.

Karzul ducked as the dragon passed overhead, the force of her wingbeats nearly knocking him from his feet.

When he rose, the prisoner was gone. The brilliant green had snatched her up as if she were prey. He'd lost his prisoner before he'd even had a chance to find out what she knew.

"Looks like we should have tied her up," Yarak said.

Rising above the lake, the brilliant green dragon carried the missing prisoner in its forefeet. It paused its flapping, executed a steep dive, and released the woman. She spread her arms and legs wide, and the dragon shoved its head beneath her. Karzul would have sworn she would fall to her death, but she had managed to go from being carried to riding the majestic creature. She was much more of a rider than he ever would be.

At least she no longer had her fire lance.

"How did you find me?" Karzul asked after the rider disappeared into the rising sun.

"When you dove, I followed you. The others told me not to, that it was too dangerous, but I knew you needed me.

"We had our orders, but I couldn't let that stop me. I saw what your dragon did. I've never seen that before. I was shocked. There was no way I could convince my own dragon to free-fall. She glided down in her own good time."

"Did you take my fire lance?" Karzul asked.

"Took them both. I was worried she might wake before you and kill you. Figured she might try to take yours, so I grabbed that too." Yarak gestured toward the trampled grass. "They're over there."

"Please fetch them." Karzul wanted to try something with the captured fire lance.

When Yarak returned, Karzul first examined his own fire lance. No damage. At least not anything he could determine.

Yarak handed him the woman's lance. It was identical to his. He wasn't certain he could tell them apart.

He handed it to Yarak.

The lad studied it. "How does it work?"

"There's a trigger," Karzul explained. "You press it. The further forward the stud, the stronger the fire. Our hope was to find more fire lances and see which of you could operate them. You may soon be training with one of them. Might as well start now."

Karzul gestured to some stones nearby. "Try it. Aim for a rock. Think about how much power you wish to use, then press the trigger forward only just a bit."

Yarak leveled the fire lance at the stones, his face contorted with concentration.

Karzul worried that he had chosen poorly. Was the lad capable of operating the lance? Were any of his new recruits?

Yarak grunted.

Fire leaped from the lance and vaporized the stones.

Karzul felt the drain on him much the same as he did when Nephim fired her lance. He'd thought he recognized strength in Yarak, but perhaps it was more like Nephim, and he was the one providing the power. He stepped a few steps back and gestured to Yarak to try again.

The fire leaped from the lance once more, this time with very little drain on Karzul.

"Looks like you have a natural talent," he said. "I'll be looking to you to help the other. Not all of them will have as much strength with the lance as you."

Yarak beamed. He held the lance above his head and let out a scream.

A burst of air knocked Karzul to the ground.

When he recovered, Yarak was lying on the grass on his back.

The Daresh fire lance was gone.

Off in the distant horizon, a brilliant green dot bobbed up and down.

Karzul cursed.

It was not long before Kin'tara and Yarak's dragon returned. Karzul climbed onto Kin'tara's back without a word. He felt shame for allowing the Daresh rider to escape, but also a bit of relief that he was not responsible for her death or captivity. He did not look forward to what Rodan might have to say about it. He almost wished there was a way to avoid that conversation, but as they approached the grand stairs, Karzul's heart sank. Standing at attention was the entire squad. Nephim stood two paces ahead of them with Rodan beside her. No doubt one of the dragons had sensed their approach and warned the troops of their imminent arrival.

Karzul's heart raced as he scrambled down from Kin'tara's back and strode more boldly than he felt up to Rodan.

"I sense things did not go as well as you hoped, but the mere fact that you are here says you had some success."

Karzul nodded. "We captured the Daresh rider. The one with the fire lance. But she escaped."

Nephim stepped forward. "You what?"

"She escaped." Karzul tried to keep his voice as calm as possible.

"What's wrong with you?" Nephim demanded. "You could have ended this war. How many people will die because you were too timid to take a life?"

"She was my prisoner," Karzul stammered.

Nephim snorted.

Rodan gently touched her shoulder. "The lad has had a time of it. Let's find out what transpired before making any judgments, shall we?"

"What's there to learn? He captured an enemy combatant and then allowed her to escape. He should have killed her and brought the fire lance back here. They wouldn't have stood a chance against us with two fire lances in our hands and none in theirs."

"Enough," Rodan held up his hand to silence her. "Let him tell us what happened."

Karzul stood on the steps in the chill wind and recounted the events of the prior evening and the morning. He left nothing out of his telling. Nephim huffed and snorted as he told the tale. Rodan asked pointed questions and asked for clarification whenever Karzul omitted any details. It seemed like an eternity, but eventually Karzul arrived at the point in his tale where he and Yarak mounted their dragons and headed for the citadel.

He glanced at Nephim. "She wasn't an immediate threat," Karzul explained. "And something about her told me she is not just a cold-hearted killer. She seemed genuinely ashamed when I told her that she had destroyed my hometown. I had no reason to kill her."

"Enough. Let us think about this," Rodan said. He seemed satisfied with Karzul's story, but Nephim never lost her angry scowl.

22

______

A FLICKER OF HOPE

*A*fter a restless night, Karzul woke early, grabbed a light breakfast, wrapped himself in his cloak and headed out to sit on the grand stairs, his legs dangling over the edge. He let the wind chill him to the bone. Perhaps the cold would blunt the sick feeling he had in his gut. He'd let the Daresh rider and her fire lance escape. The death and destruction they would rain down on the Theren troops was on his head.

Off in the distance, the dragons arose. Usually, it was Kin'tara who took flight first, launching herself from the mouth of the cave to plummet toward the valley below before letting the wind catch her wings and tuning to the distant plains to hunt. This time, dragon after dragon leaped from the ledge, catching the wind almost instantly and joining the flying V headed by Kin'tara.

He watched them as the thunder disappeared into the distance.

Footsteps, strong and confident, told him he was no longer alone.

"Not hungry?" Rodan settled himself beside Karzul.

"I'm so sure I'll ever eat again. I'm supposed to instruct the recruits in how to use their fire lances? But I'm not even sure any of them can, besides Yarak. What if I can't help them? How am I to know who can and can't wield a fire lance?"

"You can't. You have the blood. More than Nephim does. All we can do is hope that it's enough."

"What if none of these do? How are we to defeat the Daresh without fire lances? I should have killed the Daresh rider when I had the chance. This is on me."

"Are we the ones who kill prisoners?" Rodan asked.

"No."

"So, you did what you thought was right. It's all anyone ever asks."

"But with Kin'tara keeping me from the fight, and Nephim barely able to hold her fire lance, what are we to do?"

"We'll do our best. It's all anyone can do." Rodan rose. "Come. They should be ready. Time to see how many fire lances you can bring to the fray."

Karzul followed Rodan into the great hall. Eight fresh faces in uniform stood in a rank. Eight dragon riders, who each had that indescribable something that Karzul sensed might be what they sought.

"When I call your name," Nephim explained, "head to your quarters. Karzul will follow you there and see if you have what it takes to be a flame rider."

The recruits stiffened.

"Noraca." As Nephim called out her name, the woman stepped forward, saluted and turned to follow Karzul. She was a few summers older than him. Her face was reddened from exposure to the sun, her hair fair and tied back in a single queue. She followed a pace behind Karzul.

"No need to treat me special," Karzul said. "I'm no different from you."

"But you are. You found your fire lance. You wield it like the flame riders of old. I can only hope to be as powerful as you."

"It's nothing I did. Like the color of my hair or the color of my eyes. It was born with it. I did nothing to earn it, and I hope you were also born with it. If so, you will probably do better than I do."

Noraca stopped before a door much like any other. She opened it and gestured for Karzul to enter. Her quarters we nothing like Nephim's. They were sparsely decorated with only one personal item in evidence: an intricately woven wall hanging crudely depicting the mountains with snow on them.

Noraca blushed. "My gran made that. She said she had always known I'd be a rider. She had high hopes for me."

Karzul didn't know what to say to that. He had never had anyone who had hopes for him, high or otherwise, not even his mother. He pushed the memory of her death down and turned to the desk.

"Here. You can open this?" He gestured to the drawer.

"Never could," she said.

Karzul frowned. This was not starting off the way he'd hoped, but then Nephim had not been able to open her drawer either.

"Let me try." Karzul easily opened the door and withdrew the glass plate. He located the now-familiar image and touched it. The plate came to life.

"Your hand." He gestured to the plate.

Noraca placed her hand on the glass, watching open-mouthed as it scanned her and left behind the imprint of her palm.

"Now the locker," Karzul said.

Noraca placed her palm on the wall as indicated. With a slight pop, the locker opened. Inside was a fire lance, just like Karzul possessed.

"The drawer will open for you now," Karzul said. "I hope you're as good with this fire lance as your gran thinks."

He stepped back into the hall and gestured back the way they had come. "Report to Nephim and have her send back the next candidate."

Perhaps things were looking up. This was a good start, or had Nephim chosen the one she thought had the best chance first? He hoped not. They needed all the lances they could get.

The tall young man in a crisp uniform strode up to Karzul and snapped to attention. He saluted. "Virankel, sir."

Karzul recalled examining him earlier. He had the lines of the aristocracy to him. If Rodan was correct about the power being in the blood, the rider before him should be their best candidate. Karzul felt a little intimidated. The rider definitely had the bearing of one raised in the manor or even the castle, and probably looked down on the likes of Karzul.

"Let's see what you've got." Karzul followed the rider to his quarters. They were stark, but not blank. On the wall were a number of weapons. A crossbow with short bolts hung beside a heavy, curved-bladed sword. On the adjoining wall, an array of knives formed a herringbone pattern that stretched almost to the ceiling.

"Your desk drawer," Karzul asked. "Ever open it?"

Virankel shook his head ever so slightly.

It gave Karzul some relief. Perhaps the blood was not all that thick in him. He caught the thought and flushed. They needed all the help they could get. He should pray this man had the blood, not the other way around.

To cover his embarrassment, Karzul quickly withdrew the glass and touched the image. The grid pattern appeared. He handed it to Virankel. "Place your hand on the glass."

Virankel did as instructed, but nothing happened. No green light, no scanning. Nothing.

Karzul flipped the glass and tried again with the same result.

He placed the glass back into the drawer and slowly shoved it closed.

"Report back to Nephim. Let her know you were unable to secure a fire lance."

"But I did what you asked," Virankel said. "I can do it. Give me a chance."

Karzul drew a breath to give himself time. "I will allow you to try with my lance after all the candidates complete their trials. If you truly can use a fire lance, I will find a way to secure one for you, even if that means stealing the one from the Daresh rider."

Virankel straightened up, snapped a salute, turned and fled, leaving Karzul standing there alone. Had he somehow influenced the test with his attitude? He hoped not. He would have to be better at hiding his feelings in the future. Being down one of eight already was not a good sign.

Thruth was a lad that reminded Karzul of himself. The lad had grown up on a small farm outside of Chayak. He was certain he'd seen the lad more than once in the market selling eggs. One market day, the lad had been absent. He had been a dragon rider for just a summer and seemed bold and timid at the same time. He was confident in his dragon, a mature creature with two pairs of wings that he claimed would be budding her third pair soon. Soon being within the lifespan of Thruth and his grandchildren. He was rumored to be one of the better riders, having taken down three enemies with his sword.

The Karzul had to open the drawer in his quarters for him, much like the rest. He touched the image on the glass, and the grid appeared. He handed it to the lad. "Put your hand here, and it will scan your palm print. That's how you get into your locker."

"I've been briefed, Sir." He placed his hand on the grid.

Karzul waited for the brilliant green light to appear and scan the lad's hand, but nothing happened.

"Sorry," Karzul said. "It appears you don't have the blood."

"Let me try again." Thruth rotated the glass and placed his hand on it again. Again, it showed the grid, but did not scan his palm.

"Curse you," Thruth said. He shook the glass and placed his hand on it once more. Still no brilliant green line.

"Maybe it's broken. We should try another," Thruth said.

He rubbed his hand on his leg as if trying to warm it up from the winter cold. He placed his hand on the glass again, this time pressing hard.

The brilliant green bar appeared, swiped down from his fingertips to his wrist and then back again.

Karzul breathed a heavy sigh.

"See," said Thruth, it just needed a bit of encouragement. Must have been dusty." He blew on the glass as if to whisk away the dust.

"Let's see about your locker." Karzul escorted the lad to the locker and showed him where to place his palm, half expecting the locker to remain firmly closed, but when Thuruth placed his hand on the indicated spot, the locker popped open.

The lad plucked the fire lance from the locker and gently fingered the controls.

"Careful. I'm not sure what would happen if you fired that in here, but I'd rather not find out. Go tell Nephim you passed and ask her to send the next candidate."

Karzul stood in the empty hall waiting. He'd already lost two of those he had tested, and had he not had patience, might have lost a third. He reminded himself to be more careful. He'd hate to eliminate someone who could be the one to turn the war.

A figure appeared down the hall.

Karzul smiled. Nephim must have decided he needed a success and sent Yarak. The lad had proven he could wield a fire lance, but could he open his locker? Karzul was not sure, but he suspected he would.

"Let's get this over with," Karzul said.

Yarak's quarters were a mess compared to the others. He had haphazard decorations shoved into every corner of the room. While it was clean, as was no doubt required of every rider, it was poorly organized and have one the appearance of having just been robbed.

On the desk rested the fire lance.

"Already opened it?" Karzul asked.

"As soon as we learned how it was done, I knew I could do it."

"I expected no less," Karzul said.

Karzul worked his way through the rest of the riders. All but one of them were able to open their lockers and secure a fire lance. Only Achen had failed, similar to Virankel. He had hoped she would make it. The woman was old enough to be Karzul's mother, with a scar across her cheek that she claimed as an honor earned in combat where she had dispatched half a dozen enemy riders single-handedly. She did not protest the way Verankel did. She simply shrugged and departed.

23

A CRUCIBLE OF CHOICES

The next morning, Karzul was instructed to help Nephim train the new recruits. He felt inadequate, having only slightly more experience with a fire lance and much less experience as a rider. The morning was colder than usual in the mountains, and a heavy fog shrouded the citadel. The dragons refused to emerge from their den, even to eat.

The taste of the morning meal lingered as he emerged from the grand entrance to see the recruits already gathered. Six remained.

He regretted having to send two of them back, but they couldn't even open their lockers. They were never going to be able to use a fire lance.

Yarak had been the only one to open his drawer before Karzul arrived. The lad would do well if he could keep his head clear. He tended to let his ego get in his way.

Nephim and the six remaining recruits were standing at attention before the grand stairs. Nephim nodded as he emerged and took position to the left of the recruits.

"Don't let possessing a fire lance go to your head," she said. "You have the blood. That's all you've proved so far. Today, you must prove you have the strength to wield a fire lance in battle. If not, you are of no more use to us than those who failed to open their lockers."

Nephim glanced over at Karzul and asked. "Are you ready?"

"Ready." Karzul considered what the goals were. Nephim had briefed him on what was to transpire. The first goal was to see who had the ability to fire their lance while he was absent. That would dictate strategy, or at least that's what Nephim had told him. She had plans for the squad that she had not shared with Karzul.

"First, I'd like to test each of you individually to see how you can handle the lance," he said.

Karzul looked them over. All of them had successfully opened their lockers. Was that all it took? He chose Noraca as his first test. He had a feeling that she was one of the weaker ones, and he wanted to get that out of the way as quickly as possible. If she could handle her lance, then perhaps they all could.

"Noraca," he called. "You're first. Step over here." He gestured to the steps beside him.

"Aim at that stack of rocks. Focus on the top rock and touch the trigger on your fire lance, just a bit. I want to see how fine your control is."

Noraca cradled the fire lance in her arm, and aimed at the rocks as instructed. She touched the trigger, and the brilliant blue-white light flared. The top rock vanished.

Karzul was impressed. He expected her to struggle, but she had not. Still, he had a nagging feeling in the pit of his stomach that told him not to get too excited. The unsettling feeling in Karzul's stomach flashed as she fired. Was she drawing power from him?

"I'm going to withdraw a bit and let you try again." He stepped back a dozen paces and called to her. "Once more."

This time the flame was not nearly as strong, but still it was sufficient.

Karzul glanced over at Yarak. The lad was shifting his weight from one foot to the other.

"Something wrong, Yarak?" He called out.

"No, sir."

Clearly, something was bothering him. Had Noraca drawn power from Yarak as she had done with Karzul?

"Come stand here." Karzul gestured to Yarak to join him. When the lad had complied, Karzul once more called to Noraca. "Try again."

This time there was no fire from the lance. Noraca's face turned red as she jabbed at the fire lance's trigger.

Still no fire.

Karzul glanced over at Nephim and shook his head.

"Noraca. You're dismissed," she said. "Return your fire lance to your locker, pack your gear and head back to the front."

"But I can do it. Please. Give me one more chance." She jabbed at the trigger again, but the lance refused to fire. She hung her head and headed through the great doors, vanishing into the shadows.

Karzul tested each in turn. Only Thruth failed to produce any fire. He accepted his failure and departed just as Noraca had. They were down to four.

"I don't like sending anyone home," Nephim said. "We need every lance we can get in the air, but you're right to dismiss them. They would have dragged the rest down." She jutted her chin at Yarak. "Looks like you have some competition there. The lad's got talent."

"A burden shared is a burden lightened," Karzul said. "I'm glad to have him. What about the rest? It appears that Belban is emerging as the leader of the group. What do you think?"

"She's able to manage a decent fire even when solo. Not like you two, but more than me. She'll make a good second, if she can keep her pride under control."

"Looks like you have competition," Karzul said.

Nephim scowled. "Riders need to learn respect, but I can work with her." She turned toward the distant mountain. "I think the dragons have emerged. Are you ready to see what they can do in the sky? I want you to keep Yarak out of the fray for a bit, just to get a feel for how they'll operate without either of you near."

"Are you expecting either or both of us to fall so soon?"

"No. But Rodan may be planning for that eventuality. It's our job to train them for whatever their commander decides is the best at the moment, and something you'll learn soon enough, is that strategy can change in a heartbeat and you best be ready for whatever you're called on to do."

"Do you think they'll be ready?"

Nephim tapped her foot as if lost in thought.

What was she thinking?

It looked like there was more on her mind than dismissing a pair of failures.

After a hand of heartbeats, she turned to Karzul. "Why didn't you kill her when you had the chance? You could have ended the war right then and there."

"If military commanders started executing prisoners, where would they be?" he asked. "The whole point of war is to wear the enemy down. Sap their will to fight."

"And killing enemy combatants is part of that," Nephim said.

"Granting quarter is also part of that. Surrender your arms, and the war is over for you. That makes it more attractive to surrender than to fight to the death. If that becomes 'lay down your arms, and you die', no one will comply. No one will surrender. They'll fight to the death every time. The war will never end unless one side is completely wiped out."

"Or one side has a distinct advantage," Nephim said. "You could have taken away that advantage once and for all. "

"It's not right. You're asking me to kill someone who's helpless. Maybe it makes me weak, but I can't do that. Just the thought of it makes my insides knot up. We don't kill prisoners. It's not done."

"The Daresh do. If they catch you, they'll hang you. From the nearest tree, for everyone to see. You're not a prisoner to them. You're an enemy combatant."

"Because she's an enemy combatant, I'm justified in killing her? Even as a captive? Is that what you're telling me?"

"We're soldiers," Nephim said. "We take up arms, we're prepared to die."

Karzul shuddered. Was he prepared to die? "What about the ground troops?" he asked. "Does the same go there? After a battle, do we execute the soldiers on the losing side?"

"How many will die because you let her go?" Nephim demanded.

She had a point. How many indeed? But if one made exceptions in extreme cases, those exceptions would be made for less and less reason. That road led somewhere he didn't wish to go. "We don't kill prisoners," he repeated.

Karzul turned his back on Nephim. He should not have. He knew that, but she was wrong. She was too harsh. He would not kill an unarmed prisoner. No matter what anyone said.

"Rodan's back." She gestured to a dot on the horizon growing by the moment. "He'll want to see the squad in action. I'll command them. You can watch. Let's see how they do without you. Then after you and Rodan have seen enough, you can join them. Pick a side, either side, and demonstrate how that changes things."

Nephim divided the squad into three. She said that that was the best way to get the most out of the limited resources. In pairs, they could watch out for one another. More than that, and one faced a choice of who to protect. It led to no one being totally confident that someone had their back when they needed it the most. In pairs, they always knew who to trust, and that made them more deadly.

He would leave the training up to Nephim. She had much more experience than he did.

Karzul joined Rodan and his dragon above the fray. The dragons glided silently, almost as if they were a pair of leaves carried on the wind. It was a pleasant afternoon with the sun warm enough to drive away the chill. The lazy flight made talking possible and gave both Karzul and Rodan the vantage point they needed to assess the battle playing out below.

"She's in a lot of pain," Rodan said without preamble.

"Is that why she's so short with me?"

"Could be. I hear she had words with you earlier."

Karzul braced himself for a dressing-down. "We don't kill prisoners."

"That rider killed her father."

"That rider killed my mother." He'd never thought it through before, but of course she had. The Daresh only had one fire lance. He'd let the person who killed his mother go free. How many others would lose a parent, a friend or family member because of his decision?

"For her, it's like a blood feud," Rodan said.

Karzul took a moment to imagine how things could have been otherwise. Should he have tied her up? Hamstrung her? Killed her dragon. What he really wanted was to talk to her. Find out what motivated her. Find some common ground to stop the fighting. There had to be something he could have done other than kill or imprison her.

"We don't kill prisoners," he said, but as the words left his mouth, he felt his resolve faltering.

"I'm not saying you should. She should have been held captive."

"That was my plan." Karzul's stomach turned. His very first assignment, and he'd failed. Was Rodan about to send him packing? Discipline him?

"But?" Rodan demanded.

"Her dragon is my dragon's daughter. Kin'tara refused to attack. She struck her daughter only to disable her. Sent her into the lake."

Rodan paused as if in thought. When he finally spoke, it was as if he found humor in the situation. "Challenging, isn't it?" he said. "We depend on our dragons. They become a part of our lives, but they are the masters, not we. It's well that you learned this early on, but it does limit your effectiveness in battle."

"Will I never be able to engage the Daresh rider then?"

"Probably not. You'd need a different dragon, and it means we will have to limit your access to certain sensitive information. Those two will have a link stronger than most dragons. We don't want our plans revealed to the enemy, now do we?"

"The Daresh rider, she kept calling me a noble. Seemed to think I was going to force her to become some kind of servant."

"That sounds like the Daresh."

"Is that why we're at war? They think we're some sort of heathens?"

Rodan sighed. "They have a very different view of the world from ours. They believe that the individual comes first. Everyone is in it for themselves."

"Aren't we?" Karzul asked.

"You grew up in a town. I forget that. It's not like the manor or the castle. In Daresh, they only work together when there's a clear advantage, and even then, they don't trust each other. When they do business, they write words on parchment to say what they agreed, then they argue about those words and try to get out of doing what they said they'd do."

Karzul snorted. He could not imagine the blacksmith writing down words and trying to hold his customer to them. The man would simply take his hammer and have a talk with anyone who tried to cheat him.

"That's not all," Rodan said. "They don't have proper royalty. They have folks who take turns ruling. They get chosen by the people to say what the laws are, and when the people change who they pick, everything changes."

Rodan jabbed a finger at Karzul. "That's why we fight. They hate the nobility. Hate the system that feeds us all. More people starve over there than here, and they blame us. As if we were doing something to take the bread out of their mouths."

Karzul had heard rumors that the Daresh were different, but he had no direct experience with them. "So, why do they want to win this war? Doesn't sound like they want to rule us. What do they want?"

"They want to get rid of the nobility. Kill off the royal family. Empty out the manor houses. Put everyone to work. No more nobles. No farmers. Everyone is the same. Imagine that? Everyone gets an equal say. As if some illiterate townie with pig dung on his boots knows what's good for the realm."

Karzul listened to Rodan go on for a while, but he soon stopped paying attention.

He was one of those poor illiterate townies.

24

WINGS AGAINST THE STORM

Karzul sat astride Kin'tara as they circled high above the ground. For some reason, he found it easier to breathe at altitude now. The air was crisp, cold, odorless and thin. He could feel that thinness. So did Kin'tara. She worked hard to stay aloft, the heat of her exertion offsetting the frigidness of the air.

Nephim glided alongside him and took station off Kin'tara's left wing. She'd assigned the first two pairs of riders and chosen the area they were to patrol. It was important to see how the new recruits did on their own. Nephim had stopped wearing the sling, but she was still favoring her right arm.

"Ormwor and Belban," Karzul remarked. "Cahat and Yarak. Matching capabilities?"

"I think so. Belban is a strong leader, but Ormwor is better with the lance. I think they'll do well together. Cahat is the weakest. She needs to be close to someone strong like Yarak if she's to do any damage."

"You're not expecting them to go up against Daresh riders, are you?"

"Not troops, scouts. Look." Nephim pointed down and off to the east. A pair of dragons were gliding along close to the ground. Bright blue, almost sky blue, and brown. So brown, the dragon blended into the plowed fields below.

"Let's hope your friend doesn't show up," Nephim said.

Karzul flinched. If anything happened to the Theren riders, that was on him. He'd let her live. All he could do was hope she wouldn't show up at this battle. "I don't see any sign of her," he said.

"Let's hope it stays that way." Nephim leaned forward. "Do you think our folks have seen the scouts?"

"Yarak's already turned toward them," he said.

Yarak, for all his bravado, was relatively untrained. He might be equal to the challenge of a rider without a fire lance, but how could he be expected to stand against a fire lance with what little training he'd received?

Should he attempt to enter the battle? Without the Daresh rider, Kin'tara had nothing to hold her back. He could call upon her superior experience. "Should we help?" he asked.

Before Nephim could respond, a searing blue-white light streaked from the dragon Karzul had identified as belonging to Yarak. The bolt of light stabbed at the distant scout, but the rider was too far away. The bolt did nothing.

"He should have waited," Karzul said.

"Impetuous," Nephim said. "We knew that. Hope he learned his lesson."

The enemy riders broke formation, one heading to the north, the other to the south. Karzul tried to keep an eye on both of them, but splitting his attention made him lose track of the brown one. That was the tactic. Separate. Fly wide. Divert attention. Karzul's squad would have a much harder time tracking them both when they took off in opposite directions like that. Nephim instructed the squad to stay in pairs and watch in opposite directions. Karzul knew that of all the riders, he was the greenest, the least experienced. He reassured himself that they knew what they were doing, even if he didn't. Still, he could not help but wish there was something he could do to improve their chances of survival.

Karzul flinched as a brown streak came barreling out of the north and swept by Cahat. Cahat had her sword out. Hopefully, she was as deadly with the sword as Yarak was with the staff. If not, the battle would soon be over.

Swords flashed, chrome glinting in the sun as the riders clashed.

Cahat ducked beneath the flashing blade and used her own to make a cut across the enemy's leg.

Bright red appeared on the rider's leg as he flashed past her.

"Good girl," Nephim shouted.

The sky-blue dragon appeared as if out of nowhere.

It sped toward Cahat, coming up from beneath her.

She would never see the strike from where she sat.

"Where's Yarak?" Karzul yelled. "Isn't he supposed to be on the tail of that rider? Isn't that what you said he should do? Did he run off after the brown and leave her alone?" If Yarak had abandoned Cahat and she had died, how would he ever live with that? He'd been told not to abandon his partner.

Suddenly, a brilliant blue-white beam sliced through the rider and dragon just before they reached Cahat.

The separate halves twirled toward the ground even as Yarak flashed past Cahat, now in pursuit of the brown dragon.

"Strike a blow for our side!" Nephim shouted. "Remind me to reward Yarak when we get home. He gets a medal for downing his first enemy rider."

Cahat turned to follow Yarak. Her dragon was larger than his, and she quickly caught up. They made a good pair. She had more sense than Yarak did. Karzul hoped that her sensibilities would rub off on him, hopefully before he did something that got them killed. He wished she had used her lance, but that was not the only way to win a fight.

She had performed well.

"How far should they be following the scout?" Karzul asked. "Surely not all the way to the border."

"I told them not to leave the area. The other two are still out there. There might be more. Better to keep to this area than spread ourselves too thin."

Kin'tara let out a snort.

Something Karzul had never heard her do before.

Had she sensed something?

What is it? He pressed the question on Kin'tara as she dove straight down, gaining speed like a falling stone. Suddenly, she banked hard to the left and pulled up, making a steep turn in the air.

A brilliant blue-white bolt sizzled past Karzul.

"Watch it," he screamed to no one in particular. Was Yarak going wild with his staff?

He glanced down.

The brilliant green dragon was winging its way toward Ormwor and Belban.

Karzul leaned forward, encouraging Kin'tara to enter the fray. Before the dragon had a chance to move, Nephim pulled alongside.

"Stay out of it."

"Why?"

"Because of her." Nephim nodded at Kin'tara.

The dragon was breathing hard. She shook beneath him.

"She won't let you harm her kin. You're out of action. You have to let the squad handle this on their own."

"They'll be killed."

"Look over there," Nephim said.

Karzul followed Nephim's gaze. Streaking out of the east were a pair of dragons. Yarak and Cahat were winging their way toward the green dragon.

"This is what they were training for before you selected them as fire lance wielders. The Daresh rider thinks she has the upper hand — the element of surprise. She's arrogant. She won't even think of looking behind her. They'll be on her before you know it."

Karzul held back, but it was difficult. Kin'tara was agitated. Wisps of smoke shot from her nostrils as she kept her eye focused on the brilliant green dragon. Was she angry that her daughter was helping his enemy? Or worried her daughter could be injured while he held her back?

A blue-white bolt blazed beneath them, headed straight for the rider seated on the brilliant green dragon. Would this be the end for the Daresh rider? Karzul didn't think she had time for evasive action.

He was wrong.

The brilliant green rolled over. Once, twice, three times. Then, it arced hard to the left and raced for the sky.

Karzul gripped Kin'tara with his legs. Had the Daresh rider seen Karzul and Nephim above her? Was she even now changing her focus to attack the commanders and abandon the combatants? Or would she have the same hesitation to fight Kin'tara that Kin'tara showed?

She had only risen a few hundred spans when she arced over and performed a perfect inverted loop. The great wings snapped and rippled in the wind as the brilliant green sped through the vertical circle and pulled out directly behind Cahat.

"Watch out," Karzul couldn't stop himself from yelling even though there was no way she could hear him.

The Daresh rider leveled her lance.

Karzul wanted to close his eyes, but he couldn't. He needed to see what happened. The hair on his arms stood on end. He was impotent. Helpless.

He loathed the feeling.

The brilliant blue-white light raced from the Daresh rider. A heartbeat before it struck, Cahat's dragon twisted in mid-air. It opened its maw and shot fire. Straight at the oncoming beam.

The beam struck the dragon in the mouth, feeding the already ferocious fire.

Was that it? Would the dragon flash into nothingness?

No.

Was the dragon fire somehow counteracting the lance?

Karzul had no time to think. Almost as quickly as the beam from the brilliant green started, it ended.

Cahat's dragon was tumbling.

Without warning, another flash from a fire lance appeared, aimed at the brilliant green and its rider. Yarak had fallen in behind her.

"Go, Yarak," Karzul shouted.

A wave of fear and anger washed over him. For a half a heartbeat, he thought Kin'tara was about to join the fight, but pushed the thought aside, distracted by Nephim, who was hunched forward on her dragon's neck shouting, "Come on. Pull up."

Karzul followed her gaze. Far below, Cahat's dragon was tumbling like a leaf falling from a tree. Had it been stunned by the lance fire? Could Cahat get it under control before it hit the ground? Was there anything she could even do about it?

Kin'tara sensed his concern. She let out a screech and dove. Not with her wings folded, as he'd seen her do before, but with her wings spread wide, stroking wildly even as they picked up speed heading straight down.

Karzul questioned her intent but got no answer. She was focused single-mindedly on her goal.

The stunned dragon had its wings spread wide now.

At least with its wings wide, it had slowed its descent. No more diving. Perhaps that was good. It would give Kin'tara a bit more time to do — what? Intercept the falling dragon? He wasn't certain that that was her plan. What then? To snatch Cahat from her dragon before they hit the ground?

Karzul hung on. It wouldn't be long before he found out. The ground rushed up at them even as Kin'tara pulled alongside Cahat's dragon.

It was unconscious.

Kin'tara nudged the stunned dragon. Gently at first, then harder. Cahat's dragon opened its eyes, blinked, looked around, then pulled its legs beneath its body and nosed down. It caught the air and started on a gentle curve. Would it be enough? Karzul wasn't sure.

Kin'tara furiously beat all three sets of wings, showing a power the smaller and less mature dragon didn't posses. Their path changed from a vertical descent to horizontal. Karzul's head grew heavy, hard to hold up as his weight increased with Kin'tara's effort. His feet burned from the extra weight as the dragon struggled to avoid the ground rushing up at her. He could feel his heartbeat in his rapidly swelling ankles. His back flared with pain. It was as if he were suddenly carrying a load of bricks. His vision narrowed. Great swirling masses of gray and green erupted in a hurricane, blocking out his vision.

It grew hard to breathe.

The ground below was a blur.

Kin'tara had her legs out.

Was she going to try to land?

He grabbed onto her neck even as she pulled harder.

His vision dimmed.

His heartbeat echoed in his ears.

What would it be like to die?

Kin'tara let out a mighty screech, flapped her wings even harder and Karzul felt his weight increase.

It was overwhelming.

He surrendered to it.

The last thing he noticed was the smell of hay before the darkness enveloped him.

25

UNEASY TRUCE

Karzul woke in darkness and silence. Was this what death was like? He had never truly believed in the afterlife. He was never quite sure what to expect, so he expected nothing. They said unworthy souls were consigned to the vast darkness for all eternity. Was this where he was?

The scent of alcohol and iodine tickled his nose.

He was alive, but where was he?

He blinked and opened his eyes. In the dim light, he could make out his surroundings, but just barely. He lay in a bed not his own, surrounded by soft white lights and green walls. His feet stuck out from beneath the blanket, exposing his bare flesh to the cold air. He tried to pull them in, but he could not. The idea that he was alive seemed uncertain. He worked his mouth. It was sour. As if his teeth hadn't been brushed in days. How long had he been here?

Where was here?

"I think he's awake." Nephim appeared and looked into his eyes. "Yes, definitely awake."

"You did a brave thing," Rodan said. "Brave, if not foolish. You saved your rider. I'll have to give you that, but we almost lost you in the process."

Karzul blinked. "What happened?"

"You struck the ground," Rodan said. "Going mighty fast, from what I hear."

Karzul tried to raise his head from the pillow. Pain sizzled from his left ear to his right, as if it were on fire. He ignored it. "Kin'tara?"

Rodan put a hand on Karzul's shoulder, gently pushing him down. "She'll heal."

Karzul looked to Nephim for confirmation.

She glanced at Rodan and nodded.

"Who's caring for her?" he asked.

"She's being attended to by her own kind." Rodan stepped back from the bed. "I need to speak with Alchua. I'll be back to check on you later."

"Stay down," Nephim said. "I've still got some stitches to check on."

"Kin'tara?"

"Ripped a wing, maybe broke some ribs, just like you did. She tumbled pretty hard when she hit the ground. She's not doing any flying in the next thirty days or so."

"Cahat?" Karzul asked.

"Fine. Not a scratch on her. Whatever you did, you pulled her dragon out of it just in time. A heartbeat or more, we'd have two of you in here to attend to, or one of you and an urn."

"The others?"

"All fine."

"The Daresh rider?"

"She got away. The other two Daresh weren't as lucky. Yarak and Belban chased them down and lanced them right out of the sky. Pretty impressive, that lad of yours."

"What's been happening? How long have I been asleep? What did I miss?"

"Only a night. And we do what we've always done. We keep pushing." Nephim peeled a bandage from Karzul's leg, wiped the abrasion beneath it with a dark, foul-smelling liquid, and replaced the bandage. "I did some digging. That rider friend of yours. She has a name. Turns out she's not even Daresh. Imagine that. She was born right here.

Wrong side of the sheets. Her mother was a servant in the castle. Died right after the girl was born. No one claimed the girl, so they shipped her off to Daresh."

"Why Daresh?" Karzul asked.

"Her mother had kin there. Distant kin, but when they discovered that, no one in Thera wanted her."

"Is that why she hates us so?"

"Maybe."

"You found out her name?"

"Dari," Nephim said. "Not the sort of name you want to have in Daresh. I'm surprised they didn't change it. Hide who she was. It couldn't have been much fun carrying that name all her life.

"The Daresh are massing troops on the border. Word getting around is that as soon as the reinforcements arrive, they'll push forward, burning and pillaging."

She waved her hand toward Karzul's legs. "I can't believe you didn't break your legs. You received only a few stitches for all your trouble. The only thing that's broken is your ribs. Bandage them up, and you're good to go. Just don't catch a cold while they're healing. You won't be able to cough it out, and it could turn deadly. But you should be able to ride as soon as Kin'tara is ready."

"And then what?"

"Then we burn those Daresh where they sit."

Nephim refused to allow Karzul out of bed for two days. When she did, it was with a strict admonishment to only walk as far as needed and to sit down if he felt any pain or grew dizzy or nauseous. It was just before midday. He was hungry and eager to see how the troops had fared in his absence.

The aroma of cooking wafted from the kitchen, making his mouth water.

"Here he is. The mighty hero." Belban, Yarak, Ormwor and Cahat jumped to their feet as he entered.

"Sit," he said. "I'm no hero."

Cahat rushed over to him and hugged him.

Pain flared in his ribs.

"Cahat," Belban said. "You're hurting him."

Cahat released Karzul. "Sorry, sir. I just. If you hadn't done what you did, I'd be dead."

Karzul let her help him to the table. "It was nothing," he said. "I'd have done it for anyone."

"But you did it for me," Cahat said. "I'll be forever in your debt."

Karzul glanced at the empty table. "Maybe you can repay that debt by bringing me something to eat. I'm famished. All Nephim allowed me was mush and some sort of fruit juice. Said it would help my bowels. Tasted like dirt."

"Right away, Sir." Cahat rushed off.

Yarak sat down beside Karzul.

"I heard you chased down a couple of scouts and lanced them out," Karzul said.

Yarak nodded solemnly. "Yes, sir."

"First kill?"

"People. Yes, but not my first kill."

"Don't get used to it," Karzul said. "It's not something you should come to enjoy. It's a necessity, not a sport. Remember that." He placed a hand on Yarak's shoulder. It was clear that he was shaken, but was putting on a brave face. "It was necessary," he reminded the lad.

He glanced around the room. The squad seemed tense, nervous. He felt responsible to do something, but what would Nephim do? He had no idea, but he needed to do something to lighten the mood. "So what's the gossip?" He asked.

Belban leaned back in her chair and looked up at the ceiling. "You didn't hear this from me, but..." She glanced around. "I heard that Nephim isn't really all that true blooded. Turns out her family has roots in the countryside. Some say that her real father was a commoner. That's why she spent every spring and fall in some small town. She will tell you she was just getting a taste of life outside the manor, but in truth, it was more than that."

"That's just a rumor." Cahat turned as if she had heard something behind her. "Let's not talk about our folk like that." She threw a look at Belban and then turned to the door just as Nephim came rushing in.

"Dragon!" she cried. "Not one of ours."

The squad dropped what they were doing and rushed outside.

Karzul was hard-pressed to keep up with them as they raced to the great entryway.

"There." Nephim pointed to the darkening sky.

High overhead was a small dark dot. How had she even seen it? Was it really an enemy dragon or was it a wild one? How would one tell?

"Belban, Yarak. Go check it out," she ordered. "Do not engage. Just find out if it's friendly, wild, or are we in hot water?"

"Right away, sir," Belban replied. She called out for her dragon, and in moments, she and Yarak vanished.

To Karzul's eyes, they were simply black dots in the sky. He could not make out who was who other than there were two dots close together and one alone. Was it a lone scout? How had they found this place? Had they followed someone home from a raid? Or did they have some other way of gathering information? Was there a spy in their midst? Someone who couldn't hold their tongue? He hoped not.

A blue-white flash streaked between the riders.

Karzul couldn't tell who was firing. Almost immediately, the blast was returned, followed by another, and another. Then, almost as if some agreement had been reached, both lances fell dark.

The dots merged for a hand of heartbeats, then separated, the solo dot vanishing into the darkening sky. It seemed like forever before Belban and Yarak returned.

"I told you not to engage," Karzul said.

"I tried not to, but she left me no choice." Yarak yanked his left sleeve away from his arm. It bore a charred streak that, had it been half a digit closer, would have seared his arm open no less than Nephim's attack had done.

"Did you get her?" Karzul asked.

"No, sir. She's a very skilled flyer. She never gave me an opening."

Yarak shuddered. "She had me in her sights. I saw her staff pointed right at me. That's when she holstered it and saluted me."

"And?" Karzul asked.

"You told me not to engage. I was no longer in danger, so I holstered my lance. That's when she came alongside me. She motioned me closer. At first I thought it was a trap, but she was desperate to tell me something. She wouldn't take no for an answer."

"What did she have to say?" Karzul asked.

Yarak shifted his weight from one foot to the other.

"She wants to talk to you."

26

___

A SHADOW OF PURPOSE

Karzul slept fitfully, tossing and turning throughout the night. His room was warm compared to the sickroom he'd been confined to for his recovery. He sat carefully in his chair and leaned back. He usually thought better with his fingers interlaced behind his head, but his ribs hurt too much for that.

Dari, the Daresh rider, had been very specific about where they were to meet. A shrine in a forest on the Daresh border. Had she chosen the location because dragons were at a disadvantage in the trees? Was she aware that Kin'tara was injured?

Was this a trap?

"It's your decision," Rodan had told him the previous night. "I will not force you to go."

Dari had asked for him by name. Why? She was the enemy. She had killed his mother. How could he trust her? Was it just a ruse to get him alone so she could kill him? What that her plan? He thought long and hard, but decided that perhaps, just perhaps, he could find out what drove the Daresh, and maybe find a way to end the war, or at least slow down the killing.

He stood up and dressed.

He found Yarak in the kitchen.

"I need your help. You're the best person for it, but I'm hesitant to ask," Karzul said.

"Help with what?"

"I think there is something to be gained by meeting with the Daresh rider. I hope I can find some common ground. At least open a discussion. Maybe find a way to end the war without more killing. I have to try."

"Kill her and take her lance," Yarak said. "That'll end the war."

"No. I want your word that you'll provide transportation, but stay out of any fight. If another rider shows up, leave me there and come back when it's safe. No engaging the enemy. This is a peace mission we're on." Karzul glared at Yarak. "Can I trust you?"

Yarak nodded, but remained silent.

"Good," Karzul said. "Let's get going."

It took a bit of coaxing to get Yarak's dragon into the air so early in the morning, and Karzul found straddling a strange dragon to be quite discomforting. He was accustomed to a much wider straddle and longer spikes and scales to grasp. Without the constant communication between himself and the dragon, every move, every dip, every turn was unexpected and unsettling. The ground below was indistinct, hazy. Was his own perception of the land somehow enhanced by Kin'tara's own senses? He would have to ask when he had a moment.

Far below was the dividing line between the forested hills and the flat plains.

"This is it," Yarak said. "The dragons know it."

Without warning, Yarak leaned into his dragon, and they fell.

Karzul's stomach lurched.

Thankfully, the fall was brief, and the glide of the dragon over the meadow to land near the edge of the woods was almost comfortable.

A narrow, timeworn path meandered away from the meadow and slipped into the shadows beneath the ancient oak trees. Karzul followed along the path, mindful of the dead leaves and gnarled roots that might trip him up. Deep in the woods, the air was still and stifling. No bird sang, no insects buzzed. The silence was eerie. Tucked among the trees, an ancient relic stood. Rough-hewn stone stacked together stood testament to builders long dead. The mortar crumbled in places, leaving gaps like missing teeth. Squat, brooding and covered with lichen, the small building bore the weight of the slate roof as if about to collapse beneath its burden, yet somehow the roof still held. The place smelled of moss and decaying leaves. The hair on Karzul's arms rose. Whatever the place had been, it had not yet surrendered its purpose.

The entrance to the structure was narrow.

A trap? He hesitated, peering into the shadows.

Inside, a small altar stood on bare earth. More stones held together by mortar. No trimmings. No paintings. No tapestries. No words engraved on anything.

What sort of shrine was this?

"You came," said the figure in the doorway. "I half expected you not to."

"Dari." He nodded slightly. Deference one paid to an equal. "Why me?"

"You saved me from drowning."

Karzul remained silent.

"You could have killed me, and yet you did not.."

"You called this meeting," Karzul said. "Why?"

Dari lowered herself to the floor, ignoring the dust. She motioned for Karzul to do the same.

He brushed the dust away and sat across from her.

Out of knife range.

He folded his arms.

And waited.

She took her time before speaking. "I have learned of plans that are ... disconcerting. I called you here to propose an alliance of sorts. I believe our interests are the same."

"What plans?"

"The Daresh intend to push for the old mine in the next few days once their reinforcements arrive. They have overwhelming superiority and will easily take the ground needed."

"So you say, but this is not news."

"Do you know why they want the mine?"

Karzul had no idea, but he wasn't about to show his ignorance.

"When I first encountered you, I believed that you had discovered a fire lance as I did not long ago. I assumed you had done the same as I had. Stumbled across a lance in one of the forbearers' abandoned structures and somehow learned how to use it. It worried me, and the Daresh, but one fire lance alone is not enough to turn the tide. But when more fire lances appeared, it became less and less likely that you'd found them. The Daresh believe that you've located the secret to constructing fire lances and are hard at work making them for every soldier in your army."

Karzul bit his lip. Let her think what she would. She might reveal more than she planned if he appeared more knowledgeable than he was.

"The old mine. It's the secret to building more fire lances. There are ores down there that are used in their construction."

"Are the Daresh capable of building fire lances?"

"Not yet. They have old records — instructions from the forbearers. That is why they want the mine. So they can perfect their knowledge and manufacture fire lances in great quantities."

"I see," Karzul said. "And if they capture the mine?"

Dari shook her head. "They plan to kill you. Every man, woman and child."

He imagined a dozen flame riders attacking one town after another. The image of the burning buildings and his own mother dying in the flames flashed before his eyes. He swallowed. No quarter. Just what he had argued against not so long ago. "And what do you want me to do?"

"I want you to stop them."

"How do I do that?"

"Destroy the mine," she said. "If you destroy it, I give you my word that I will not harm you or your squad. I'll find a way to be elsewhere when the battle begins. Mind you, I will not do anything to harm the Daresh troops. Nor undermine them. I simply want you to destroy the mine. If you do, there's no reason for the Daresh to invade."

She rose. "You have three days."

By midday, Karzul was ready to gather the recruits. He and Rodan had yet to work out a plan.

"How does one destroy a mine?" Rodan asked.

"Collapse it?" Karzul suggested. "Fill it with earth?" That seems impractical. "We have only three days."

"There might be a way," Nephim interjected. "If we can get into the mine, we can collapse it from within. My uncle lives near the mine. I used to visit it as a child. He warned me of certain dangers. Said they could kill me or trap me in there. We used to sneak out and go there when no one was looking. There are a lot of strange and wonderful devices still operating that may lead us to a means to thwart their plans to use the mine, and ultimately destroy it.

"There are pumps that keep the mine dry. The water flows out of one of the buildings to empty into the river. If we destroy that, the mine will fill with water. Another building contains huge fans that blow air into the mines. If we destroy those, perhaps that will make the mine unusable. I'm certain that the application of a fire lance on one of the critical pieces of equipment would destroy the mine, at least make it unusable."

"Do you know where these weak points are?"

"I do, but my knowledge is limited to what I just revealed. We need to find out more before we can say for sure. There are lots of ancient artifacts down there that no one understands. Tunnels that go so far into the ground that there's no light. It's scary. But it's our only hope."

"So you can take me there?"

She nodded.

"You and Yarak can join me. He's my ride until Kin'tara is healed enough to bear me aloft. You're my guide."

The trip to the mine was uneventful. Karzul was growing accustomed to riding behind Yarak, even though the lad was a bit reluctant to be his chauffeur. On foot, the mine was a full day's march from the border. In the air, it was a quick trip. He had seen this place before. It was where Kin'tara had first stopped for a drink.

"Barracks," Nephim pointed to the remnants of walls on one side of the road. "Temple of the Winds." She gestured to the building where Karzul had heard the mighty rushing winds. "Temple of the Waters." She indicated the building where Karzul had noted the thrumming. "And the Temple of the Forbearers. It's filled with machines abandoned by the forbearers. And that's where the mineshaft starts. It's where the opening is."

Karzul looked at the scene with fresh eyes. What he saw below was strange and wonderful. The temple of the forbearers was situated next to the river, just beside the great square pond. A great fan of brownish-green spread out from the pond to embrace the river. Rivulets of bright green ran through the duller green like veins in a leaf. The temple of the forbearers bore a strange mark on its roof that could only be seen from the air. Was it a signal to the dragons and their riders? The mark was a common symbol. One that Karzul had learned as a child.

Poison.

Yarak landed beside that building.

"This is the entrance," Nephim said. "Inside here." She pushed open a large door that swung easily at her touch. Karzul would have expected it to protest at the very least, but some trick to the forbearer's technology made it glide as if it had only yesterday been installed. Inside the building, it was dusty and empty. There was evidence that heavy machinery had been removed. Something had worn a path into the stone floor. But it was a large iron-framed doorway that caught his eye. It was here that Nephim led him. Beyond the door was a tunnel carved in the earth that quickly became rock as the passageway worked its way deeper and deeper into the earth. After what seemed like ages, they came to a side tunnel that glowed with an eerie green light.

Karzul was eager to see what was down there. He'd never seen such a light before. He peeked his head around the rocky corner.

The glow seemed to intensify in the distance. What they were seeing was a feeble light compared to what must have been further down the tunnel.

Karzul turned to head down the side tunnel, but Nephim grabbed his arm and pulled him back. "Not down there," she said.

"I won't be long."

"That's poison." Her grip on his arm grew tighter.

"I don't plan to eat or drink anything."

"You don't have to," she said. "That light is poisonous just to look at."

27

WHISPERS IN THE BORDERLANDS

arzul stared at the greenish-yellow light reflecting off the walls. It didn't flicker; it was steady, just like the lights in the citadel. Whispers erupted, calling out his name. The light was steady, but somehow, the impression of shadows came through, as if someone was standing just out of sight beckoning him to join them. He longed to answer that call. He took a halting step toward it, then another.

"Don't." Nephim's grip on his arm was insistent. She hauled him bodily from the tunnel. It wasn't until they were inside the large building that the draw faded, and Karzul could once more think of anything else.

"Poison. I spent my summers near here. One day, someone from the village went down there. A girl. Just entering womanhood. She said the light called to her. She visited whenever she could. Within a moon, she had the appearance of an old crone. Gray hair. Wrinkled skin. Shortly after that, her hair fell out, and she fell ill. She was unable to eat or drink anything. By the time she died, it was as if she had lived a hundred summers in just a few moons. It's not a healthy place."

Karzul tried to make sense of what he was hearing. He only half believed it. How could someone age so quickly? It must be a tale told to frighten the children and locals, keeping them away from the mine.

"I went down there myself once. Only for the briefest moment, but when I came back..." She ran her hand through her hair, highlighting the white streak she bore. He had never given it much thought. He thought it was natural. He opened his mouth to ask her about it, but before he could, Yarak stuck his head in the doorway and called out to them. "We have to leave now."

"But we just got here," Karzul remarked.

"Soldiers are coming," he said. "On foot, from Daresh."

Karzul didn't hesitate.

Soldiers.

Dari said he had three days.

Had she lied?

Three men in Daresh uniforms appeared from behind the crumbled wall of the first barracks. "You there!" one of them shouted. "Stay where you are."

Before Karzul could think of a response, a brilliant blue-white beam flared, and the three men disappeared.

"Come on," Yarak shouted. He was already holstering his fire lance and straddling his dragon.

Karzul hopped behind him even as the mighty dragon leapt into the sky.

"There. More." Yarak pointed to a small group of soldiers. "Half a dozen. No more."

"We can't let them have the mine," Karzul said.

"I can take them." Yarak un-holstered his fire lance.

"Where's Nephim?" Karzul looked for her. He expected her to be in the air, but she was not.

"They have her." Yarak pointed to two men who held a struggling Nephim between them. Several more Daresh troopers had arrayed themselves around the mine complex. It appeared as if they had been camped there for some time already.

"We've been betrayed. Find a place to land." Karzul gestured to the

Daresh soldiers. He couldn't believe they were already trying to take over the mine. He would put a stop to that.

As Yarak's dragon, the whistle of an arrow sped past Karzul's head.

"Archers!" he cried out.

The dragon pulled up hard and shot for the sky, as the soldiers beneath her dwindled to the size of ants.

"We have to save Nephim," he said.

Yarak's dragon banked over, giving Karzul a clear look at the soldiers holding Nephim. They were surrounded by archers. There was no way a dragon or rider could attack directly.

"Lance fire is our only hope," Yarak said.

"No, I can't aim that well from this distance. I'd hit Nephim."

"I can do it." Yarak leveled his lance and, before Karzul could stop him, fingered the firing stud. A brilliant blue-white light jabbed from his fire lance, taking out first one and then the other of the archers.

"The archers!" Yarak shouted. "You didn't think I was going to get close to Nephim, did you?"

Karzul felt his face go flush.

He leveled his fire lance and aimed at the next archer. He fingered the stud, and the archer vanished in a puff of smoke. As the lance discharged, a tingle flowed through Karzul into the lance. Was that how the lance was powered?

"One more." Yarak took aim, and another archer vanished.

He leaned forward. "It's clear enough now."

Yarak's dragon dropped like a stone, Karzul struggling to hold on.

Karzul aimed at the two men holding Nephim even as they streaked for the ground. "Take the one on the left. I'll take the right."

Before Karzul had a chance to respond, the brilliant blue-white light streaked out to embrace the man on Nephim's left. Karzul followed suit, his own beam of destruction striking the man on the right.

The two soldiers vanished.

Nephim shook her arms and ran for her own dragon.

She was away, and airborne, but not before two more men appeared from behind the barracks walls.

Archers.

"There," Karzul pointed.

Two more bolts flashed. The two archers vanished.

"Are there any more?" Karzul asked.

"Over there." Not far up the road, a triple line of Daresh soldiers marched in unison. There must have been two dozen. Karzul called out to Nephim. "Follow us. Take the center column."

Nephim nodded and positioned her dragon right behind Yarak's. Together, they turned and lined up on the road. The first pass saw three blue-white bolts cut through the troops, scattering the men. After that, it was chasing them down one by one and eliminating them until there were no more. After the shooting was over, Karzul noticed that Nephim's dragon had taken several arrows through one of its wings.

"You've been hit," he called to her.

She nodded. I have to go back to the Citadel and get her sewn up."

"I expect them to send troops," Karzul said. "Tell Rodan that Dari lied."

He tapped Yarak on the shoulder. "Let's go find her and have a word."

Word had come that Dari and the brilliant green had been overflying Alchua's camp several times a day. Karzul donned a nondescript brown cloak to hide his uniform and set out to find her. Yarak had sent his dragon away to hide until she appeared. As soon as she turned for Daresh, he called the dragon back and they were off. Before he knew it, they were three leagues into Daresh territory, just outside a mid-sized town. The green dragon circled the town twice, then landed in the square.

Dari hopped off and disappeared into the town.

Karzul instructed Yarak to land outside of the town so that he could follow Dari. Following his orders, Yarak immediately took flight after the drop-off. No use putting Yarak and his dragon in harm's way.

Yarak had wanted Karzul to take his fire lance, but Karzul refused.

The weapon would attract attention he wished to avoid. He had his knife in case he ran into trouble.

He checked his cloak to make sure it completely covered his uniform and unsnapped his sheath so nothing would be in the way, should he need to get to his knife in a hurry? Still, he was on edge. The town, like every town, had its own unique scent, but those scents were odd. Freshly mown hay, nettles, cattle dung, wood smoke, frying pork bellies and a hint of wild flowers made their presence known. It smelled as if there was a market nearby. As good a place as any to start.

Karzul entered the street where he'd seen Dari disappear. It was narrower than he expected, with the second floor of the buildings jutting out over the street. The homes were of wood and mortar construction, well maintained but not ostentatious. All the doors and walls were the same color. No flowers or herbs growing in boxes. No stained windows or colorful signs. Not like home.

"You there."

Karzul turned in the direction of the voice. Two men blocked the way behind him. One held a pitchfork; the other a pike.

"I'm looking for a woman," Karzul said.

"I bet you are," the man with the pitchfork said. His face was ruddy and red, as if exposed to the sun frequently. His arms were thick and strong. A blacksmith?

"No. Not like that. Her name's Dari."

"Why would a stranger like you be looking for one of our own? You lost?"

"I just need to find Dari. We have business."

"What sort of business does a Theren have here?" He took a step closer, lowering the pike. The blade was sharp and glistened. "Did you really think your cloak was going to fool anyone?"

Karzul glanced behind him. That way was blocked by three more men. How had he been so foolish? He'd let Dari lead him straight into a trap. For a moment, he held out hope that Yarak would see what was happening and pluck him from his predicament, but the building all but obscured him. Besides, did he really expect Yarak to be watching that closely and risk his own life to save Karzul from himself?

"Let's string up this sorry sod of a Theren," the blacksmith said. He prodded Karzul with the pike.

Karzul backed away, straight into the hands of the waiting men. They grabbed his wrists and bound them with a thick rope. They placed a noose around his neck and used it to pull him along through the market square. In the center of town, was a large grassy area, filled with stalls selling all manner of items. Produce, meat, and home goods occupied a large portion of the market, but one stall caught his eye. It was filed with weapons. Knives, throwing stars, pikes, poles, lances, almost every kind of weapon Karzul had ever seen or heard about, and back in the shadows, was that a fire lance?

Beside the weapons seller stood a stout oak tree. Its branches overhung the street and provided shade for the shoppers. It was there that they took Karzul, threw the rope over the lowest branch and positioned him beneath it.

The blacksmith stepped beside Karzul and whispered. "Today is my lucky day. I can use a few coin." He glanced at the patrons and raised his voice. "We have ourselves a spy here. Who wants to bid on hauling him into the air?"

A young man held up a single copper.

"You think I'm going to sell you the right to execute a spy for a measly copper?" the blacksmith asked. "Besides, with arms like yours, you couldn't haul him up, and even if you did, you'd just shimmy up the rope. He outweighs you by a bit, I'd venture." The blacksmith surveyed the crowd. "Any takers at all?"

A hand raised above the crowd. Slender fingers held onto three coppers. "I'll give you three to let him go. Go get yourself an ale."

The blacksmith laughed. "Why would I let him go?"

The crowd parted, and Dari stepped forward. Her black uniform was crisp and neat, her boots coming up to her thighs. Her black hair had been tied back and bound in a single queue that fell over the cape that swirled when she turned. "Because he's *my* prisoner."

"Then why's he running around free? Where's the regular guard?" the blacksmith demanded.

"I had my eye on him. He wasn't going anywhere. Tell you what. I'll still give you three coppers. Just for your trouble."

Dari dropped the coins into his outstretched palm.

The blacksmith removed the noose from around Karzul's neck with a shake of his head. "Next time it won't go so well, you hear me?"

"Yes, sire," Karzul said meekly.

"Come on," Dari said. "You must have something on your mind. You found me, we should at least have a drink."

She led Karzul to a small public house that bordered the market.

When the server arrived with their ale, Dari nodded to Karzul. "Six coppers, and you owe me three from the square."

Karzul fished out the coins and placed them on the table.

"What am I supposed to do with these?" The server demanded. "These foreign coins are worthless. No one will take them. Don't you have any real money?"

"I..." Karzul stuttered.

Dari handed the coins to the server. "Take the man's coin. Soon enough, every soldier is going to have a pocket full of these."

"Suppose you're right." The server pocketed the coins and set down two flagons of ale.

"So, why've you come here? You know how foolish that was? If I didn't need you, I'd have let them hang you."

"I came to see why you lied to me. To see your face when I ask you if you set a trap and led my people straight into it. You said three days. When we got to the mine, they were already there. Half a dozen or more. We barely made it out with our lives." He leaned forward. "Did you send us there to get us killed?"

"Karzul," Dari said. "They told me three days."

"So you said." Karzul emptied his mug of ale and pushed back his chair. "I'm not sure I believe you. You certainly have given me no reason to."

Dari glanced around. "Don't look around. Follow me. We have to leave," she said. "Now."

Karzul hesitated, but Dari was already on her feet.

She bent down to whisper in his ear. "Come with me now. There are soldiers outside, and they're looking for you."

28

BEYOND THE EDGE OF TRUST

Karzul followed closely on Dari's heels. He winced in pain as he twisted to squeeze through a narrow passage behind some discarded wood that partially barred access to a side alley. The place smelled of must and rot, not just wood rot, but food. Pig slop. The air was filled with smoke, and the ground was slick beneath his feet. How could they not be followed after this? Karzul was certain they would be leaving tracks that even a blind man could follow.

Behind him, the sound of a hound barking set his hair on end.

"What's the matter?" Dari asked.

"Hounds. I hate them. I was bitten as a child. Never got over it." He turned to glance behind him. "They'll scent us."

"We Daresh do love our hounds. Can't live without them. Every contingent has its own. Does make it a bit hard to hide from them. We'll need a place they won't go. "

Dari indicated a low doorway in the mud-brick wall. The beams that formed the doorway were weather-stained but looked to be sturdy. The door itself was formed of planks that had weathered and warped. The floor consisted of ill-fitting stones that threatened to trip him. A few barrels stood against the far wall, and the place smelled of ale and stale vomit.

"What is this place?" Karzul asked.

"They won't follow us in here." Dari settled onto the floor, tucking her legs beneath her.

Karzul tried to follow suit, but his ribs hurt too much. He winced in pain, using his hand to steady himself as he sank to the ground, facing her. "Why are you helping me?"

"Kin'tara. She says you are to be trusted."

"Kin'tara? My dragon? What do you know of my dragon?"

"I know a lot about you from Sar'tia. The next Queen of the Thunder." Dari glared at him. "You've only been a rider for how long? A moon?"

Being a rider, had become his life. It was who he was now. It hardly seemed possible that he'd been doing it less than a moon. Karzul began ticking off the days with his fingers.

Dari smiled. "If you're counting the days, it can't have been long."

Karzul let his hands drop to his lap. He'd never seen Dari smile. In his mind, she was a cold and ruthless killer, not a human.

"What are you staring at?" Dari demanded.

Karzul shook his head. "I never thought of you as human."

"What did you take me for?"

Karzul shrugged. "You're right. I haven't been a rider for long. All of this is so strange. I hardly know what to make of it. I suppose you're accustomed to all of it."

"Not really. I haven't been a rider all that long myself," she said. "I'll never forget." Dari paused, as if searching for a memory. "I was an apprentice. Seamstress. I was good. I could sew with the best of them. Garments for the locals mostly. Shirts and trousers. That kind of thing. I got a reputation for being quick. It got me business. One night after I'd finished for the day, an old man came to the door. Ancient, white-haired. He didn't come in. Just stood in the doorway and said, Dari, it's time. Come with me."

Dari paused and took a deep breath.

"For two days, we walked until we came to the mountains. We rested there, and at sunset we started. We hiked up that mountain all night. It was sunrise when he took me onto the bridge and told me to wait. 'Wait for what?' I asked, but he just said wait. After a while, I felt a pull. Like someone was calling my name. I looked into that swarm of color. The dragon thunder was leaving their caves at first light. And there she was. I'd never seen a color so brilliant. Green. Like no green I've ever seen before." Dari paused again as if waiting for an interruption, then continued. "When she drew close, I leaped. Closed my eyes and jumped." Dari looked over at Karzul. "You recall the feeling."

Karzul nodded.

"We bonded. At first, all I got was a feeling that she wanted something from me, but after a while I started hearing her voice. That's when she told me what she truly wanted."

Karzul had never thought about what the dragons wanted. Kin'tara definitely had her own desires. Was that the way of it? Riders were only a means to an end for the dragons? Was Dari's story so different from his?

"And what does your dragon want?" he asked.

"To be the next queen. To take over from her mother. To evolve"

"How do you think Kin'tara feels about that? She seems hale and hearty. I don't believe she has any plans to die soon."

"Not as dragons go, but soon enough for them."

Karzul shuddered, but tried to rationalize the idea. Kin'tara had given him the impression that he would grow old in her company. Her death would not come for a long time as humans go, yet the idea that she would one day perish made his insides knot.

"Kin'tara is worried that Sar'tia won't be ready in time," Dari explained. "There's something she needs. Something that used to be plentiful, but now is rare. Without it, Sar'tia will not mature properly."

Dari glanced at Karzul as if assessing his competence. "She believes you are the key."

Karzul snorted. "Inexperienced as I am?"

Dari shifted her weight. "Anyway, we're safe here until dusk. We should be able to slip away after dark. Is Kin'tara nearby?"

"She's injured. She's roosting. Hasn't come out since the accident."

"Then how did you get here?"

"Yarak," Karzul said. "He's waiting for my signal to return and pick me up."

"You left a dragon circling overhead?"

"How else was I supposed to get home?"

"Do you know nothing of dragons? They're territorial. The sky above this town belongs to Sar'tia and her thunder. If they find another dragon here, they'll attack. I thought Kin'tara brought you. They would never attack the queen."

She stood and brushed the dirt from her clothes. "Come. We can't wait until nightfall. We have to go now, or your friend will be killed. And we can't have that. I need you. You still have a mine to destroy."

"But the soldiers."

"We'll have to take our chances."

Karzul followed Dari through a warren of alleys and narrow streets until they came to the edge of town. Across the road from the last building, was a grove of fruit trees. Karzul had never seen the likes of them. The leaves were large and flat, dark green and shiny. Fruit grew in clusters, in varying shades of purple. The sun was warm and directly overhead in a clear blue sky.

"Come on," Daris said. "My riders will not see you from above because of the trees. The soldiers and townsfolk won't see us because the grove is thick enough to mask our presence. I think we've avoided being seen by anyone. We should be safe here. Call your friend. There's a clearing over there where the dragon can land and take off safely." She pointed to the barn nestled in a clearing. The road that led up to it was straight, and the trees had been trimmed back.

Karzul looked to the sky. Four dragons churned and dove as they harried Yarak and his dragon.

The brilliant blue-white flare told Karzul that Yarak was still in the fight, even though the beam went wild and did little to deter the pursuit.

A dragon swooped close to Yarak.

The blue-white beam stabbed at it, but not before the dragon pivoted in mid-air and took the lance blast on its stomach.

The next dragon was not so fortunate. Yarak caught that one on the wing and sliced off part of the thick leather that stretched between her wing bones. The dragon reeled in the midair and then began tumbling earthwards. Good for Yarak. He'd scored at least once.

Karzul turned to Dari, but she was gone. She was running along the path between the trees.

Within seconds she emerged from the trees, stopped and raised her arms. A brilliant green flash swept by, and she was gone.

Dari had joined the fight.

He screamed at Yarak. There was no way the lad was going to survive, not even with his fire lance.

"Yarak. Go home," he screamed, knowing it was useless.

Yarak's dragon plunged, spun, and tore through the sky in furious loops, turning and pivoting with a speed Karzul only envied.

The four pursuing dragons were joined by the fifth. The brilliant green.

A flash of blue-white lanced out, but Yarak was prepared. He turned his dragon, as Karzul had seen Dari do. His mount took the brunt of the blast on its stomach, then pinwheeled and dove for the ground. This too was a tactic he'd seen Dari perform. Was this something Karzul had not had time to learn? Why did they head for the ground? A dragon flying low was nothing more than a target for archers on the ground. A dragon flying high was only a target for another dragon. So why go low?

Karzul didn't have long to wait to learn the secret. As the blue-white light from Dari's lance stabbed at Yarak, he pulled out of the dive and skirted the ground barely a man height above the trees.

The blue-white light winked out.

Of course. Dari wasn't about to lance her own people. Yarak was using them as a shield to make his escape, and make his escape, as he did. His dragon sped away like an arrow from a bow, and soon he was lost to sight.

Karzul heaved a heavy sigh. At least Yarak was safe.

He waited just beneath the edge of the grove for the brilliant green dragon to land. When she did, Dari sent her on its way and walked toward him. He wished he'd brought his fire lance, or a sword, or a knife, anything. She had sent his squad into an ambush; she had attacked Yarak directly when she said she would not. So far he was learning that she was the enemy, not some misunderstood kindred soul.

"What was that?" Karzul demanded when Dari reached him.

"You see, but you do not understand," Dari spat. "I told you we were allies, if not friends. What did you think I *was* doing?"

"That you were trying to kill Yarak."

"If I had wanted to kill Yarak, he would be dead. You've seen me with the fire lance. Do you think I'm that poor of a shot? If I had wanted him dead, he would be dead. But I had to put on a show for my own folks. If I hadn't joined the fray, they would have cut him down. Maybe they would have lost a flyer or two, but they would have had him before he could escape. This was the only way to keep him alive and not lose face with my people. They won't suspect I did what I did on purpose. They'll just think I was a bit distracted, or tired, or something. They won't think I missed by intent, and once I was there, they pulled back, so your friend could escape. That's what I was doing."

She made a motion in the air with her hands, then turned to him. "Go home, Karzul. Think about what sort of friend you want to be. I just demonstrated what kind of friend I am."

She jutted her chin toward the sky. "I called your dragon for you. She's not completely healed, but she's well enough to carry you home. Think about what I just did. I thought you were my friend, but now I'm not so sure."

29

THE SHATTERED LANCE

Karzul had time to ponder what had happened as he winged his way back to the citadel. The air was crisp and clear. The rhythmic beat of Kin'tara's wings did little to soothe his troubled mind. The occasional twinges of pain from his ribs reminded him that neither he nor Kin'tara were completely healed. As it was, he had time to think. If his entire squad descended upon the mine at the same time, how could a few ground troops stand against that? Under the assault of six fire lances, there was little they could do. Once the Daresh troops had been dealt with, Karzul and his squad would descend into the mine as deep as they dared, right down to the eerie glow. Even now, it nagged at the back of his mind, calling to him, demanding he make his way toward that green glow. It was almost like a hunger he could not satisfy. Just when he thought it was gone, it cropped up again.

But they had to destroy it. Nephim had said there was something in the mine they could use to bring it down. They would use whatever it was, but failing that, the squad would use the combined power of their fire lances to burn away the pillars that supported the mine. It would collapse and seal the shaft. That should end the Daresh push to take the mine.

Even as that thought crossed his mind, Karzul felt a vision of Kin'-tara urging him to wait. To hold off until she had satisfied some urge that nagged at the back of his mind. She didn't want him to destroy the mine just yet. He pushed a thought to her, but what came back made no sense to him. It was a jumbled set of images, ranging from dragon's nests to butterflies. He shook the image off and headed inside as soon as they landed.

Rodan, Nephim, and the squad were already debating his plans when he arrived.

"We can destroy the pump station. Let the mine fill with water," Belban offered.

"That would not bar them from entering, not for a while," Nephim replied.

"Stop the ventilation?" Cahat asked.

"Same as the pumps. It won't bar entry immediately." Nephim said.

"Burn the beams. Let the mine crash in on itself. That's the only hope of ending this quickly," Yarak said.

"That might be the best way," Karzul mused, "but do you want to be down in the mine when the beams are cut? How do we know that it's not a suicide mission?"

Yarak huffed. "I'm all out of ideas then."

"No, you're right," Karzul said. "Burn the beams. Bring the shaft down on itself. It will bar them from entering the mine immediately, then destroy the air system and the water pumps. That will keep them from reopening it in the future. I don't see a better path."

Karzul was proud of the recruits. They were eager to engage, and he was glad to be back on Kin'tara, even though she was still recovering. The squad broke their fast together in the morning and allowed their dragons to feed before departing. Now, after a quiet flight, they were ready. The mine was in sight just below.

Karzul signaled his squad.

Nephim nodded, and as one, the dragons fell from the sky.

Karzul held back. He was the strongest with the fire lance, and with Kin'tara not fully recovered, it made sense to run cover rather than join the attack.

He didn't like not being down there with the squad, but he was learning that being in command meant making difficult decisions. And holding himself in reserve in case his squad needed him to power their lances was the right choice.

From his vantage point, Karzul could see the extent of the Daresh presence at the mine. There could not have been more than two dozen soldiers. Not insignificant, but surely a small enough crew that the squad could handle them.

They had set up camp between the remnants of what Nephim said were the barracks and the woods. While this gave some cover, it also obscured their view of the temple of the forbearers, where the mine entrance was. It seemed that fate had smiled upon them this time.

Belban initiated the first strike. She picked out two soldiers guarding the temple of the winds and dove at them. Her lance strike was stronger than he expected.

The two soldiers were engulfed in her blue-white flame and vanished. She let out a yell and banked hard to rejoin the squad.

Next came Cahat. She chose three soldiers who were patrolling in front of the temple of the forbearers. She took out the closest soldier first. With ease. The second one, not so brilliant. The soldier vanished — burst into flames and screamed in pain — but he vanished. The third one fared poorly. He screamed, but he did not burst into flames. But he did not vanish. He dropped to his knees and screamed in agony.

Close behind Cahat came Ormwor. He was the weakest by far, but Yarak was right on his tail. Ormwor targeted a lone soldier, one who was loitering near a tree. It should have been an easy kill, but it was not. The light from Ormwor's lance barely chased away the shadows the man stood in. Karzul was not certain the soldier even knew he'd been the subject of a lance attack.

Yarak pulled ahead of Ormwor and leveled his lance at the solitary man. Karzul waited for the soldier to vanish, but nothing happened. Had Yarak decided not to make the attempt, or had he and his lance failed? This is what he had held himself in reserve for. Karzul chose his own target. A pair of soldiers raced along the road side by side. He banked Kin'tara and dropped toward them, leveled his lance, and touched the stud.

Nothing happened.

No flame, no fire, and no brilliant blue-white light. His lance was dead. "Come on, let's get out of here," he called to the squad. One by one, they fell into formation. The entire squad winged its way back to the temple.

Karzul and Nephim rushed to find Rodan.

"It was as if the lances had exhausted their power," Karzul explained. "We managed only a few shots. Have you ever heard of such a thing?"

Rodan shook his head. "No. This is the worst news we could receive. If the lances are unreliable, how are we to win? We've never seen this happen in battle. Did you see anything that could have caused it?"

"Perhaps there's something about the mine that affects our lances, or maybe it's the dragons. Without the fire lances, our plans will no longer work."

"There is a town, Easton, near the mine that we can call upon to supply troops," Nephim said. "They have no love of the Daresh, and they are known to be tough, especially on outsiders. They know the area better than Alchua's men. They would help us."

Karzul glanced at Rodan. "Is this true?"

"As we pledge our lives in service as soldiers, so do most folk. They pledge to defend their manor or castle in times of war. When we need more troops, we levy the towns, and they send young men and women."

"Who will we send?" Karzul asked. "Rodan? Will they follow you?"

"They will follow you," the old man said. "Not me. I may convince them with help from Nephim, but not lead them into battle. Nephim knows the town. She will best know how to persuade them."

"Can you do it?" Karzul asked Nephim.

"I think I can, but I would feel better if you were with me. The young me will listen to me, but the elders may not. They may listen to you."

"You are a better candidate for this than I am," Rodan told Karzul.

"Kalnis," Nephim said. "He's the one we want to talk to. Oftentimes, the rest rely on his judgement. He has no love for the Daresh, not a drop. Nobody would blame him either. Lost his son in the war summers ago. Then, three summers ago, he lost his grandson, a boy barely old enough to shave. Went off to fight the Daresh and never came back. His blood lies buried in unmarked graves on Daresh land.

"Even after all that, he still had his pride. He used to run a trade wagon. Real caravan. He had a dozen wagons, armed guards, the lot. He brought spices from the north, blades from the east. Made real coin.

"Then one day, about a summer ago, they were heading home after a very successful trading session. Spirits were high. Kalnis was as happy as a man could get until they were stopped by the Daresh at the border. By law, the tax was to be one in ten, but the Daresh soldiers must have seen what the wagons were hauling, because they decided to tax them heavier. Not the proper tax of one in ten, but half. Claimed it was for the good of the people and that those goods belonged to everyone.

"Kalnis told them to go hang themselves. They put him in chains, took his wagons, and killed his guards. They let him live only because he promised them gold as a ransom. Cost him everything. Since then, he has raised maize and beans. Barely enough to keep his body and soul together. We can count on him to do whatever he can against the Daresh."

Karzul mounted Kin'tara and followed Nephim out. Easton was in the foothills southeast of the mine. The dragons were able to glide most of the way. Nephim led Karzul through the streets that were much like the streets in every other town. Houses nestled against cobblestone, the second story hanging over the first to obscure the sun. The section of town where Kalnis lived was neither wealthy nor impoverished. The houses were well built and reasonably well maintained. Nephim said the room they sought was above a tailor shop, that Kalnis chose it as the least likely to have noisy patrons, and most likely to be helpful to him in his advancing age.

The doors of the tailor shop had been thrown open. A woman and a young girl sat on the floor, hard at work. They sewed together a large quilt. A third woman worked at a dress form, carefully stitching together a white gown, her needle plunging into the cloth again and again, dragging a white thread behind it.

"Hoy," Nephim called. "Is that old coot around?"

The woman working on the dress looked over from her task, stuck the needle into the form, and stood. She glanced at the other two and clicked her tongue as she walked over to Nephim and paused. Her shoulders drooped, and she stared down at her hands. "I'm so sorry, little one. If only you had been here three days ago."

"Three days ago? What happened? Where is he?" Nephim pushed past the woman and headed into the shop toward the back.

"He's not here."

"Where is he then?"

"He's gone. Dead."

Nephim staggered, grasping the door frame for support. "What..." she paused, took a deep breath and started once again. "What? What happened? He was hale and hearty the last time I saw him."

"Truth, but it was no illness that took him," the woman said. "It was the Daresh."

"Daresh? Here?" Nephim asked.

"They had the nerve to come onto our land, they did. Half a dozen fliers landed up near the mine. Kalnis and a few others decided to have a talk with them. Things didn't go so well." The woman looked up. "Got caught up with a dragon. Didn't even leave enough for a proper burial."

30

KINDRED IN THE SHADOW

*K*arzul stood at a short table. Seated across from him were the elders. Seven of them. Five of them appeared as Karzul would have expected of elders. White hair, thinning or in one case, gone. White beards trimmed neatly or, in one case, long and unkempt. The sixth elder was a woman. Not nearly as old as the men, but gray and grizzled nonetheless. It was the seventh who seemed out of place. Cerol He couldn't have been more than a summer or two older than Karzul. Nephim explained that with the passing of Kalnis, Kalnis's tribe had elected Cerol to represent them.

Ashtai was speaking.

He fit the image Karzul had of an elder. He also bore a large scar across one cheek, possibly from a war injury. Would that make him more or less inclined to commit his folk to battle? Karzul didn't know.

"What you claim, Karzul," Ashtai said, "is hard to believe. We have no records that confirm your story. Fire lances have always been the purview of a few with the blood strong in them. You expect us to believe that common foot-soldiers can wield fire lances and are asking us to go to war so you can prove it." Ashtai touched the scar on his cheek. "Do you know what war looks like?"

Karzul nodded. "I have seen it."

"From the air," Ashtai said.

"From the air."

"Then you don't know what it looks like."

"I do not."

"I do. And I'm not convinced we want to bring such an experience to our townsfolk."

"We faced down the Daresh at the mine not three days ago," Karzul said. "They are not coming. They are here. They are in the process of taking the mine. Next, they will take Easton."

"That's not their way. They take a town here; we take a town there. They fire a field here; we fire a field there. The war has been going on for generations without either side gaining an advantage. Why would that change?"

"They want the mine. They intend to use it to build more fire lances."

"Then they're fools."

"Fools with an army. Right now, there are two dozen Daresh soldiers garrisoned at the mine. If we can defeat them and destroy the mine, then we remove their reason to invade. No min. No rare ore. No Daresh."

"But your informant's a Daresh rider. Why would you believe her? She'd have us walking into a trap."

How could he argue against that?

"You received a piece of tantalizing information from a beautiful Daresh woman, and she has swayed you into dragging us into a war that does not concern us." Ashtai looked around the room. "Is there any reason to continue?"

One by one, the elders shook their heads. All save Cerol.

"I believe him," the young elder said. "We know the Daresh have taken the mine. We know Karzul and his squad tried to retake it and failed. Just three nights ago we had to drive away a Daresh scout party on our land."

"The mine is dead," Ashtai said. "Useless. It was abandoned summers ago, with good reason. Anyone who spends any time there falls ill."

A few of the elders nodded, but some shook their heads. They were no longer of one mind.

Karzul took a breath to speak, to plead his case, but Nephim placed a hand on his shoulder and whispered. "Let Cerol speak. They don't trust you. They trust him."

Cerol looked at Karzul. "You said two dozen soldiers?"

"Yes. I counted them from the air."

"You had six fire lances and six dragons. Why did your attack fail?"

His face flushed with heat. How much should he admit? He was supposed to be the last hope for the Theren troops, but he'd let them down. The fire lances seemed to be of little use near the mine, and he could not explain why. So much for being the leader of the flame riders. Would his ineffectiveness cost them an ally? He hoped not, but he had no choice but to be honest. Lying would surely cost him the chance to recruit these men.

"We attempted to destroy or demoralize them from the air. At first, our fire lances were devastating, but quickly, they became ineffective. We managed to kill four and disable two, but unless we kill all of them and destroy the mine, they'll call for reinforcements."

"That's magic for you. Runs out when you most need it. How can we depend on you to deal with them from the air if your lances give out?"

"It only seems to happen near the mine. If we can drive away the Daresh, we may yet discover what happened, but they should last long enough to give you some cover while you deal with the foot soldiers"

"It is a lot to ask," Ashtai said. "The harvest is just in. The farmers are busy. No one wants to fight. I say we give it some time. See..."

"There are Daresh on our land," Cerol said, cutting off whatever Ashtai planned to say. "You propose we simply allow them to make themselves at home?"

"I do not, but forcing men to die is not the answer."

"Let's ask for volunteers then," Cerol said. "A man choosing to fight is not the same as a man forced to fight. Would you agree, Ashtai?"

Ashtai sat back and exhaled deeply. "If that is your wish, let us vote on it." He glanced around the table. "Who is in favor of Cerol's plan?"

One by one, the hands went up. The only one who refrained from endorsing Cerol's plan was Ashtai.

"Cerol, you may call for volunteers," Ashtai said. "Please make certain you're asking and not persuading. There are enough adventurous young men in this town to form a decent squad. You just might succeed. I certainly hope you do. I've seen enough war. I wish to see no more, and I do not wish it on any of our folk."

"I understand," Cerol said. "It will be as you wish."

"It will be as it is destined to be," the elder said. "I only hope your fate is not as grim as I fear."

"Come on," Nephim whispered in Karzul's ear. "I think I know where Cerol will begin. And I can use an ale."

Nephim led Karzul to a large public house not far from the center of the town. The ceiling beams were coated in black tar from a fireplace that could have used more draft. The counter was well polished, if not by craftsmen, then by the hands of those who clouded around it to vie for drinks. The server was a young woman with a sly smile and a quick hand.

"What you having?"

Nephim turned to Karzul. "Your treat?"

"Always is," he answered.

"Two gold ales. And a plate of those." Nephim pointed at a patron who had just received a platter of fried fowl gizzards.

"Be right up."

As the server vanished into a back room, a minstrel struck up a tune. It was a song Karzul had heard once or twice before, only the words had been changed to reflect the name of the town. And the names of the people had been changed. The minstrel was fair of voice but adequate on the lute. Altogether, Karzul could have gone for silence or conversation.

As the song was finished, Cerol entered with three young men in tow. They were well-dressed. Tradesmen perhaps. Not farmhands, judging by their clothes. They seated themselves at a table in the corner and spoke in hushed tones. After a while, Cerol rose and joined him and Nephim at the counter.

"Neff," he said. "You look great. How's the life of a rider treating you?"

"I'm not just a rider. I'm a flame rider," she said. "I have my own fire lance."

"I'm impressed."

Nephim blushed.

"She's the squad leader," Karzul added. "And modest. She's a deadly shot with a fire lance. And there are only a few who can manage anything at all. That's why we need your help."

"We have a few men. We meet in secret. Train like soldiers. With swords." He held up his hand. "I know we're not supposed to have swords, but we feel that it is our right to protect ourselves and our families." Cerol paused as if challenging Karzul to disagree with him before continuing. "Whatever weapon may be used against us, we may use to defend our families and our land."

Karzul chuckled. "I care little how you came by your weapons. I am just glad that you have them. Going up against trained arms-men with farm implements and pikes is never a good strategy. At most, it's a holding strategy even with proper weapons. We might even have a chance of winning, and that means stopping the Daresh before they take the mine. I appreciate what you are doing for us."

"Not for you. For us," Cerol said. "I have a bond-mate, two daughters and a son. I'd like to see my children grow up. I don't know you except through Nephim's words. I'm not a soldier, but I'm a family man. I won't have foreign soldiers strutting around our land as if they own it. Neither will my friends. We will fight."

Cerol motioned to his friends, who came over and faced Karzul and Nephim.

"Neff, I think you know these men."

She stretched her hand into the air, then raised three fingers, signaling the server, raised her glass to her lips and drained it without pausing to take a breath. "Glad to meet you all. The ale is on Karzul."

As the evening wore on, Karzul and the locals debated the best approach.

Cerol maintained that there were vantage points that he was

familiar with that would give them the advantage over the Daresh. Even so, that advantage would not last long.

There would be a battle.

There would be casualties.

Karzul only hoped that casualties were all on the Daresh side, but feared they would not be .

Finally, they were in agreement. "We're set then? First light?" Karzul asked.

Cerol grasped Karzul's forearm. "First light."

31

WHISPERS IN THE VEINS OF STONE

Karzul woke before daybreak. The morning was crisp. The smell of wood smoke permeated the inn. A quick morning meal of dark tea and hard bread was all he had time for. They were to head out before sunrise in order to ensure that there were no Daresh dragons around when they took on the ground troops.

Karzul was optimistic about the upcoming battle. Even though he lacked much in the way of military training, he still recognized the deep thinking and insight of Cerol and his men. They had an innate feel for where in the mine compound the Daresh would be able to take cover, and where they would be exposed. When Karzul asked where they had learned these tactics, Cerol blushed and said that they spent their leisure time playing a game that sharpened the wit and taught tactics. Perhaps when this was all over, they would teach Karzul and the squad.

Nephim had chosen to accompany Karzul on the raid. The two of them were to stay back, fire lances in hand. He had tested his before setting out for the mine and found it fully charged and functional. Had the last time been a fluke? Even if the lances eventually ceased working, at least they had some limited advantage. There was so much he didn't know, and he feared the cost of failure.

Karzul and Nephim flew low over the trees, keeping out of sight of the Daresh and their archers.

Nephim pointed. "Here, see that one?" She whispered. "He's alone. I'll deal with him."

The sky was starting to lighten, but it was still full dark. "Wait," Karzul said. "There may be more."

As if to confirm his words, a second soldier stepped from the shadows. He paused before the first and saluted. The first man departed into the shadows.

"I think he's alone now," Karzul said. He turned to Nephim, but she was already gone.

He peered into the shadows. Nephim was making her way toward the lone soldier, her back against the wall of the temple of the forbearers. He held his breath, hoping that her lance remained effective until she completed her task, but she carried it as if it was an afterthought.

She edged her way through the shadows until there were no more shadows to hide her.

Heartbeats passed.

The man turned his attention back to the fire.

Nephim drew her knife, slid from the shadows, caught the man from behind, and quickly sliced through his throat. She held him while he bled out and stopped moving. There was more blood than Karzul would have thought.

While she was busy, the first man returned. Karzul had thought they were watching a change of guard, but perhaps it was simply a necessity break for the soldier. He hissed at Nephim, but she didn't appear to hear him. She continued to advance, heedless of the man approaching her.

Karzul slid his back along the wall. The returning soldier was going to realize his relief was missing a heartbeat from now. Karzul stepped out of the shadows to avoid tracking blood as he crept to the side. If he could take the soldier from behind, he would have the advantage. Karzul had no illusions about how much of a fighter he was. He could swing a sword without cutting himself or those near him, but that was about it. Any trained arms man would outclass him. Surprise was all he had.

The soldier paused, bent, and stuck his finger in the blood.

Karzul leaped from the shadows, aiming a blow at the back of the man's neck.

The blow struck armor, sending a shock wave up Karzul's arm.

The man straightened up and drew his sword from its scabbard in one smooth motion.

Karzul instinctively raised his fire lance to deflect the sword.

Metal clashed as the sword struck the fire lance.

A sharp ping filled the air. Sparks jumped from the point of impact. The vibration from the contact stung his fingers, and Karzul nearly dropped the lance, but he held on.

Again, the sword swung toward him. This time, from the side.

Karzul used the fire lance to block it. He fended off blow after blow, barely escaping serious injury. He felt a sharp pain in his forearm as he failed to deflect one blow. Blood seeped from the wound onto the fire lance, making it slippery. The man was strong. His blows stung, even though blocked. He hacked away at Karzul, giving the impression he was playing with his opponent, and not yet ready to deal the death blow. What other reason was there that Karzul was still alive?

On the next blow, the Daresh soldier turned his blade to the side and knocked the fire lance from Karzul's grip.

Karzul raised his hands in surrender, even though Dari had assured him they would not take him prisoner. Perhaps he could stall his demise just a little while.

"How many of you are there?" the soldier demanded.

Karzul remained silent.

"Where are your forces encamped?" the soldier asked.

Karzul glanced around. Was Nephim nearby? Could he depend on her to step in?

He didn't see her.

"Make peace with your gods. You will soon be standing before them," the soldier said.

Karzul closed his eyes. Best not to see the blade coming. He should have been brave. He should have stood there, eyes wide, face composed. That's what the songs said about those brave men and women who fell in battle.

Karzul heard a rustle, then the clang of metal on metal.

He opened his eyes.

Nephim stood facing the man.

He had turned his attention to her.

Karzul stepped to get behind him, and the man shifted with only the briefest of glances toward Karzul. He was much more of a fighter than Karzul would ever be.

"Are you prepared to die?" the man asked Nephim.

"Are you?" She responded with a quick slash of her knife. She had jammed her fire lance into the dirt behind her to free her hands as she shifted the knife from hand to hand. A trick Karzul had heard of but never seen. She slashed with her left hand, spun and slashed just as quickly with her right.

The soldier slashed with his sword, but she caught the blade on her knife guard and turned it aside.

Karzul jammed his own staff into the dirt and drew his knife. He was nowhere near as accomplished as Nephim, but he could at least distract the man. Perhaps make an opening for Nephim.

The soldier took another step to keep Karzul from getting behind him, even as he slashed at Nephim.

The clang of metal on metal rang out as his sword met her knife. She nearly crumpled under the impact, but sidestepped just in time to let the blade flash past her arm.

The soldier turned to follow her.

Karzul lunged.

The man's blade came around in half a heartbeat, striking Karzul's knife even before he knew what was happening.

Karzul's knife flew from his hand.

"I should have killed you when I had the chance," the soldier was breathing hard.

Karzul hoped his meager efforts had tired him out enough to slow him down.

"Playtime is over." The man's sword arm twitched.

Karzul flinched.

The soldier paused and took a step toward Karzul.

Karzul jumped back.

A thin red line appeared on the man's leg. Nephim had drawn blood.

The man spun to face her.

Nephim screamed at Karzul. "Get your lance. Reinforcements are here."

She backed away from the soldier and raised her own staff to turn another sword thrust.

Karzul grabbed his fire lance and fired. The light that it emitted was bright, but not as bright as it should have been. Rather than turning the man to ash, it simply blinded him.

The soldier threw his arm across his eyes and screamed. "You son of a whore." He swung his sword wildly, blindly, taking a halting step toward Nephim.

"Come on," Nephim said. "Quick."

She ran along the side of the building.

Karzul raced after her. Pausing when she stopped against the crumbling wall of the barracks. He couldn't believe he'd survived that battle. He'd never been in battle before. It was nothing like he had imagined it. He said a quick prayer to give thanks to whichever god had spared his life.

"This way. I think it's clear." She indicated the temple of the forbearers that was in shade now that the sun was starting to make its appearance. No more cover of darkness.

The sound of swords clanging against one another erupted from around the corner. Cerol and his men had met the Daresh.

They turned the corner to see a sight that made Karzul's stomach knot. Half a dozen soldiers were engaged in a pitched battle with Cerol's men. Several soldiers and townsfolk lie in the dirt surrounded by blood.

"We have to help," Karzul said.

"No, you'll only get yourself killed. We need you." She yanked on his arm, but Karzul brushed her off.

As he stepped from the shadows, Cerol called to him. "We have this. Go. You're too valuable to lose in a fight."

Karzul backed up and let Nephim drag him along until they reached the temple of the waters. The thrumming noise drowned out the noise of battle. She pointed to the great doors of the Temple of the Forbearers. "We'll be safe in there. At least for a while."

"But Cerol and his men."

"If they win, they'll seek us out. If they lose, wouldn't you rather be somewhere safe?"

"Are we cowards, then? Folk who cower under cover of the shadows and hide while others do the fighting?" he demanded.

"You are the commander. You knew this was a risk. You need to live. You need to come up with another plan. You're too valuable to lose in the first skirmish of the war."

"I don't like it." Karzul felt responsible for Cerol and his men.

"Good. You're not meant to like it. You're meant to feel bad when your troops die. If not, you would make a terrible commander. Never forget how it feels to send men to their deaths."

After a moment, Nephim pointed to the doors once again. "When I say so, make a run for it."

"What are you going to do?"

She ignored his plea. "When I say go, you run."

Nephim slipped from the shadows and leveled her lance at the melee.

"Close your eyes!" she screamed. Her fire lance came to life. To Karzul's surprise, the closest Daresh soldier glowed brightly, then vanished in a puff of smoke.

"Go," she yelled.

Karzul rushed for the great doors, passing between them and into the shadows.

"They're behind us." Nephim appeared in half a heartbeat. "Down the mine. They daren't follow."

"I thought it wasn't safe."

"You want to risk the mine or the Daresh?"

"The mine shaft," he said.

"Good. I know of a side shaft they won't think to look into. It's dark, and the entryway has partially collapsed. We'll be safe there if we hurry."

Karzul followed Nephim deep into the mine. When they arrived at what looked like a collapsed section, she dropped to her hands and knees.

"It looks tight," he said as she squeezed between two fallen beams and vanished into the shadows.

"You'll fit," she called back. "It gets wider."

Karzul dropped to his knees. The gap was narrow. It made him shiver. He hated being trapped in a small space. He'd always had this fear. It made no sense, but he could not shake it. But what were his options?

He crawled into the gap, wriggling to get his arms ahead of him to help pull himself along. At one point, he had to turn sideways to squeeze through. His belt caught on something.

He was stuck.

He felt panic rise, but pushed it back down. Panic would gain nothing. Breathe. He had to breathe, calm himself.

He reached down, sliding his hand between his stomach and the beams that encircled him. His belt was caught on a splinter in the beam.

He yanked at it, but could not free it.

"What's the matter?" Nephim called back to him.

"I'm stuck." He pulled at the splinter, but it jabbed into his flesh as he tried to break it free.

"Back up," Nephim said.

She was right. If he backed up, he could guide the belt past the splinter and free himself. He took a deep breath, let it out and pushed himself back. He felt the belt snap free of the splinter.

He reached down and guided his belt away from the splinter as he crawled forward one more.

He was free.

He kept crawling until he emerged into darkness that was so black he almost forgot what it was like to see.

"This way." Nephim's hand slid into his. "Once we turn the corner, I'll light a lantern. Then keep one down here for emergencies."

Soon enough, Nephim released his hand.

The scratch of something on stone was followed by a brilliant flare that faded quickly into a soft yellow glow. The lantern flared to life as she touched the flame to its wick and trimmed it down to a gently flickering flame.

The mine shaft they inhabited sloped down into the darkness too far to see, yet Karzul felt more than saw a faint yellow-green glow far off in the distance. He felt the pull. It called to him.

Nephim pulled his arm, drawing him back to the main shaft. "Don't, she said. "Not the light. No good ever came from anyone going down one of the tunnels that led to the light."

He let her stop him, but the echoes of a thought in his head said the light was precisely where he needed to be.

32

THE THRESHOLD OF FIRE

Karzul settled in. It was going to be a long day. He wondered how they would know when the day ended. At night, one could always see the stars. Even when the sky was overcast, some light filtered through the clouds. Down here, there was nothing. The lamp lit a circle of space a little more than a yard across. Nephim had trimmed it low to conserve oil. The eerie glow from the side passage appeared to be growing stronger, or was it just because his vision was adjusting?

"We should be safe enough here," Nephim said.

Hearing the sharpness in her voice, he asked, "Did you hide here often when you were a child?"

"I did. It was one of our favorite places. Safe from the grownups."

"Ours?"

"Me and my cousins. We would come down here, turn off the lantern, and just let the glow soak into us. Worr said that the glow would impart magic. That's what happens to those who venture down the mine shaft. They become wizards and witches. And leave."

"Do you know anyone who went down there?"

"No. Bu there were rumors. You know how it goes. The children tell tales, but not everyone believes them." She explained. "They say a woman several summers older than me decided to seek out the magic. She headed down the mine shaft, and never returned. Her folks claim they saw her in visions on the anniversary of her disappearance. They say she looked old, with white hair, wrinkled skin, and all shriveled like a crone."

Karzul shuddered. He had no belief in wizards and witches. Whatever was down there, it certainly wasn't magic. "Do you hear something?"

Karzul stilled his breathing. Off in the distance, he could hear voices. Faint, too distant to make out the words, but definitely voices. "Daresh?"

"Probably," she said. "They won't find us."

"Should we go deeper into the mine? Chance the light?"

Nephim made no reply.

A new sound was joined the voices.

Howling.

"Curses," Nephim said. "They've brought hounds."

Karzul shuddered. "Should we extinguish the lantern?"

"And fight them off in the dark?" Nephim grabbed her fire lance and tapped the end on the floor of the mine. "They'll smell us."

"Best be prepared for a fight. Sounds like more than one, a lot more than one."

Karzul backed against the mine wall. His fear of hounds surged. He still carried a faint scar on his leg and a deep scar on his soul. It itched as if in anticipation. Hounds could tell that he was afraid. They smelled it. It emboldened them.

A hound stepped from the shadows. It was squat, muscled and covered in short hair. Its ears had been bobbed, so that they stood at attention, like soldiers on parade.

The hound hunched low to the ground.

Light washed over the hound from Nephim's fire lance.

It whimpered and took a step back.

"Come on," Nephim said. "That should hold it for a bit." She stood there, fire lance in hand. Had she intended to cause discomfort? Or kill it?

"Hounds are bad news," she said.

"You're telling me. I hate hounds."

"A few soldiers would not bring hounds. This means that there are a lot more troops here than we thought. They're already settling in."

Another snarl sounded.

A pair of hounds rounded the bend. Neck hair bristling. Teeth bared. Snarling.

Karzul stiffened, his back against the wall.

The hounds hunched down, preparing for the leap that would end Karzul's life.

Karzul put his hand on the wall to guide himself as he slid along it, trying to put distance between him and the hound.

This wasn't going to end well.

The hounds advanced.

Karzul took another step. The wall behind him gave way to the side passage. He was in the side tunnel, the one that glowed.

The hound stopped, sniffed the air and paused.

"They're afraid," Nephim whispered.

"Afraid of what?"

"The light — you're standing in the light."

Karzul glanced to his left. The tunnel was lit with an eerie yellow-green light.

"Will it stop them?" Were the hounds afraid of the light? He took a step toward the hounds, not wanting to go any farther down the tunnel than he had to.

Both hounds crouched down as if preparing to lunge.

He stepped back into the light.

They relaxed.

"Looks like we're trapped here," he said.

Nephim stepped into the light and settled to the floor, legs crossed beneath her. She faced one of the hounds, eyes locked.

He would like to have sat beside her, but his fear of the hounds kept him on his feet. "Now what?" he asked.

"Now we wait."

For a while, it seemed as if they were at a standoff. Karzul stood watching the hounds as Nephim sat quietly beside him. But the calm was short-lived. Before long, the sound of more hounds became noticeable, then the voices returned. Far off and muted, but definitely voices. Several loud noises were accompanied with puffs of dust wafting down the mine shaft.

The voices grew louder.

"They've found us," Karzul said.

Nephim jumped up. "Come on. Deeper. There might be a side shaft we can use that will take us out of the light"

"If there's not?"

"I'm not in favor of heading into the light, but would you rather take your chances with very real hounds, with the soldiers, or with the imagined magic?"

"I don't believe in magic." Karzul backed away from the hounds until he was certain they were'nt following, then turned toward the strange light. It was a hundred yards away down the mine shaft. Faint, steady, yellow-green. No warmth emanated from it. No flickering. It called to him once more, a whisper in his thoughts. Go toward the light. He needed to go down there. He longed to go down there. It was his destiny to go down there.

He took several steps toward the light.

The sensation grew stronger until it suddenly ceased.

No longer was it calling to him; now it was cautioning him.

Told him to hold off.

An echo in his mind tasted of Kin'tara. He glanced around.

The mine shaft was cut through rock that changed from the dark gray of the upper mine to a lighter shade as they descended. The walls were coated with a thin layer of powder. He swept a finger through it to reveal the same dark gray color of the upper mine beneath the dust.

Where had the dust come from? Did the light affect the stone, turning it to dust, or was there something else at work here? Is that why the mine had been abandoned?

The sound of voices grew louder behind them. "This way. They can't escape."

The hounds might fear the glow, but the soldiers did not. Wildly swinging beams of light stabbed down the tunnel, casting their glow on the walls behind Karzul and Nephim. There was nowhere to hide.

"Stay close to the walls," Karzul said. "Maybe they won't see us."

He slid his hands along the wall as he moved toward the eerie yellow-green light. They came to a narrowing of the shaft. The walls closed in, then the ceiling; then abruptly, the shaft ended in rough rock that sported several holes as if someone had drilled into the stone. They were at a dead end.

Tiny specks of yellow-green were embedded in the walls. Not like gold ore that came in nuggets, or like iron ore that appeared in veins. The glow came from a light dusting of powder scattered around the mine shaft. Tiny pinpoints of light.

"There's no way out," Karzul said. "Get ready to fight."

Nephim lowered her fire lance. "I hope the rumors are true, that we will be reborn as wizards, even if that means we emerge aged and infirm."

"I would rather live out my days and earn my gray hair," Karzul said. "But if we must die, then we must die. I only hope you have some fire left." He matched her stance. If they were to die, he would try to take as many Daresh as he could with him. Not that he was prepared to die. How could anyone ever be prepared to die?

Two Daresh soldiers turned the corner. They stood side by side, their lanterns casting a brilliant light on Karzul and Nephim.

The man on the right drew his sword and called back to someone around the bend. "Only the two, what do you want me to do with them?"

"Kill them," came the reply.

The soldier advanced. His blade glinted in the lamplight.

"You'll not have me so easily," Nephim said.

Light flared from her fire lance. Both soldiers vanished in a brilliant shower of sparks.

Karzul blinked. Just moments ago, Nephim's lance was depleted. Now it was fully charged. Why was it so much deadlier now?

Karzul touched the stud of his own fire lance. Just the merest touch.

He didn't want to bring the full force of the device to bear so deep in the mine.

The light that flared from his staff was enough to illuminate the entire mine shaft, exposing the wooden beams that shored up the ceiling.

"Our lances," Nephim remarked. "I thought they were dead. Maybe we're not going to die today."

Karzul started toward the entrance. From the sound of it, there were still several soldiers there, and the hounds were whining.

Karzul rounded the corner.

A trio of soldiers stood behind a pair of hounds.

The hounds crouched down, snarling, but as Karzul approached, they backed away.

"Get them out," one of the men shouted. He drew his sword and rushed for Karzul.

The fire from Karzul's lance was brilliant. Blinding. When his sight recovered, the soldiers were gone. The hounds were gone. The debris that had partially filled the entrance was gone. All that remained was the mineshaft and its stout wooden beams. It was clean, as if the shaft had been constructed only that morning.

"Good shooting," Nephim remarked.

"Let's see if the lances still work above ground." Karzul carefully stepped out into the main shaft. Nothing had changed there. The shaft angled upwards until they emerged from below ground. He had expected more soldiers, but maybe their number had been thinned. He wondered what had happened to Cerol and his men. Had they all been slaughtered, or were some still alive? Had they retreated to save their lives?

He hoped they had survived, because with the change in his plans, he was certain they could win against the Daresh.

"There." Before Karzul could react, a blue-white bolt raced out and consumed a pair of Daresh soldiers who had turned the corner.

Another pair of men appeared.

Another blue-white bolt.

"We need to do this from the air," Karzul said.

A screech echoed off the distant hills.

Kin'tara must have been waiting overhead for him to emerge. She fell from the sky like a stone and landed mere yards from Karzul. Half a heartbeat later, she was joined by Nephim's dragon.

"Looks like our rides have arrived," he said, climbing aboard.

33

A BATTLE TO RECHARGE

Karzul's stomach lurched as Kin'tara took to the air. The sun was halfway to noon, the air still cool but starting to warm. Nephim and her dragon were close behind him. The pall of wood smoke hung over the mine complex. The Daresh had indeed moved in in force. A dozen tents lined either side of the road that granted access to the mine. Soldiers were assembled in ranks, preparing to march toward the mine. Was that because of them? Dozens of soldiers for two lowly riders and a handful of townsfolk?

He would show them what two riders with fire lances could do. "You take the left side. I'll take the right." He pointed to the row of tents.

Nephim shook her head. "Soldiers first. Tents can't fight."

Of course. What sort of soldier was he? They could always return for the tents.

He guided Kin'tara into position, lowered his fire lance, and waited until Nephim and her dragon were ready.

"Fire," he cried out.

The twin beams of blue-white light streaked toward the line of soldiers. Before they even realized they were under attack, most of them had vanished, leaving behind tiny piles of dust. The few that remained scattered.

As he fired, the lance grew hot in Karzul's hands. As if he were grasping a metal rod heated in a fire. He almost dropped it.

He examined his palms. They were red, as if he had indeed touched something hot.

"There." Nephim pointed to a pair of soldiers running from behind the temple of the forbearers.

Karzul took aim and released the deadly light. It flared, but not as intensely this time. The pain in his hands grew stronger. He half expected to see the fire lance glowing as if it had been thrown in a fire, but it remained the same.

More soldiers appeared, rushing from behind the tumbled wall of the barracks. One of them drew back his bow.

Archers.

Archers were the last thing he needed.

Kin'tara could withstand arrows, in small quantities, unless one hit a vulnerable spot, but with a dozen, they were sure to bring her down.

Karzul fired again.

More pain.

The soldiers burst into flame, consumed in an instant, leaving only ashes in their wake, but the fire lance was losing its effectiveness and the skin on his hands was steaming.

Beside him, Nephim took aim at a solitary soldier making for the temple of the waters. The light from her lance didn't even slow him down. She released her grip on her fire lance, holding it almost gently with her fingertips.

Karzul took aim at the soldier and pressed the trigger of his fire lance. The soldier burst into flames and screamed. The fire lance had very little power left, and the staff was so hot in his hands he could no longer hold on to it. He tucked it under his arm.

What now? Back to the mine? Recharge the lances? A handful of archers had appeared from behind the barracks wall. Flying had its advantages, but archers tended to dampen that advantage. They could either rise above arrow height or take their chances with the archers.

Head for the doors, Karzul bid Kin'tara.

She banked, pulled into a tight turn, and shot for the mine. Nephim and her dragon landed heartbeats after Kin'tara.

Karzul dismounted and headed for the great doors. He glanced back at Kin'tara, pressing a thought toward her.

Archers.

In response, she snorted flame into the air, but it was weak and gave him the impression she was a bit worried herself. When Nephim's dragon rushed for the great doors, Kin'tara raced to intercept her, hissing at the younger dragon.

The immature dragon hissed back and crouched down just as the hounds had.

Kin'tara hissed and spread her wings — all three sets — as if showing off her age and power.

The younger dragon snorted. Wisps of smoke came from her nostrils.

Kin'tara motioned to Karzul. She needed no words or images. Her intent was clear. Karzul and Nephim should enter the mine.

She would deal with the insolent younger dragon.

The smaller dragon screeched as Kin'tara snapped at her.

"She wants to come with us," Nephim said.

"This is no place for her. Kin'tara wants her out. They are safer away from here. They can return when we summon them. If the archers get a clear shot at them while they're in here, there is no place to escape. We should hurry. Who knows how many Daresh are really here, or when more will arrive? We need to recharge our fire lances and finish them off."

"Do you think they'll last longer this time?"

"I am not sure, but at least we can dispatch more troops. I have an idea. A way to end this war, once and for all. It's time to bring down the mine. We can't afford to have it fall into Daresh hands. But before we do that, we need to charge up as many lances as we can to give us the advantage in the coming fight."

Karzul led Nephim back into the mine, straight to the tunnel where the dust glowed.

How long had they been here last night? Had they done anything that caused the fire lances to charge?

He'd touched the wall.

His hands had been covered in gray powder then.

He grasped the fire lance and waited.

Soon, a solitary soldier rounded the corner.

He touched the stud.

Nothing.

The soldier stepped out of the way, exposing a pair of archers behind him.

Karzul slapped his hand on the wall, gathering the gray dust. He grabbed the staff once more and fingered the stud. The soldier and archers flared under the brilliant blue-white light and vanished.

That was it.

The powder that coated the walls.

Could they take some of that with them?

Karzul cupped his hand and ran it upward along the wall. He managed to collect a small amount of powder. Fine and insubstantial.

"There are more coming," Nephim shouted.

"Rub your hand on the wall," Karzul said. "Then, your staff will work."

Karzul went back to examining the area, thinking of ways to collect the dust. There was nothing. The dust was too fine. He could see the tracks where they'd removed it from the wall with their hands.

Nephim's lance flared. "There are too many," she cried out.

"Let's get out of here." Karzul advanced, his staff held before him. His stomach turned only mildly at the thought of incinerating any more Daresh. Even though they were trying their best to kill him. Was he growing inured to the violence? Did that make him a hardened soldier?

By the time they exited the mine, his hands were blistered from the heat. They had dispatched half a dozen soldiers and just as many archers. Just how many Daresh were there? How many would he have to kill?

They burst through the great doors into the daylight.

Karzul's heart sank.

They were surrounded by Daresh. At least a dozen. Karzul took aim, but what was the point? He could take out a few, but there were too many. His lance would be depleted before he had dispatched them all.

There was no way out.

"Hold your lance over your head," Nephim said.

Karzul glanced over at her. She held her lance high over her head, gripping it tightly. Was that a sign of surrender? What was she doing?

He imitated her gesture.

Before he had time to think, his arms were grasped in mighty talons and he was jerked from the ground with such force, he felt as if his shoulders were about to separate. Kin'tara had not grasped his staff as Nephim's dragon had done, but rather, had his forearms in her grip. As they rose from the ground, Kin'tara tossed him into the air and flew beneath him, just as he'd seen Sar'tia.

Kin'tara flew close to the ground. An archer appeared ahead. An arrow twanged; it pierced her left wing, sending her into a wobble, before she righted herself and quickly placed herself out of easy range of the archers. She flow for a league or so, then rose above the clouds. They were safely away, but Karzul was not so sure they'd escaped unharmed. His hands were raw. Red. Bleeding.

"We should have checked out Easton," Karzul said. "See how many survived. I'm worried about Cerol and his men."

Karzul leaned over, pressing his concern onto Kin'tara. The Daresh had overrun the mine. Had they also taken the town? How could they? That would be an invasion, and Dari said that was still days away. He needed to know. But the pain in his hands was growing stronger.

"Go," Nephim said. "We can't risk you if there are Daresh archers near Easton. You need to report back. Tell Rodan what we learned. I'll find out what happened."

"Those men followed me." Karzul felt responsible for their fate.

"Go. That's an order," Nephim shouted as her dragon banked sharply away from him.

Karzul urged Kin'tara to follow, but she refused.

"Find out what happened, then report back," he called to Nephim.

Nephim peeled away and dove for the town. He hoped that some of Cerol's men had survived. It had been his idea to attack the forces guarding the mine. The townsfolk would blame him for their loss. Why not? He blamed himself. He should have scouted before committing to the action. They would have seen that there were more troops than expected. He was failing as a military commander right from the start. He wondered how many more would die because of his ineptitude.

Before he realized it, he was back at the citadel. The squad had gathered for the midday meal and looked to him for information. Even Rodan was in attendance and had just seated himself when Karzul arrived.

The squad held their peace as he seated himself, but from the strange looks they gave him, they were anxious about something.

"From the look on your face, I see that things did not go as expected," Rodan said.

"There were a lot more Daresh than we thought. Not just a handful. Dozens, maybe more. And archers. I hadn't planned on that.

"We attacked at dawn. Killed a few troops, but quickly found ourselves outnumbered. Nephim and I took refuge in the mine. They followed us down. We thought we were safe, but they brought hounds. We went deeper. Where the mine glows. When we did, our lances were more powerful than ever before, but it didn't last. We barely escaped with our lives."

"Let me look at your hands."

Karzul glanced at his hands. His palms were covered in gray powder, the flesh beneath bright red and blistered. He should be in the medical section, not the kitchen. He had planned to go straight there, but he knew Rodan and the squad were eager for news.

"There was this gray powder," Karzul muttered. "I got some on my hands."

"Go wash up," Rodan said. "Put some of that salve on it. Should take the sting out of it."

Karzul was hungry, but Rodan was right. He should tend to his wounds first. He made his way to the medical section and scrubbed his hands as well as he could. The gray powder seemed to have worked its way into his flesh. The blisters were not as bad as he first thought, but try as he might, he couldn't get the gray out of his palms. It was as if the powder had worked its way under his skin.

He wrapped his hands in bandages. At least he couldn't see them now.

He returned to the kitchen to eat. With both hands bandaged, feeding himself was a challenge. He had to tear the bread apart with his teeth.

Rodan joined him as he was attempting to cut a wedge of hard cheese. "Here. Let me help." Rodan glanced at Karzul. "Do you want to tell me what happened to your hair?"

"My hair?" Karzul ran a hand through his hair. The bandage kept him from feeling too much, but it was much the same as always. Short, neatly trimmed.

"From the looks of it," Rodan said, "you could be nearing your hundredth name day." He ran his hand through his own thinning gray hair. "Your hair is completely white."

34

THE FORBEARER'S CHARGE

arzul spent the day sitting on the grand stairs, letting the chill wind numb his flesh. He worried about Kin'-tara. Taking an arrow like that. In the back of his mind, was an echo of the pain she continued to feel. He worried about Nephim and what news she would bring. Was he ultimately responsible for the deaths of the townsfolk? Surely some had died, but how many?

The wind stirred the surrounding dust. He blinked it back, noticing a distant dot bobbing its way toward him.

Nephim.

She had returned.

He watched the immature dragon emerge from the distance, and execute a perfect landing on the great stairs. It lowered its head just long enough for Nephim to dismount before taking to the air and flying south. "He survived," Nephim said without preamble as she pulled her cap lower about her ears. She must have been feeling the cold as much as he was.

"Cerol?" Karzul asked.

Nephim nodded. "And most of his men. They took out a few archers, then fell back. There were too many. Surely, you didn't expect him to waste his men on nothing? Did you?"

Karzul heaved a sigh of relief. "At least I don't have that on my conscience."

Nephim snorted. "Your conscience? Every military commanded takes that risk with every mission. If you live long enough, you'll come to accept it as part of the job. The better you plan, the better their chances of surviving are, but there is always risk, and the foot soldiers and riders alike take that risk on themselves. It's not on you. Don't look so glum," Nephim said. "We learned much. Did you see how powerful my lance was after we came out of the mine?"

"The fire lance did little to change the outcome."

"But it shows us that we have more power than we thought."

"That's what I've been struggling with all day," Karzul said. "If we charge all the fire lances, we stand a much greater chance of wiping out the Daresh. Not just a few, but the whole army. Perhaps those we sent home might wield fire lances as effectively as Yarak after being charged up in the mine. What more could we do, even with half a dozen?"

Nephim settled beside him. "I thought you were going to destroy the mine?"

"I was. At least I thought I was. No, I am, but not right away. Kin'tara is pushing me to wait. Even though Dari thinks that if the Daresh capture the mine, they can make as many fire lances as they wish, we could not. We don't have that secret, but we know we can charge ours up, and maybe field a lot more than the meager handful we have now. Imagine if we did. Would that not turn the war in our favor? End it once and for all? Imagine a corps of riders all wielding fire lances. As it must have once been."

Nephim drew a deep breath. "Be still, my beating heart," she said. "A return to the olden days, with us leading the troops. You do paint an attractive picture."

"I believe it's possible," he said.

"I wouldn't have believed you until I wielded my lance at full power. It was exhilarating." She held up a hand. "And painful."

Nephim's hands were as red and blistered as his were. And she also had gray powder under her skin. She slipped her cap from her head, exposing a shocking white braid. Karzul realized that his hands and hair were not the only things affected by the mine.

He rubbed his own hands. They also carried the gray powder beneath his skin. He absentmindedly ran his hand through his hair and stopped. He held out his hand. "I suppose that limits the power we can contain. How can we wield the fire lance if every time we do, it burns our flesh? I wonder what the forbearers did?"

Nephim shrugged.

They sat there in silence for a while, neither one speaking. Nephim was usually so talkative, but not now. He sat with her for a while, not feeling the need to speak, until his stomach growled when he realized she must be hungry too. She hadn't eaten since the midday meal.

"Come," he said. "You must be starving. I know I am. You can tell the squad about our new plan."

Nephim seemed to perk up at the idea of presenting the plan to the squad. "Do you truly believe it will work?" she asked.

"If it does not, we're no worse off than we are now."

She rose and headed for the dining area where the squad was gathered, and she explained the plan. "We're going to search the citadel, and see how many fire lances we can come up with. We can charge them in the mine and use them against the Daresh. They'll never know what hit them."

The squad erupted with cheers, their determination turning into enthusiasm as they dove into the search for more fire lances.

"I'm going to find the most," Yarak said.

"No. I will." Belban elbowed him and rushed off.

They scoured every corner, flinging open locker after locker, but the halls yielded no more fire lances. Karzul had envisioned a treasure trove of weapons, imagining the squad emerging with armfuls of fire lances—enough to equip every rider in Thera and turn the tide against the Daresh, but the reality fell far short of his hopes.

They unearthed only a handful of fire lances, just enough to equip half a dozen riders, if those riders could even wield them.

Nephim remained optimistic. "Even these few lances can turn the tide of the war. The Daresh have but the one. We can target key enemy positions and cause significant damage before the power of the lances wanes."

She painted a vision of a stream of riders soaring to the mine to recharge while the remainder of the squad remained over Daresh, wreaking havoc, only to be relieved just as their lances ebbed. It all sounded so reasonable. All they needed to do was secure access to the mine.

~

The next morning, Karzul led a v shaped formation flying toward the mine. It was later than he would have liked, but the dragons had taken their time eating. How did Dari rouse her dragon at sunup and engage before the Theren dragon had eaten? What was her secret? As they approached the mine, Karzul instructed Yarak and Belban to scout ahead. They made a good pair. Yarak was deadly with his staff, but young and impulsive. Belban kept his youthful enthusiasm in check while drawing on his power to drive her own fire lance. Karzul had never figured out why he and Yarak were able to provide power to the less abled lance wielders; he was just thankful that they were.

As they drew close to the mine, Kin'tara slowed. She favored her right wing as if protecting her left from another archer attack. As she winced, Karzul felt a sharp pain in his left side. She pushed no thoughts his way, but she certainly wan't enthusiastic about returning to the mine. She roared at the rest of the dragons even as they kept low, skimming just above the treetops as they sped along. It was unsettling and made his stomach queasy. He often went without a morning meal when he was riding.

Nephim said it was only unsettling to new riders and that soon enough Karzul would grow to like it and feel slightly unsettled when on solid ground.

He caught a glimpse of color, off in the distance. The scouts were returning. He hoped it was good news.

But it wasn't.

The Daresh had reinforced their troops with even more arms men, and brought in additional archers.

"That means we can't even get close," Karzul said. "Anyone have any ideas?"

"Stealth." Yarak replied. "We go in on the ground. A few of us keep to the air to distract them while the rest of us sneak in on foot. Once we have our lances charged up, we can wipe them out."

"Who will distract the enemy archers so we can sneak in undetected?" Karzul asked.

"I'll do it," Yarak said. "I can keep them occupied for a while."

"I'll join him," Belban said. "I can raise some fire. Enough to distract them while you enter the mine."

"I can't ask this of you," Karzul said.

"You didn't," Yarak said. "We volunteered."

Karzul shuddered. Yarak was so eager to engage in battle. Would the youth be as enthusiastic if he were injured? "The rest of you, land about a league east of the mine," he instructed the remainder of the squad. "Stay low. We don't want them to see you until you're needed. Their fire lance may not be near, or she could already be overhead." He turned back to Yarak. "Wait for our signal. Try to stay out of range of the archers."

Karzul watched Yarak and Belban depart. He felt a chill, as if the wind had suddenly turned cold. He let the shiver it inspired shake him.

"Fly well," he murmured as he turned Kin'tara away from them.

Kin'tara skirted the treetops and dropped to the ground. Beside her, the three remaining dragons settled in. They shifted their weight from foot to foot, one of them swinging her massive tail, sweeping the ground behind her clear of brush. Dara'tia lurched in the direction of the mine, only to pull back when Kin'tara snapped at her.

After several snaps from Kin'tara, Dara'tia settled down, but continued to sniff the air and look around, as if seeking something that was just out of sight.

Wait here. Karzul told Kin'tara. Watch the other dragons. Hold them with you.

"Come on." Nephim gestured toward the dragons. "They'll be fine."

Karzul hoped she was right. The more experience he accumulated as a commander, the more he realized he did not know what he was doing.

They were approaching the mine complex, and they were in for a fight. More than a dozen Daresh troops were already on guard. Most were stationed along the road that led to the mine, but a handful of them walked the perimeter of the mining site. Each pair of foot soldiers was accompanied by a pair of archers.

Where had they gotten so many archers from? How had they made their way so deep into Theren territory without a fight?

"We've been spotted," Nephim jabbed Karzul with an elbow.

He turned to see Ormwor take an arrow to his shoulder.

35

THE RIVER'S RED EMBRACE

Karzul rushed to Ormwor, bending almost double to keep his own head out of the line of fire. The stream babbled along peacefully, mocking the red that had invaded it as Ormwor tumbled into the icy water.

"Take them back," Karzul hissed at Nephim. "This was a bad idea."

"War is filled with bad ideas," she said. "Some casualties are expected. That's how it works. We can't back out just because we took one arrow. He's not dead. He'll recover. We push on."

Karzul dragged Ormwor out of the water and ripped a strip of cloth from his shirt to stuff into the bleeding wound. The young man reached up and pushed his hand away. "I can take care of it myself."

"You're injured. You need medical attention," Karzul said.

"Get those fire lances charged." Ormwor reached up, grabbed the arrow and yanked it free. He scooped up the cloth fragment Karzul had torn from his shirt and pushed it into the bleeding wound. It slowed the flow of red but did not completely stop it. "Go. I'll be fine." He extended his fire lance to Karzul. "Bring it back fully charged."

Karzul hesitated. What sort of commander abandoned his own plans at the first casualty?

Still, it bothered him. It looked as if Ormwor would survive, but how could he tell?

Karzul crawled up next to Nephim. "They know we're here. What now?"

"Cahat and I will distract them while you make a run for the mine. We'll keep them occupied long enough for you to get inside. When you come back, you can take care of the Daresh. Even if you deplete the lances you carry with you, you can recharge them before we leave. It's a solid plan. Don't back out because we met a bit of resistance. We don't have an alternative."

"You're planning on standing up to archers?" Karzul asked.

"No. I don't plan to stand up to archers. That would make me daft. But I do plan to draw their fire. There are five of them, from what I counted. Between Cahat and I, we can keep them focused on us while you run." She extended her fire lance. "Take it. Bring it back fully charged."

Karzul wrestled with the fire lances as he crawled along the stream bed. They were unwieldy and threatened to fall from his grasp at every turn. He needed a way to carry more than one and leave his hands free. Karzul ripped off the pack's strap and used his knife to tear it apart. Soon he had a sling that would carry the additional fire lances. He shrugged it onto his shoulder and rushed along the stream bed until he was certain he was as close to the mine as he was going to get. He carefully peered over the bank.

Fate was with him. There were no archers nearby. Those nearest the Temple of the Winds were targeting Nephim and Cahat, who were making sure they did by taking turns standing and throwing rocks at them. Karzul shook off the image and crawled out of the stream-bed. He tried to hold his head low and still keep an eye on the archers. It was difficult, and his back ached with anticipation of the arrow that he was certain would soon find him.

He'd made it all the way to the temple of the forbearers before he took his first arrow. The shaft appeared out of the south, accompanied by a sharp whistle. Karzul turned, but not fast enough. The shaft pierced the straps of his pack, grazed his shoulder and stuck into the wood frame of the building behind him, pinning him to it.

Karzul tried to twist to free himself, but the arrow was stuck tight in the wood.

He was trapped.

He grasped the arrow. The wood had been polished to a smooth finish, making it hard to hold on to.

He yanked.

The arrow remained firmly stuck in the building.

He tried to move away. Perhaps he could snap the shaft, or failing that, slide the strap off the arrow and free himself that way. His heart raced, and it was hard to breathe. Any moment now, the next arrow would come. He was stuck in plain sight.

Only the expected arrow didn't come.

What did come was laughter.

"Look. Tonan pinned a bug to the building. It's no butterfly. It's a dirty clothes-eating moth."

A soldier approached, sword drawn. Flanking him on either side were archers, bows at partial draw. How could he have been so foolish? Was there ever hope of his plan working, or had it been doomed from the start?

"What you carrying," the soldier said in a singsong voice, "little moth?"

Karzul struggled against the arrow that pinned him to the structure. He recalled Dari's warning about the Daresh, who planned to hang him if they caught him. Would they do that immediately or take him captive first? He glanced to his left. Another archer stood ready, bow drawn halfway back in readiness. No escaping that way.

He lowered his hands.

His hand brushed the hilt of his knife.

Of course. His knife. He could cut the strap, and then what? Not simply escape. He would be shot dead before he could take ten steps.

His fire lance?

He was uncertain how much power his fire lance had left. But perhaps there was enough to distract the archers while he made his escape.

If he was fast.

If he was fortunate.

He stilled himself. Slowed his breathing. Snapped open the strap that held his knife in its sheath. He wrapped his fingers around the cold handle, letting the roughness of it rest against his still-sore flesh. Almost as if time had slowed down, he removed his knife, slashed through the strap, and raised his fire lance.

The twang of a bowstring told him the archer had not hesitated.

He swung the fire lance, fingering the trigger as he did.

Between him and the archer, a puff of smoke told him how close the arrow had come to piercing him. As the stream of blue-white light struck the archer, he vanished.

Another twang.

Karzul spun without thinking, his fire lance emitting a continuous beam of blue-white that scarred the buildings before incinerating the second archer.

The soldier between them stepped back, his sword coming up into attack position.

Did he truly expect to fight a fire lance with his sword?

Karzul took a step forward, leveling the lance at the soldier.

The hair on his neck stood up. There was an archer behind the swordsman.

He threw himself to the ground as the arrow whistled past him and stuck into the wood beside the one he'd freed himself from.

His shoulder erupted in pain.

He reached up.

Blood.

He cursed.

"Get him, you fool. He has a fire lance," someone screamed.

Ignoring the pain in his shoulder, Karzul steadied his aim.

The staff crackled and spat out a feeble beam of yellow light. The man erupted in flames, his agonized screams piercing the air before he collapsed, engulfed in a blazing inferno.

Karzul ran for the Temple of the Forbearers.

An arrow whistled past his ear and twanged into the wood beside his head.

He dove to the ground and crawled towards the opening between the massive doors. It was still several yards away, and he would probably never make it, but he had to try. He could not give up. Not yet.

More arrows clattered to the ground as it struck the stone of the building above him.

Were they playing with him, or was his strategy working?

He kept a slow pace, crawling on his elbows and knees, even though the pain in his shoulder was growing worse by the moment.

Thunk. Thunk. The arrows were getting closer.

Were they not able to see him? What sort of archer could not hit a target so close?

Did they have orders not to kill him?

But the archer who had grazed his shoulder hadn't been afraid to hit him. Perhaps it was just luck.

Thunk.

Another arrow.

This time it grazed his back, tracing a line of fire across his shoulder blades.

Clearly, this wasn't the way.

Karzul flattened his body against the stone floor, holding his breath as another arrow thunked into the wood. This one was lower. It would have penetrated his ribs. No, the archers were not intentionally missing him. They were simply not accustomed to aiming so low. His luck would soon run out.

He steeled himself for the rush to the doors. If he could move fast enough, he could be inside the entryway before the archers could get a clean shot at him. He prepared himself. Sweat poured down his arm, threatening his grip on the fire lance. He tried to put it out of his mind and drew his legs beneath him. He was ready.

Just as he began his flight, Karzul felt a wash of heat accompanied by the stench of rotten eggs and brimstone.

Dragon fire.

He threw himself back onto the ground.

He rolled onto his back, almost losing his grip on his fire lance.

The fire was not aimed at him, but at the archers.

Flames washed over them and the soldiers alike.

They scattered.

Karzul sat up.

A grip like a vise grasped his chest and yanked him from the ground. Talons as long as his arm closed around his chest, making it hard to breathe as great wings beat the air and lifted him aloft. His injuries protested.

"Kin'tara?" he offered his thoughts.

No response.

If not Kin'tara, then who?

He tried to catch his breath, but the dragon had him in a grip so tight that breathing was impossible. Stars formed and circled his vision even as he started to lose his sight.

He beat his fist against the brilliant green of the claws that encircled him.

They were brilliant green!

36

A SHATTERED TRUCE

Karzul came awake, lying in a field looking at the sky. His ribs ached as if he'd been in a tavern brawl against a much larger adversary. The sun was almost at midday and the air warm, with only a hint of chill on the breeze. It carried the scent of clover and cook fires.

"The dead have arisen." Dari stood over Karzul.

"You attacked your own people."

"You said you were going to destroy the mine. You took fire lances there. You lost them to the Daresh soldiers. Do you know what that means?"

Karzul was having difficulty coming to grips with being alive. There was little hope he could puzzle out what she was on about.

He shook his head.

"I'm not going down there. I'll not do it. You forced their hand. They'll come to me. They'll demand that I go. They'll torture me, threaten my loved ones. But I can't. I simply can not." She squared off, glaring at him, a single tear running down her face. "You've ruined everything."

"What are you talking about? You'll not go where?"

"They will make me go down the mine," she said. "Charge the lances. The ones you left behind."

"Left behind?" Karzul searched his addled mind. Lances? Left behind? The image of his cutting the strap on his pack to free the fire lances flashed before his eyes. Karzul's face grew hot as he realized the truth of Daris' words. He'd lost the lances. And he'd lied to Dari. She asked him to destroy the mine, and he'd decided to use it against her people.

He cursed. "I would rather you not go down the mine and charge fire lances, either. Not for the Daresh."

"You realize what you've done? Not only to the cause, but to yourself? Surely you know what your white hair means?"

His hair was snowy white; he knew that. His skin around his jaw was slack, and there were deep lines on either side of his mouth. He looked like a middle-aged man.

"You see it? See what just a brief exposure to that mine did to you. They will expect me to go," Dari said.

"Why?" Karzul asked.

"Because I'm not a true Daresh. They consider me expendable. If I had not found the fire lance, and been the only one who can wield it, they would have disposed of me long ago. I will demand that they make you do it, but they won't trust you. They'll insist I do it unless you destroy the mine first." Another tear slid down her cheek. "Don't you see why it's so important?"

"How? Do you have any suggestions? There are soldiers, archers. I was trying to get to the mine when you abducted me."

"Abducted you? I was saving you. You were not trying to destroy the mine. You were trying to exploit it. I thought we were friends. I may not be a native Daresh, but it is my home. Everyone I care about is there. I can't let you tip the scales in favor of Thera. I trusted you."

Karzul winced. His shoulder hurt, but not as badly as her words.

"I'm sorry. Kin'tara wants me to wait, and I let my people talk me into it. You're right. We have to destroy the mine. Fire lances on either side is a bad idea."

Dari leaned in. "Let me look at that shoulder of yours. We don't want you dying from a simple flesh wound before you complete your mission." She stretched out a hand and tugged at Karzul's shirt.

Pain flared. His stomach churned.

She leaned in and pulled the edges of the wound together.

She reached into her bag and withdrew a small glass cylinder and touched it to the flesh of his shoulder.

Karzul tried to get a look at what she was doing, but all he could see was her hand pinching his flesh together. After a few heartbeats, she released it.

He reached for the wound, but she gently shoved it out of the way.

"Don't touch it until it's had a chance to set. Touch it now, and your finger will be stuck to your shoulder. Let it heal. When you're up to it, I have a task for you. A way you can fix what you just did."

"How?"

"By risking everything like I did to save your sorry hide. You strike at the archers from a low altitude. They expect you to attack low, but they can't see you until it's too late. Come in hot. Dragon fire blazing. You'll have a hand of heartbeats before they can warn the archers positioned on the roofs of the nearby buildings. Don't wait too long. Those men can see you coming even low, and can pick you off like birds in a nest. Don't give them the chance."

She nodded to the west. "Enter the mine and bring the shaft head down. On yourself if you must, but bring it down. Once you're inside, and your lances are powered up, you can melt iron with them. The longer you stay in the mine, the longer the lances will last. Just don't stay there any longer than you must."

"So, I'm to bring the mine down, even if it means my own death," Karzul said. "You said I had already done damage to myself." He ran his hand through his hair, recalling how white it had been when he last looked into a mirror.

"Karzul. You say you want to save your people. I've told you that that is also my goal. To save our people. I thought you agreed. Thought you saw the necessity. Are you willing to sacrifice yourself if you must, to save your people? Everyone you've ever known or loved is at risk. Is this not a noble cause? Something worth dying for?"

"Everyone I ever loved is already dead," Karzul said. The squad were becoming his friends, but as Nephim kept reminding him, he must be ready to sacrifice their lives for his plans. No, he loved no one who remained alive. Yet he did have distant relatives. His mother's sister still lived, and her children. Would he wish to see them dead or enslaved? Not really. Maybe Dari was right. This was something worth dying for.

"I'm ready. But I sincerely hope it doesn't come down to choosing between my life and those of my fellows."

"I hope not either, but war is an ugly business. You have to be prepared to do what's necessary, and it's necessary that the Daresh not hold on to any more functioning fire lances than the one I wield. The cost to the Theren people will be high if they do."

Dari made a motion in the air with her fingers. Almost immediately, the brilliant green dragon descended to land beside her.

"Call your dragon," Daris said. "There's something I need to show you."

Karzul copied the gesture that Dari had made. It was similar to the one he used to coax Kin'tara into the bond. Was that how the riders all called their steeds? Kin'tara seemed to appear when she wished, and not because he needed her, but this time, she came almost immediately. He hopped onto her back and pressed a thought at her to follow Dari and Sar'tia.

He needn't have bothered.

He looks down. He was still trying to accustom himself to how to judge height while flying. It was more difficult than it appeared, especially when there were no familiar buildings to give him an idea of how far he was from them.

What he did notice was lines of tents. Hundreds of them. All along the road, tents stood in straight lines, three deep. There must be a thousand Daresh troops stationed on the border. Alchua and his troops would be no match for them. They would all be killed in the first assault, and then who would stand against the Daresh? Karzul had no idea what they might do, but they needed time to plan. He could give them that, if nothing else.

"Is this what you wanted to show me?" He called to Dari across the sky between them.

"You'll see when we get there." She didn't even turn to look at him.

He was done playing along.

Karzul pressed a thought at Kin'tara to take him to the front lines where the battle was about to begin.

Kin'tara pushed with a series of images of dragons. Blue, red, yellow, gold. All small. All dead. Except the last one. Brilliantly green. Alive. Dari's dragon. The only one of Kin'tara's offspring who had survived.

"Come on, Kin'tara," he pleaded with her.

The image of her offspring wavered.

Kin'tara banked sharply and descended toward the ground like a stone, pulling into level flight a dozen yards above the ground.

Karzul's stomach turned. He held its contents in if only by sheer strength of will.

Before he knew it, they streaked across the Daresh camp and across the border back into Thera. A wave of relief washed over Karzul as they crossed the border.

It was short-lived.

The Daresh were already on the move.

37

AN UNEASY TRUCE

It didn't take long for Karzul to locate the Theren troops. They were camped across the road from the advancing Daresh. The road that used to be packed with trade wagons, but since the outbreak of hostilities, was vacant.

Alchua had been too worried about the advancing Daresh to spare troops for the assault on the mine, but had decided since that this was their best chance. The tents were arranged not in rows as the Daresh did, but in a great semicircle that centered on the road as if there were some invisible marker there stating where the battle was to take place. Was it a historical site that Alchua was memorializing, or was it just personal preference?

Cook smoke rose from the camp, and Karzul's stomach growled to remind him that it was getting late and he had last eaten well before dawn. He searched for the tent he knew to be Alchua's. It was no larger than the rest, and not centrally located, but off to one side, in the fifth rank, as if it were an ordinary troop tent.

Kin'tara dropped Karzul near the outer perimeter of the camp and nestled down as if she intended to take a snooze while waiting for his return. He wondered how she had sensed his intent. Was she sensitive to his moods, or could she actually read his thoughts? He might not live long enough to find out.

When he reached the command tent, Karzul found Alchua there with Rodan seated behind Alchua's writing desk, stacks of parchment at either elbow.

"The duties of a commander never relent," Rodan said.

"Don't you have an assistant for that?" Karzul nodded at the stacks of parchment.

"To organize and catalog them, not to write them. That's my job." He placed the quill pen he'd been using into the inkwell and looked up at Karzul. "I thought we'd lost you. You were carried away by the Daresh rider. Your squad returned home empty-handed, and leaderless."

Karzul flushed. He had lost the fire lances and been taken captive all in one morning. What kind of leader was he? "Did they all make it back safely?" he asked.

"Ormwor took an arrow and perished. Belban fell in a skirmish near the mine. Your squad is no longer a squad. Just a couple of riders with a pair of lances. Things are not looking good."

"Sorry to hear that. I should've known better. It's my fault."

Karzul drew a breath and held it. What he feared had come to pass. He'd sent his people into harm's way and lost two of them. The guilt settled in his stomach like a stone.

"Karzul," Rodan said softly. "There will be time for that later. Right now. We need a plan."

"We can recharge the remaining fire lances at the mine. They don't last too long, but they are powerful. We can continue recharging them while the rest of the riders keep the enemy distracted. We can drive the Daresh away from the mine, push them back to their stronghold. With the threat of unlimited fire lances, the Daresh will be forced to retreat or be exterminated."

"Where are you going to get the fire lances?"

"Yarak still has his?"

"He's the only one."

Karzul shook his head. "Maybe we can recover the ones I lost. I was carrying them to the mine when I was shot. Pinned the bundle of fire lances to the building I stood before. I had to cut away the strap that bound them to my back to free myself. There were archers. More than I could counter in one go. No doubt the fire lances are in their hands already. If we are fortunate, they will not have enough riders to wield them. Dari said that she was the only one who was able to wield the one she possessed."

Rodan nodded. "Nephim said as much."

"She survived." Karzul stated it as fact, hoping it was true.

"She survived. Nearly lost her life trying to rescue the fire lances, but she made it out. Another sword wound. But she'll heal."

Karzul heaved a sigh of relief. He wasn't sure how he would be able to carry on if Nephim had fallen.

"We need her for this next part of the plan. I need a flame rider I can trust."

"Not Yarak then?"

Karzul carefully considered his response. He had plans to destroy the mine, but Kin'tara pushed him to wait. Was she encouraging him to charge the fire lances? Was that why? Or was there something else? They had to destroy the mine, or the Daresh would just keep coming.

"So what to you plan to do?" Rodan asked. "Storm the mine?"

"No, we use stealth to enter the mine. We can come in low, spitting dragon fire from as many riders as we can get. The first pass will be the most dangerous, but if we are fortunate, it will take time for the Daresh to respond to the attack. While the rest of the riders are harrying the soldiers, Nephim and I will sneak into the mine and charge up whatever lances we can. If we can rescue the lost lances, that'll give us that much more firepower, but only two will be sufficient for what I have planned."

Karzul paused to see if Rodan had any questions, but the old man simply nodded.

"Once the fire lances are charged, we'll take the Daresh on from inside the temple of the forbearers to avoid the archers as best we can. We can drive them into the open, and the riders can take them out with dragon fire while the foot soldiers pick off any stragglers. Once they are defeated, we'll go back and bring the mine down. If the foot soldiers can hold them off long enough."

"It'll take too long to move enough men," Rodan explained. "Dragons will have to do. We still have a few of those."

The old man seemed distracted.

"You agree then?" Karzul asked.

"Provisionally. There's still a lot more to decide. Why don't you dismiss your dragon? Spend the night here. There are a lot of plans to be made before we attempt this daring attack of yours. You're going to get a firsthand look at what it is like to be a true commander, not just a glorified squad leader." He gestured toward a chair across from him. "Sit."

Karzul took his seat while Rodan addressed his aide. He instructed the sub-commanders to assemble as soon as the evening meal was finished and ordered food for himself and Karzul to be brought to the tent.

They ate alone while Alchua and Rodan questioned Karzul about enemy troop placement and every detail he had witnessed while behind enemy lines. Karzul realized that he had missed a lot that was important. He hadn't considered assessing the enemy. He had a lot to learn.

Before the two men ran out of questions, his men began to arrive. Strong brandy was brought and served to the staff while Rodan explained what Karzul had told him. At first, the men seemed against supporting the effort at the mine.

"It feels like cowardice," one of the men said. "Turn tail and run away from the front lines when the enemy is preparing to attack."

"Supporting the mine effort will provide us unprecedented fire lance power," Rodan explained.

"Not to be contrary, but the dragons and the fire lance have done little to turn the tide so far. What makes you so sure that they will now?"

The questions flew, the brandy flowed and eventually the men began turning toward Karzul's plan. Rodan was obviously selling the idea to his men by asking for their opinions. Was that part of being a good commander? Soliciting input from your subordinates even when you had already decided on a plan of action?

He finally wrapped it all up with, "I want this camp broken by nightfall. Pack heavy. We will not be returning. I want this site to look like a ghost town by the time the sun rises and the Daresh get a chance to put their dragons in the air. We should arrive at the mine complex just about the time Karzul and his riders arrive."

"Sir." The sub-commander saluted and departed, taking with him those who had simply stood there in silence.

"I hope your plan works," Rodan said. "But if the information you provided is accurate, and I have every reason to believe it is, then there's little we can do here. It's best to get moving. I'll leave this tent behind. Bunk here. When your dragon rises, get your people and get under way. It will make for an amusing spy report when the Daresh riders alight and find a single solitary tent in the field where the bulk of our forces had been the night before."

"I thought you said it would take too long to reach the mine." Karzul said.

"If we followed normal procedures. By marching overnight, we keep the men occupied. Rumors buzz around here like flies on dung. The troops already know what you reported. If we remain where we are, they'll be up all night worrying, wondering what we're planning. This way, they're out of harm's way, they're occupied, and they just might get to the mine complex by the time you need them. At least, that's my fervent hope. You and your fire lances can deal with the bulk of the advancing Daresh, and we will save uncounted lives."

"I wish we still had all the fire lances. Two is hardly enough to make a difference. Let's hope the Daresh kept the fire lances near the mine. If we can defeat the soldiers, retrieve the fire lances, charge them in the mine, and confront the Daresh as they cross the border, we might just win."

Rodan laughed. "The optimism of youth." He motioned to Karzul's ripped uniform. "Let's get the medic to take a look at your shoulder. From the slash on your uniform, you must have taken quite a slice. Arrow, you said?"

"Yes."

Rodan called for the medic. A stout woman of middle age who wore a crisp uniform despite her unmilitary build. She trimmed away Karzul's uniform shirt and probed the wound that Dari had attended.

"She use the old world magic to seal this?" the medic asked.

"Yes."

"Don't suppose you saw where she got it?"

"Her bag?"

"You know what I mean. This is magic from the before times. Lets you seal the flesh without stitches. Makes a perfect seal too. Keeps the flux out. We'd lose half as many of our own men with even a few of them."

"Sorry. I have no idea where she got it from."

"Same place she got the fire lance from, is my guess," the medic said. "I'd ask you to look the next time you are at the citadel, but it doesn't seem like you'll be there anytime soon."

She covered the wound with a clean bandage and handed Karzul a fresh uniform shirt. "Looks like it's well on the way to healing," she said. "I'm jealous. We sure could use that sort of help. Tomorrow is going to be a rough day."

38

A DRAGON'S RESOLVE

arzul woke to the sound of silence. He half expected there to be some sign that Rodan and his troops had departed, but he knew better. As soon as the evening meal was complete, the camp had begun the process of packing heavy, as Rodan put it. Under cover of darkness, the entire camp vanished. Tiny holes in the ground bore witness to the absence of half a hundred tents. The trampled grass had yet to recover from countless footsteps. The place truly felt like the ghost town Rodan wished to portray for the Daresh scouts when they arrived.

Stretching his legs, Karzul emerged from his solitary tent. Should he pack the tent when he left? Was there even room for him to carry such a thing? No, best to leave it behind, just as Rodan wished.

Outside the tent, Karzul found a small sack. It contained a few hard rolls, some white cheese and jerked meat. He heaved a sigh of relief. He'd completely forgotten to make arrangements for his morning meal.

He was totally unprepared.

For everything.

Karzul wondered where Rodan and the troops were. He imagined them trudging across dark fields and over rock-strewn hills with only the light of the moon to guide them. After midnight, the moon would have set. Karzul wondered how they had managed it in the dark.

Karzul made the sign to summon Kin'tara. In response, he received the image of a lamb. Still warm. Still running with blood. She was still feeding.

Now, he pressed the thought to her. I need you now.

He had never used that tone with Kin'tara before. He received an image of her tearing open the lamb's ribcage and snatching its heart.

She pushed the image of her spitting out the remains of the carcass and taking flight.

As he awaited her, the outline of Dara'tia, Nephim's dragon, emerged from the clouds, with another pair close behind it. Yarak and Cahat. Nephim still favored her injured arm. Would she be able to wield her fire lance? He was not proud of himself for thinking it, but should he have chosen Yarak instead?

"We thought you were dead," Nephim said, stepping down from her dragon.

"Not even a little bit dead. Kin'tara says I'll be a thorn in your side for a long time, but if you thought me dead, why are you here?"

"We expected to find Rodan and his troops, but instead we are met by the ghost of our fallen squad leader. Care to share what transpired since we last saw you?"

"I sold Rodan on our plan," he said.

"To recharge the fire lances?" Nephim glanced at Yarak.

"Yes." Karzul turned to the younger man. "Yarak. I need Nephim with me. She's already been down the mine with me once and shows the signs of it. Just look at her hair." He ran his hand through his own hair to emphasize that he too had taken the risk along with her. "I can't ask anyone else to place themselves in harm's way like that."

"I'm not afraid," Yarak said.

"No, you're not, but I don't want to inflict what happens in the mine on more than one person. Nephim and I have already been exposed to whatever is down there. There's no reason to take a chance that it might be fatal."

"I'm a soldier," Yarak explained. I'm willing to die for the cause."

"Only if necessary," Karzul said. "I've made my decision." He nodded to Yarak's fire lance. "Please."

Yarak hesitated.

Would he resist? Would Karzul need to insist on his compliance? What if he didn't?

As it turned out, his fears were unfounded. Yarak handed his fire lance to Nephim, but his eyes remained firmly on Karzul. "Don't lose it."

"You'll have it back."

Karzul's gaze took in Cahat, who seemed to be waiting to be told what to do. She shifted her weight from foot to foot, glancing around as if looking for something only to let her gaze drop to her feet.

"Do you really think this will work?" she asked.

"I can't think of anything else to try," Karzul admitted.

"Call my name at the next planting?" Cahat asked.

"You call my name," he said.

That brought a slight smile to Cahat's lips that soon faded.

A tingle pulled at Karzul's mind.

Kin'tara had arrived.

"This is it. We're either heroes who live forever in song, or we're respected fallen spirits called to bless the planting season. Let's try to make it into the songs."

Karzul slung the fresh pack over his shoulder and mounted up. Kin'tara leaped into the sky, and they were soon winging their way across the land, the treetops just beneath his feet. The mine was only a short flight by dragon. Would Rodan's men be arriving by the time they did?

"Yarak. Up high. Scout out ahead. I want to confirm what we're up against before we get there. Cahat, you join him. You decide which direction we should approach from. You can coordinate with Alchua's riders. I want dragon fire concentrated where it will do the most good."

"On it." Cahat pulled her dragon ahead of Yarak as the two raced for the clear morning sky.

"Have you made up your mind?" Nephim asked when Yarak and Cahat had vanished.

"If we do destroy the mine, will the Daresh simply pack up and leave, or will there be a fight? I can't imagine the Daresh will slink away quietly. No matter what happens, there will be bloodshed. Lots of it. On both sides, but we have to beat them back first."

"I worry what exposure in the mines has done to us. Our hair is as white as snow. I'm not sure what that means. Will we survive another trip down there?"

"Let's hope so." Before Karzul could say more, the air ahead swarmed with arrows. Archers on the ground were shooting at something above. Karzul hoped it was not Yarak and Cahat. The two of them should have remained out of arrow range, but one never knew.

"Behind us," Nephim shouted.

Half a dozen dragons were winging their way toward Karzul and Nephim. For a moment, Karzul thought it was Rodan and his riders, but at the head of the thunder was the brilliant green of Dari's dragon. They were on course to drive Karzul and Nephim into the path of the archers.

"We had best move," Karzul cried. "No time to waste."

He urged Kin'tara forward.

The dragon dropped even lower, her claws brushing the treetops as they rushed along the ground. So great was her speed that Dara'tia was hard-pressed to keep up. The younger dragon started to fall behind as they emerged into the clearing that housed the mine and its buildings.

Arrows ripped through the air, more than one piercing the thick leather of Kin'tara's wings.

"The mine," Karzul shouted.

Kin'tara banked hard and shot for the temple of the forbearers.

The great doors had been rolled shut by the Daresh. Were they trying to prevent the dragons from entering?

Karzul thought of Kin'tara. "Force the doors open. I don't want you in the air."

Kin'tara landed with a skid and struck the great doors. She grasped them with her massive claws and pulled.

Ever so slowly, the doors rolled back. When they were wide enough for Kin'tara to squeeze through, she folded her wings tight and shoved her great bulk through the crack. She stepped aside and made way for Dara'tia.

Once both dragons were inside, Kin'tara grasped the doors and shoved them closed with a thud, and not a heartbeat too soon. The sound of arrows striking the wood was thunderous.

Karzul leveled his fire lance at the seam where the doors met and fired. Smoke filled the room, the metal glowing red, then flowing together to seal the doors, at least for now.

Karzul turned toward the mine.

Kin'tara rushed to block his path.

"Get out of my way," Karzul muttered, attempting to circle the dragon.

Kin'tara nudged him away from the mine, her great head shaking.

Karzul had to dodge her horns as they swung past him.

"Why not?" He pushed the thought to the dragon.

The dragon ignored his words and shifted her bulk to prevent him from entering the mine shaft.

"We have to recharge the lances," Karzul screamed. Why was Kin'tara behaving this way?

Karzul glanced over at Nephim. She was similarly facing down Dara'tia. The smaller, immature dragon was not trying to block her path but was rather attempting to squeeze past Kin'tara and enter the mine. She'd done the same thing the last time they were here. Dara'tia seemed determined to enter the mine, while the Kin'tara was equally insistent that she not.

"Karzul," Nephim screamed.

He turned to see Dara'tia disappear down the mine shaft.

39

THE DRAGON'S CRUCIBLE

arzul's ears rang as Kin'tara let out a screech. It sounded for all the world like a child screaming in frustration. She nudged Karzul toward the mine with her snout and quickly followed him.

Why had she changed her mind?

Perhaps she'd decided it was time to abandon their position. The temple of the forbearers was filled with smoke from Karzul's fire lance.

From down the mineshaft, Karzul heard a high-pitched squeal, followed shortly by another.

It was Dara'tia.

It was not a cry of pain or of frustration, as Kin'tara had expressed, but rather a squeal of delight, like a small child would make. Why was Dara'tia so desperate to get down the mine, and why did Kin'tara want to stop her?

Kin'tara roared and turned toward the mine shaft. Her tail brushed the ground, sweeping Karzul from his feet. He jumped up and raced after as she disappeared down the mine shaft. The faint light ahead barely illuminated his path, and more than once he stumbled over shards of rock or debris.

They had no lanterns this time. He wished they'd had time to find and light one. The mine shaft made him uneasy. Every step down was a step into deeper darkness.

Karzul caught up to Nephim standing dumbstruck in the middle of the tunnel.

"Dara'tia put me down as soon as we turned the corner," she said. "She's out of control. Screaming like a child on its name-day celebration. I don't know what's gotten into her."

Behind Karzul, Kin'tara snorted impatiently.

"Come on," he said. "Nothing to do but follow her. That's where we wanted to go, anyway."

Kin'tara screeched, growing more impatient as she started after the younger dragon.

Karzul flattened himself against the rocky wall, dragging Nephim behind him. "Go after her," he said.

Kin'tara was clearly agitated by the smaller dragon being down the mine. He stepped aside to let her pass. They would have to take their chances with the archers and Daresh soldiers behind them.

Kin'tara shook her head and nudged Karzul toward the fleeing dragon. She sent him an image of himself looking like a hedgehog, arrows protruding from him like spines on a porcupine.

He laughed.

Kin'tara was developing a sense of humor.

"Come on," he told Nephim. "She's protecting us from the archers."

They raced after the smaller dragon, Kin'tara close behind. The huge dragon barely fit through the mine shaft. Her tail smashed into a supporting timber, shedding sparks. Karzul worried that she might be weakening the structure of the shaft, risking collapse, which meant a slow death, trapped in the mine, either suffocating or starving. Or would Kin'tara eat him to save herself?

Best not to dwell on it.

They followed Dara'tia down the mine shaft and hoped their fire lances charged.

Had he really thought this was a good plan? They should have destroyed this place the first time they entered it.

Karzul nearly tripped over Nephim, so lost was he in his own thoughts. Nephim had stopped mid-tunnel, and was kneeling down to observe her dragon. Dara'tia had reached the glowing chamber and was licking the walls as if they were made of honey. The dragon paused to roll on the floor of the mine just as a dog rolls in the dust to clean its fur. Only dragons don't have fur. What was she doing?

Karzul reached out to touch the wall. This was the place where they had encountered the powder. He was certain the powder was responsible for the fire lance performance. Was this why Dara'tia was relishing it?

As his hand neared the wall, Kin'tara shot fire at him.

"What's wrong with you?" he demanded.

The image that came to Karzul's mind was of an old man, bent over and wrinkled.

That is what the dust does?

Kin'tara nudged him away from the wall.

What about the fire lances? How did the ancients charge the lances if the powder killed them?

Kin'tara rubbed her snout against the wall, then licked the powder from it. Her eyes narrowed, the vertical slits turning orange, then brilliant white as if Karzul was looking into the noonday sun.

He blinked, shielded his eyes and took a step back.

You eat this?

Kin'tara turned her massive head, a single horn striking the solid wall. The horn dug into it, shattering the stone as she dragged it along.

A shower of tiny particles fell to the floor.

She backed away as Dara'tia let out an ear-piercing squeal. The younger dragon knocked Karzul to the ground in her hurry to get to the small shards of stone. Her forked tongue emerged and swept them all up in one go.

Karzul had completely forgotten Nephim was there.

"Kin'tara had been keeping Dara'tia away, but now she's helping her. I think it's something they need."

"The images I get from Dara'tia are hunger and desire," Nephim said.

"Not Kin'tara," Karzul said. "Whatever she just exposed on the wall, she doesn't want for herself."

As if the mention of her name had awakened something in her, Kin'tara let out an ear-splitting roar. She turned back toward the mine entrance, scattering rocks from the wall as she did.

Light streamed past her.

The Daresh had found them, and they had lanterns.

"This is it," Nephim said.

Karzul reached out for the wall.

The image Kin'tara had pushed into his mind returned.

Aged, wrinkled, white hair.

He shivered.

"Don't touch the wall," he said. "Get your staff ready. You can draw on my power. We're either going to fight our way out of here or bring the place down on our heads."

Before he could move, Kin'tara roared and knocked him to the ground. Fire shot from her maw, licking at the Daresh.

The soldiers pressed themselves against the wall.

A volley of arrows rained down on the dragon.

Kin'tara bellowed once more and crouched down.

Behind her, the young dragon was squealing with glee. Dara'tia squeezed past Kin'tara, heedless of the arrows that raced her way.

Suddenly, the mine shaft flared to light.

Blue-white light.

Like a fire lance.

Karzul glanced over at Nephim to see if she had activated her fire lance, but she stood there as dumbfounded as he was. It was not Nephim's fire lance that was the source of the blinding light. It was her dragon.

The rain of arrows ceased.

"What was that?" Nephim asked.

"I've never seen anything like it," Karzul said. "Dara'tia — her eyes — they work like fire lances."

"More likely, fire lances work like her eyes," Nephim remarked.

Before Karzul could reply, the earth shook beneath his feet. Dust rose from the floor, and the beams supporting the ceiling creaked. A large rock ripped itself from the ceiling ahead, crashing to the floor, partially blocking their path. An image materialized in his mind of himself and Nephim squeezing through a narrow passage. Kin'tara curled her tail around Karzul and nudged him forward.

Karzul shook his head.

No.

Kin'tara pushed him with greater force.

Yes.

How are you going to get out?

Kin'tara closed her mind to him.

You'll die down here.

The tail shoved him toward a small gap between the fallen rock and the wall of the mineshaft. This time the image that came to his mind was of the mine shaft collapsing with Karzul and Nephim trapped behind Kin'tara. Clearly, the dragon was trying to save their lives. But who would save her?

"She wants us out." Nephim pushed past Karzul and disappeared into the tiny opening.

He knelt down to follow her.

The passage was tight. Too tight. And his fire lance was getting in the way.

He tossed the fire lance ahead of him and squeezed into the gap.

For a moment, all he could think of was being stuck there. The weight of the stone surrounding him made him sweat. What would he do if he got stuck? There was no way he was moving that huge stone. It was simply too heavy. What if the passageway grew narrower? He could not turn around. Was he to back out? That seemed unlikely.

His heart beat faster, thundering against his ribs. He panted like a dog on a hot day. His breath came in short gasps. He was trapped. This was his fate then. He struggled against it, but it was no use. He was going to die. He resigned himself to death. He had lived a good life. Short, but good.

He was a soldier now, in truth, sacrificing his life for his country. They would call his name in the spring so that his spirit would come and bless the land. Perhaps he would see his father and mother. They had preceded him in death. Surely they would guide his spirit to its final reward.

"Karzul! You're almost there," Nephim called from ahead.

"I'm stuck." He tried to move, but his arms were pinned beneath him. He'd thought to crawl on his arms, but the gap had closed in on him and now he could barely move them, much less use them to push his body forward.

"My fire lance. Can you grab hold of it?" Nephim asked.

Karzul felt the cold of the fire lance thrust beneath his body.

He let his fingers brush the inert metal.

"Got it," he called, hoping that he truly did.

Nephim pulled.

At first, it did nothing but jam the staff tighter against him. Karzul raised onto his toes to give himself just a bit more space. Slowly, digit by digit, Karzul edged his way along the narrow passage. Before long, fresh air made its way to his lungs. He might just live after all.

With a sigh of relief, Karzul emerged from the narrow passage. His flesh was raw and red. He had scratches all along his back from contact with the rough stone, but he was alive.

"Welcome to the world of the living," Nephim said. She settled against the wall. They were near the mine head, but still deep beneath the earth.

"Where's Dara'tia?" Karzul could see a light ahead. Brilliant blue-wine light. It hurt his eyes after so much time in the dark.

Nephim nodded ahead. "I think that's her. The mine seems to have energized her just as it energized our fire lances."

Karzul shook his head. He would never have suspected that the fire lances were patterned after the dragons, and he certainly had never heard of a dragon that brandished anything like that sort of power. Perhaps there was something back at the citadel that would explain what happened. For now, they probably should make their way to the surface. Stones and dust still occasionally dropped from the ceiling overhead, and Karzul had yet to think of a way to save Kin'tara.

"Is your lance charged up?" he asked Nephim.

"Karzul. You can't blast your dragon out of the mine. All you'll do is bring the rest of the shaft down on her. Maybe we can find enough men to dig her out."

"I can't leave her behind." Karzul turned his fire lance toward the fallen rocks blocking the mine shaft. He fingered the stud. Brilliant blue-white light streaked out, washing over the stone. Noting happened.

He released the stud.

Darkness returned.

"Kin'tara. Hold on," he said. "I'm going to try again."

Before he could act, fire shot from the gap in the rocks. It smelled of rotten eggs and brimstone.

The rocks rumbled and gave way.

The fire ceased.

"Kin'tara!" Karzul rushed for the rock. He grabbed for one, but as his hand came into contact, it flared in pain, emitting a sizzling sound. He reflexively withdrew his hand, shaking it.

Dust filled the air, and the earth rumbled.

"Come on. We have to get out of here." Nephim grabbed Karzul's arm and yanked. "The whole mine is about to collapse."

Karzul followed Nephim, his fire lance dragging along the stone floor behind him.

As they exited the mine shaft, a great rumbling shook the building.

The mine collapsed, dust shooting from the shaft.

"Kin'tara?" Karzul called out.

No image came to his mind, no thoughts from the dragon answered him.

Would they ever?

40

THE WEIGHT OF WINGS

Karzul blinked at the brilliance of the sun as he exited the mine shaft. The temple of the forbearers was in ruins. The metal was twisted as if melted. The wood had turned to ash. The roof had collapsed, and that made walking difficult, but he was alive.

Kin'tara was gone.

He would never ride another dragon.

He did not want to.

Kin'tara was his dragon, and he would never want another.

"What's she doing? Get back here, you silly beast." Nephim made the sign in the air that Karzul recognized as a summoning. Would it work? Dara'tia seemed distracted, almost as if she had been set free from captivity and was finally allowed to run free.

"Dara'tia, you get back here," Nephim demanded.

The dragon altered her path and headed for the destroyed temple. She folded her wings, then extended them to capture the air just as she landed.

"There are Daresh all around. What were you doing? Joy-flying?" Nephim leaped up and onto Dara'tia's neck and laced her feet around the dragon's gleaming scales.

"Sorry. I imagined us doing this together." She reached out her hand, gesturing for Karzul's fire lance.

For a moment he hesitated.

The fire lance was his last connection to Kin'tara.

But what use would it be on the ground?

He handed the staff over. "Go kill some Daresh."

Nephim shoved the lance under her arm. She looked menacing, holding two fire lances.

He hoped she possessed the strength to wield them both. The air was filled with riders, both Daresh and Theren. They fought, not with fire lances, but with blades. On the ground, the Daresh and Theren troops battled it out with lances and pikes.

As he watched, a dragon separated from its pursuers and cut a swath through one or the other armies, but that tactic was always met with a pursuit that drove the dragon back to the sky. He mused that dragons, while impressive, were not the determiners of the battle. It would be the troops. Even Nephim with her fire lance might not be enough to turn the tide of the battle.

Blue-white light flared, not from Nephim toward the ground but from the sky, aimed at Nephim and Dara'tia.

Dara'tia twisted in the air and absorbed the staff directly into her chest. She dove for the ground and rose beneath the brilliant green dragon.

Karzul held his breath. Could Nephim defeat Dari? They had not matched weapons since the destruction of Karzul's home, and that time Nephim had nearly lost her life, and her dragon.

As Dara'tia swept upwards, three beams of blue-white light lanced out.

The brilliant green dragon turned to catch the beams on her chest, but they were spread too wide. One of the beams caught her wing tip, severing half a span.

She tumbled, recovering a dozen spans below Nephim.

Nephim fired again.

Her shot went wide.

Blue-white light lanced out from Dari, catching Dara'tia in the tail.

The young dragon screamed in pain and twisted in the air. Twin beams of blue-white shot from her eyes to catch the brilliant green square in the snout, despite the green's best effort to spread her jaws and absorb the blast.

The brilliant green tumbled once more.

Was Nephim winning?

Once again, the dual beams of blue-white snaked their way toward the brilliant green. The pursuer had become the pursued, and she didn't like it.

The brilliant green folded her wings and plummeted toward the ground. Just before she reached the earth, she pulled up.

Dari and her dragon streaked over Karzul's head. She raised her fire lance in salute before tucking it beneath her arm. Dari was leaving the fight. Without Kin'tara, her dragon would become the queen of the thunder.

Now, all they had to do was drive back the Daresh army with its overwhelming numbers.

Nephim soared through the sky, the brilliant blue-white beam of her file lance stabbing the ground, leaving flames and ash wherever it touched. Was Dara'tia powering her lance, or had Nephim absorbed enough power to wield her lance with such fierceness?

The Daresh broke lines and fell back, lacking organization as they withdrew. Nephim pursued them and incinerated the stragglers. Dara'tia's fire joined Nephim's, twin beams of blue-white stabbing the ground until the Daresh turned tail and ran.

Dara'tia banked and streaked for the ground, landing softly half a dozen paces from Karzul.

"You did it," Karzul called out as Nephim slid from her dragon. He half expected her to rush to him in excitement, but she collapsed onto the ground, exhausted.

"They're leaving," she muttered. "Can I rest now?"

Before Karzul could respond, Rodan strode up. His uniform was blood-streaked and splashed with ash and mud. His hair was unkempt, and his beard peppered with debris from the battle.

"Nephim. Great job. You turned the tide," he said.

"Not me," she said. "It was all Dara'tia." She patted the scaly side of her steed.

"When you are rested, you must tell me what transpired," Rodan said. "Did you notice?"

"Notice what?" Nephim asked.

"Dara'tia. She has started budding a second pair of wings."

Karzul turned to look. Dara'tia had indeed sprouted a set of bulges where her second pair of wings would emerge. It reminded him of his own dragon. What did the ore from the mine do to Kin'tara?

Would she sprout a fourth set of wings?

It seemed improbable.

Kin'tara was dead.

Yet.

Karzul fell to his knees as an image of a great dragon, cocooned in stone, warmed by an eerie green glow came to him. The dragon roused from its slumber, opened a sleepy eye and sent a one-word message.

Soon.

An image of the great dragon slumbering in the warmth of the eerie green glow, cocooned by stone, came to him, her rumbling snores shaking the timbers that held up the mine shaft.

The image receded.

Then there was nothing, only black.

THE END

ABOUT THE AUTHOR

James A. Eggebeen crafts epic fantasy tales brimming with dragons, magic, and fearless heroes from his home in California. Born in a Dutch farming community in Wisconsin, he served in the Navy before thriving as a tech executive. A college switch from poetry to creative writing ignited his passion for fiction, fueling a dozen captivating novels since 2011, including the pulse-pounding *Bonds of Fire and Fury*.

Now retired, James channels his creativity into worlds of swords and sorcery, inspired by his rural roots and adventurous spirit. As a dedicated mentor in writing communities, he loves nurturing new authors. When not writing, James designs intricate 3D machines and creates beautiful dresses for his granddaughters, blending precision with imagination.

ALSO BY JAMES A EGGEBEEN

Apprentice to Master

Foundling Wizard

Wizards Education

Master Wizard

Wizards's Hatchling

Origin

The Priest

Dragon Lord

The Sorceress

The Healer

Stand Alone

Reluctant Wizard

Indentured Magic

Sufficient Magic

Novellas

Kalis

Gypsy